Distant Seas

Distant Seas
by Bud Sparhawk

In-house editor: Ian Randal Strock

Cover by George Krauter

Fantastic Books
1380 East 17 Street, Suite 2233
Brooklyn, New York 11230
www.FantasticBooks.biz

ISBN 10: 1-62755-633-8
ISBN 13: 978-1-62755-633-0

First Fantastic Books Edition, 2015

Preface

These guys want you to think that sailing's a science—that it's all application of mathematical rules and physics. Listening to them, you'd think that you're constantly thinking, calculating, and plotting. Well, that's all a pile of crap, sailing isn't some branch of engineering.

Sailing's a love affair between you, the boat, the water, and the wind. Every one of them has to be balanced, held in check; let any one of them dominate and you've lost it. A good sailor has to be conscious of wind and water and responsive to the boat's needs. You have to understand the language of wind and sea and ship—you have to feel that edge that means you're running a tight line with every nerve of your body. The boat'll tell you how she wants to behave; she'll fight you when you're wrong, and support you when you're right.

Sailing is an art, not a bloody damn science. That means you have to sail with your heart, as well as your mind. When you're on the sea, managing the sails and the wheel, the rest of the universe could disappear, for all that you care. When everything works right, there's a rhythm, a reverie that transforms you, that makes you one with the universe. If you put everything you have into it, mind and body, your ego disappears—it's just you, the boat, the wind, and the water.

—Louella Kobata Parsons
Reflections 2195

"Why did I ever listen to you about *this* race? I already spend a bunch right here on Earth," protested Jerome Blacker.

The two tanned and muscular people facing him looked uneasy. A sales tag was still attached to the man's sleeve and flapped as he waved his hand as he spoke. "You already made the commitment, JB—you just have to follow through. Come on, it doesn't cost you any real money."

"You sure as hell aren't much of a businessman if you think this won't cost me anything!" Blacker replied.

"Mr. Blacker," Pascal interrupted, "the publicity about this race will bring in more than enough to offset expenses."

Jerome leaned across the desk. "What about insurance, the cost of transport, the cost of the boats? Those things aren't cheap!"

Pascal sighed. "The funds from the Jovian ventures can't be spent on Earth. Thanks to the treaty of '54, you have to reinvest at least seventy-five percent of your profits."

Jerome winced. "Don't remind me about those damn pirates! If it hadn't been for my stations and hubs, the damned Jovians wouldn't have a pot to piss in," he grumbled.

Pascal continued his attack. "GeoGlobal and the Times cartel are both outfitting ships for the race. No telling how many the Jovians are going to enter themselves. If we don't race, JBI will lose a lot—the publicity about our entry will bring in more than enough revenue to cover our expenses."

Jerome mused, half to himself, as he rubbed his chin. "Yeah, I saw your numbers and read the reports. So be it." He sighed. "What do I have to do to finalize the financial arrangements?"

Pascal spoke slowly, not wishing to reveal how anxious he was to get JB's approval. "I've already reserved *Thorn*, a used barkentine. You just need to sign the commitment for outfitting her. Once that's done, the orbital factories will start fabricating the sails—we've already sent them our specs. We'll use the Jovian funds for both of those efforts. The only cash outlay you need to worry about will be our transport out to Jupiter."

"Which leaves only the human element," Jerome said. "Even now I find it hard to believe that we can win this race." He swivelled in his chair to face the woman who sat beside Pascal. She was the best captain in his fleet and winner of more sailboat races than he could count. She'd been unusually quiet since she came in the office.

"Do you think you can race one of those barques, Louella," he asked her quietly. "Do you think you can sail a boat on the seas of Jupiter?"

Pascal held his breath as he awaited her answer. The success of their entire enterprise, and the payoff for the past year's worth of intense training, rested on her reply. The answer she gave would make or break the deal.

"I could sail a fucking bathtub on the sun if the price was right," she spat back. "Now how the hell do I get a drink around here?"

Chapter One—Earth

Sailors call everything below fifty degrees, south latitude, the Southern Ocean, even though technically, that name only applies to the water around Antarctica. Ocean temperatures there vary from about ten degrees Celsius to minus two and, when winter comes to the southern hemisphere, the water freezes as far north as sixty degrees.

Year round, eastward cyclonic storms containing the strongest average winds found anywhere on Earth rage across the water, forcing waves as high as fifteen meters or more. It is the most dangerous body of water on the planet.

When summer comes to the southern hemisphere, the irresistible lure of the Southern Ocean as the shortest way across all Earth's longitudes draws sailors into her depths. But it's not just the shortest path around the world; it's also the route Louella and Pascal were taking to get to Jupiter.

Louella was so cold that she could barely feel her fingers wrapped around the thin safety line. She concentrated on maintaining her hold. With a moment's loss of attention, a second's relaxation of her grip, or any slip of her boot, she could slide into frigid waters that would drain the heat—and the life—from her in a matter of minutes.

The ice-slick bottom of her boat, *Mistrial*, rolled slowly as another wave passed. She pressed her foot hard against the keel that stuck up beside her like the fin of a monstrous shark. Her position was precarious. Every shift of her weight on the overturned boat was dangerous.

It had been so long since she last had a drink. Her mouth felt as if it were stuffed with dry cotton. As the boat crested the next wave, she saw a range of mountains on the horizon and wondered if the mountains' melting snows produced crystal clear streams of the purest water. Her cracked lips parted at the thought.

Had it only been a day and a half since her boat had been flipped by the storm? How many hours had it been since she'd last slept?

The mountains had to be imaginary, just like the fleet of phantom liners that had steamed past hours before with their ball-gowned and tuxedoed passengers lining the rails and laughing at her.

The phantoms didn't disturb her. Hallucinations were an expected part of these extended, single-hand races. The mountains and liners were probably more vivid because of her sleep deprivation, her burning thirst, and the piercing, biting, eroding cold that burrowed through her survival suit and crept into her bones.

There was a splash and an Orca surfaced, water streaming down its glistening black body as it nosed onto the edge of the hull.

"I say, old girl," the Orca said politely in British English. "Do you need a spot of help?"

Georges Franchard's radio call woke Pascal from his four-hour nap, hours before it was expected. Georges's boat was over a hundred kilometers west and quite a bit north of Pascal's current position.

"Louella's in trouble," Georges said without preamble. "We think she's twelve hundred kilometers southeast of your location. Her emergency beacon's been beeping for a couple of hours."

Pascal swore as he studied the readings Georges sent him. The course he had plotted for his own boat, *Mon Ami*, was to have taken him around Antarctica on a more northerly route, not deep below latitude forty-nine so early in the circuit. What the devil was that damned Louella doing, going below fifty-five, where the EPIRB was insisting it was located?

"Is there no one closer," he asked hopefully.

"I'm too far north and east to be able to help her," Georges explained. "And we haven't been able to contact Randy Holiday."

"Yeah, I haven't heard from Randy for a couple of days either," Pascal replied. Randy's silence wasn't unusual, since the race boats frequently dropped out of VHF range and more often were below the line of sight for a satellite link.

"I'm turning toward her location, but *Mon Ami* is closer," Georges continued. "I'll shadow, but you'll reach her long before I will."

"What about air rescue or the navy?"

"Look at the weather map. There's a storm swinging south of Perth, Adelaide hasn't got an operational plane, and *Mistrial*'s too damn far from Christchurch."

Pascal knew that Georges was right. None of the land-based rescue crews could reach Louella until the storm passed, and that might take more time than she had if anything serious had happened to her boat. Although Georges hadn't said so, the chances of there being a navy vessel nearby ranged from slight to none.

"*Merde!*" As much as he disliked diverting his course and sacrificing race time, it wasn't a matter of choice. Nor did it matter that Louella was his potential sailing partner for the Jupiter race. He knew that the nearest boat was always obligated to help any sailor who was in trouble, just as he'd want someone to rush to his aid should he find himself in danger. This was a rule all sailors had abided by since the dawn of time.

Pascal leaned over the navigation table and plotted the fastest route to Louella's last known location. With a little luck and being able to maintain a steady eighteen knots, he should be able to reach her in three days. But after that much exposure to the freezing weather, the chances that she'd still be alive were not even slim.

Worse, he wouldn't even find a body if an Orca got to it first, damn her risk-taking hide. He was as concerned about her safety as he was mad at her making him lose time.

A glance at the latest weather map told him that there was, as Georges had said, a typhoon swinging south of Australia that would block any rescue from there. Unless it changed course the typhoon would track north of the route he could take. Weather to the southwest looked clear, although one could never be certain in the Southern Ocean, where storms could blow up in an instant.

Mon Ami was flying under full sail with three hundred square meters of main sail, ninety on the staysail, another hundred on the jib that he'd tied down on the foredeck, and two hundred in the balloon spinnaker that caught the breeze coming across the boat's stern.

He would have loved to see *Ami* sailing like this from afar, with all the sails. It had to be a beautiful sight. Instead, he had to stand in the cockpit, staring along *Ami*'s twenty-three-meter length or checking the wind indicator atop her forty-meter mast.

Mon Ami was a standard Open 70 design, nothing more than a fiberglass splinter, five meters wide and carrying far more sail than any reasonable sailor would think was even halfway rational. Had it not been for her advanced automation, the computer driven mast and keels, and the ballast tanks, no single sailor could have managed a boat this powerful. *Ami* was designed for ocean racing alone, and contained none of the amenities a cruising sailor would want: a toilet, for instance.

After doffing the spinnaker and raising the jib to better catch a quartering wind, Pascal turned abruptly south and toward the dangerous lower fifties. He swore at Jerome Blacker, at JBI, at the idiocy that put him and Louella at risk in this around-the-world race. With this delay, he'd never prove his worth, his ability to be the first across the line. If he didn't, then Blacker had every reason in the world to back out of sending him to Jupiter.

Why had he ever suggested it?

A day later, he recalled with some envy how pleasant those five indolent days crossing the equator had been, quite unlike the storm that now lashed his boat.

The rain gear he wore over his warm clothing made moving about the deck awkward. He hated the sound the gear made and its chemical scent of solvents and plastic. The inside of the suit felt like a sauna. He'd love to open the front, but to crack the Velcro seals was to invite the rain, wind, and biting cold inside—a whole other order of numbing discomfort.

What was worst about the rain gear was taking a piss, where he had to drop the front of the outer pants to get to his fly. Thankfully, once that was done he could just let go into the wind and not have to climb below to use the bucket like *la noire* probably had to do. Such was the advantage of men on boats. Well, for the two women in the race, Ann and Louella, it was either use the bucket or wet themselves. He'd wet himself more than once, when boat handling was paramount and dropping pants not an option. Personal cleanliness was not a grave concern when the safety of your boat was at stake.

To reach Louella at the fastest speed possible, he was sailing with *Mon Ami*'s main, flying jib, and staysail. All that sail meant he had to fight to keep her from heeling too much as she crabbed up and down the high waves. The wind temperature was barely four degrees above freezing. Not as cold as it was going to get, but cold enough to make standing at the wheel a miserable experience.

The steady rise and fall of *Ami* made footing treacherous. If not for his deck boots he'd probably have to lash himself to the wheel, like the wooden-ship sailors. Because of the waves and weather he wore *le pieuvre diabolique*, the octopus from hell, a safety harness whose straps and buckles, snaps and rings, made donning it overtop the cold weather gear an exercise in combative frustration. He hated the thing as much as he appreciated the need for it.

A single carbon-fiber cable snaked from the harness to a D-ring in the center of the cockpit. That was all that would keep him from being swept overboard by a rogue wave or misstep. That increased safety was purchased at a disadvantage. Moving about the boat meant tethering the line to the various D-rings, much as a mountain climber would secure belay points as he progressed up a sheer cliff.

That thought made Pascal shiver. He could never understand why anyone in their right mind would chance their lives by climbing a mountain. Hanging on a thin line off the face of a cliff even a few hundred feet up was suicidal, idiotic. A thousand feet was beyond the pale.

Better the safer ocean and seas. Even with all its dangers, from bad weather to huge waves, one still remained reasonably and sanely close to the planet.

Which was another point he hadn't thought deeply about when he bravely suggested the Jupiter race. Humanity belonged on the land and sea, not in the sky.

Just as *Ami* crested a wave, Pascal heard a distinct ping, the sound a highly tensioned cable makes when struck—or when it breaks. At the same moment, the boat lurched sideways as she lost wind.

An instant later, something on the windward side began beating against the mast. He turned the wheel over to the autopilot and, after making sure that *Ami* was holding true to course, struggled forward. It had to be one of the cables that braced the mast.

He hadn't gone very far forward when he saw the problem. The middle shroud, the one attached to the mast about twenty meters above the deck, was slack enough to flail the mast. Both the top and bottom seemed connected, so it must have stretched—but that was not possible!

Blinking against the stinging spray, he looked up and saw that halfway along the shroud's length there were only a few stands of wire holding it together.

The remaining two shrouds might be able handle the wind loading if those few wires separated, but he could not be certain. And, if the compensating shroud servos kept taking up the slack, there would be hell to pay. He didn't relish the thought of a broken steel line whipping about the deck when the cable broke. Given enough force, it could wrap itself around arms, or worse, cut him in two.

There was no choice. He had to kill the power to that servo, and then replace the cable at once. Fortunately he had another cable in the hold, along with the extra sails and other spare gear he thought he might need in this non-stop race.

Before he could do anything, he had to come off the wind and relieve the pressure. That would cost him valuable time, but it couldn't be avoided.

He turned *Mon Ami* upwind and let the boat run close-hauled. The pitching of the deck increased now that the waves were having more influence on the motion of the boat, but that couldn't be avoided, either. *Mon Ami* would continue up wind at a few knots and on a stable setting with the wind backfilling the jib and the main loose.

With the pressure relieved, the shroud hung slack, swinging only in reaction to the boat's movements. He quickly crawled below decks, found the breaker, and killed the power to the servos.

He considered the situation. Replacing the shroud meant he would have to climb twenty meters above the deck. It was insanity to climb so high in such heavy seas. Too damn much like climbing a mountain.

The fear of falling sank into the pit of his stomach. It was an icicle of fear that nearly froze him to inaction.

"You must do it," Georges insisted over the radio. Pascal had put the task off by asking him for a second opinion. It wasn't cowardice, he told himself. It was the prudent thing to do.

"It should not have broken," he snapped angrily. "Those shrouds were less than a year old." Of course, he should have had them tested, but somehow there hadn't been enough time before the race.

"I agree," Georges replied. "But you can't chance sailing with damaged equipment. You've got to replace it."

He knew Georges was right. The weather and waves he would face farther south would be too demanding for less-than-ideal equipment. "Perhaps I should drop sail until the storm passes," he said, hating the words that left his mouth. "I would lose a few hours at most."

"Hours that Louella might need," Georges replied too quickly. "Fix the damned shroud, Pascal. You've got to get to her as fast as you can."

Georges was right. He had no choice but to face that terrible height and try to conquer a fear it made him sick to even acknowledge.

Pascal pulled a cable from the spares locker and returned to the wind and spray. At the mast, he unsnapped the safety line from his harness and hooked the spinnaker lift line to it. He threaded the belay line carefully through the loops, saying a prayer with each, as if each was a bead on a rosary.

He put one foot on the boom and pulled himself up. The boat's rolling and pitching motion was already more pronounced just two meters above the base of the mast. The higher he went, the more swing he'd have to endure.

The thought of climbing any higher froze him more than the wind and rain, but putting it off wasn't an option. He fought to convince himself that he only had to climb a little way and he'd be done. He pulled the line tight and, bracing his boot on the first of the sail's tracks, pulled himself up another half meter. He let the replacement pay out behind him as he slowly climbed.

Mon Ami's swing became ever more pronounced as he ascended, almost nine meters from side to side at times. Only keeping a tight grip on the mast prevented his body from swinging wildly above the deck, like a flag waved by an excited child.

Things only got harder when he reached the lower spreader. To get around it he would have to use both hands. He tried not to look down at the angry sea and tiny deck far below him.

He secured the line before taking it in both hands, saying a brief prayer, and swinging his body to hook his leg over the spreader. He held tight to the spreader with one hand as he desperately took up the slack in his safety line with the other. When that was done, he hugged the mast in relief.

After a few moments, he composed himself and once again began his climb. Only two meters higher, the replacement snagged behind him. No amount of tugging and pulling would free it. He cursed the gods of mechanical objects and carefully lowered himself to work it around the spreader.

As he reached to free the snag, he glanced down and saw the deck and water swaying beneath him. His heart pounded as if it would leap from his chest. His stomach clenched, and he vomited, sending a splash of bile across the face of the mainsail. It took an effort of will to stop his bowels from releasing, but it was too late to keep from wetting himself. He was shivering; his sweat felt like ice water inside the overheated suit. He was going to die. He was going to fall. He should never have come up here. Who was screaming, he wondered?

Slowly, the panic attack subsided, and he could once again begin to think rationally. But his gnawing, gibbering fear of heights remained. He could not stay here, his inner demon cried. He had to get back down. He had to get to safety.

No, to come this far and stop was idiocy. Pascal took a deep breath and stood on the spreader. Carefully, deliberately, and trying to not think of the dangerous climb remaining before him, he took one careful step after another until he reached anchor point of the damaged shroud, just beneath the upper spreader. He pulled past it and then, repeating the frightening maneuver, hooked a leg and levered himself to sit on the spreader.

Before he did anything else, he ran the end of the safety line around the mast and tied himself to it. The sway was enormous at twenty meters above the deck. Despite his years on the sea, he started to feel queasy. Each time the boat rolled forward, he felt as if he were going to continue going face over into the sea.

He concentrated on the anchor point and shut out the motion of the boat and the long drop below—everything but the task of fastening the replacement.

Pascal released the spare cable from his harness with one hand, only to realize that he would have to use both hands to fasten it to the mast. That meant he had to depend only on the line holding him to the mast, a line that now seemed far too thin to hold him.

Releasing both hands was an act so simple in concept and so difficult to perform. He tried to force himself to release his hold as his eyes filled with tears of fear and frustration. His mind, always rational, was willing, but emotionally, his body knew that to let go was to invite disaster, to let go was to lose his perch and fall, fall, fall tens of meters, only to be dashed to death on the deck or, worse yet, be cast into the unkind and frigid ocean.

No. He wasn't going to let that happen, not after going through so much effort, facing so much fear, passing so much piss to get here. He drew in a breath, braced himself, and let go.

He had just released the damaged shroud when the sudden pitching of the boat threw him backward, cracking his head hard against the mast and nearly dislodging his death grip on the spare cable. Only the knowledge that, if he let go of the spare, he would have to repeat the painful, horrid, miserable, pants-wetting climb once again made him hold onto it.

On the next attempt, he synchronized his actions to the boat's motion. He leaned forward, quickly pulled the new shroud's end through the eye, slipped a clamp over both sides of the loop, and snapped it close. Three turns of the clamp's screw secured it. It was done so smoothly and quickly that he was done before the boat pitched again.

Muscles burning, and his ever-present fear still gibbering, he carefully worked his way back down to the deck.

His arms were shaking from fatigue as he wound the cable through the servos, attached the end to the deck, and took up the slack until he could tighten it no further, even using the wrench handle as a lever on the turnbuckle. He let the length of broken cable slip into the sea.

Pascal crawled on hands and knees to the cockpit. Fastened his harness to the cockpit's D-ring. And then, totally exhausted, ignoring the rain, his soiled pants, and the freezing cold, collapsed on the wet deck to cry with relief and thankfulness, and to curse Louella and JBI and the planet Jupiter, curse them all to hell and gone.

Louella wondered about the lone Orca. Didn't they usually travel in groups? Wasn't she too far from the seals' feeding grounds near the Antarctic shelf, where the Orcas usually hunted?

There was little else to think about, the Orca and her looming death. Her whole world was water, ice, hull under her, the Orca, and the bobbing orange emergency beacon.

She figured it would take a while for either location to organize a rescue mission. Until then, she had to hang on. If the EPIRB was working. How much time did she have before a rescue plane found her? Could she stay awake for however long that took? If they couldn't find her, then thirst and exhaustion would doom her even if she did miraculously manage to stay aboard *Mistrial*'s slippery hull.

She didn't have high hopes of rescue, even if someone were able to hear the EPIRB's distress signal. At her last position check she'd been at 58 South, 135 West. That was over thirty-seven hundred kilometers from Perth, about the same from Adelaide, and more than fifty-five hundred from the Christchurch rescue field in New Zealand. A rescue plane launched from any of those would only have a couple of hours of fuel to spend searching before they had to return.

Thirst would only be uncomfortable, but it would be exhaustion that did her in. The longer she was exposed to the elements, the more her strength would be sapped by the bitter cold, the angry wind, and the steady pounding of the towering waves. It was only a matter of time before the Southern Ocean took her into the sea.

"Tell me, Sheila," the Orca continued with an Australian accent. "Why would someone like you ever come to a place like this?"

Louella hadn't intended to enter the Super Grand Vendee race. She and her business partner, Scott Jamison, had been trying to raise the funds to outfit one of the ultimate British Offshore Race boats. They had a good partnership. She was the talent, the woman at the helm, the brave sailor, the pretty face of their partnership, while Scott took care of the business side.

Scott arranged her personal appearances, got writers to ghost her articles, and constantly fed the maw of the sporting press with teasers, ticklers, and occasionally, a bit of substance about the simply fabulous Louella and her races.

Keeping Louella's name in the press was important. Their sponsors— at least the ones who could throw a few tens of thousands of euros toward a sailboat race—wouldn't fund an unknown.

Together, Scott and Louella were a marketing force that could pry funds out of every wanna-be sailing enthusiast they could reach. Corporations were Scott's specialty. He'd already rounded up a dozen sponsors who would pay for the privilege of having their logo on the boat's hull. Those who wanted their icon to grace a sail, especially one of the huge spinnakers, paid a small fortune. Just having a picture of the nylon billboard plastered across the front pages of newspapers and magazines around the world was an irresistible lure to corporations of a certain type. And if Louella's boat, logo flying, were the first across the finish line, they paid a handsome bonus.

Sponsoring their next BOR entry, Groupe FP5, and gear wouldn't come cheap. Already the cost for even entering the competition went way beyond their initial breathtaking estimates—well over the eight-hundred thousand she needed just for the hull of the boat that would cross the starting line. The support crew who would meet them at each port, the spare parts, extra sail, two replacement masts and booms, travel expenses, and provisions would more than double that number.

So far Scott had arm-twisted and cajoled seventy-five percent of the total they needed.

"I think we're limiting ourselves," he remarked over dinner one evening in Brisbane, where they had been checking out the specifications on a new asymmetric jenniker foresail. "We've been concentrating on the traditional backers. You know, the global conglomerates, the networks, the web weaves, and groups like that."

Louella wondered what he was getting at as she picked at her scampi. The community that had any interest in sailing, especially high speed, long route sailing, was quite small, and the population of those who were willing to support it with real money was smaller yet. Competition for those few was fierce and, as far as she knew, there were no untapped sources, no new sponsors. Funds obtained from one source denied cash from that source to someone else. Half the battle, it seemed, was fought before the boats ever got launched.

"We tried getting public support a few years back. Penny-ante donations from the clubs aren't worth the accounting effort it takes to collect," she said.

"I'm not talking about going after the boat clubs," Scott said with a smug smile. "I'm talking about hitting another class of companies."

Louella sighed. "There aren't any others, Scott. We've hit the regional ones, the nationals, the transnationals, the internationals, and the global conglomerates. We've begged from everybody with money on the face of the Earth."

Scott grinned widely. "Yes, I agree. But there's more than the face of the Earth."

"What the hell have you been drinking, Scott? Has some alien invasion force of corporate financiers landed?"

"In a manner of speaking, yes. We've got an appointment with Jerome Blacker."

Louella shook her head. "Who?"

"Jerome Blacker, president of Blacker Industries." Seeing the puzzled look on Louella's face, he continued. "You know, JBI, the Jupiter people."

Louella nearly spit a scampi as the name finally clicked. "Are you out of your fucking mind? Why the hell would somebody in the deep space industry fund a sailboat race?" She waved toward the ceiling. "I'd think they'd be sinking every euro they have into building more resources out there."

Scott nodded. "I thought the same thing, but the other day I got a strange phone call from Blacker's secretary to set up an appointment. He was anxious to meet us, she said."

Louella tried to imagine why the president of JBI would be interested in meeting a couple of blue-water racers. The corporation founded by the father and run by the son was something one occasionally read about in the news, usually in conjunction with some space disaster in the Jupiter complex. Surely she would have heard if he had any interest in sailing—most of the corporate types who spent their company's money on sponsorships were enthusiasts. But nobody in the race business had ever mentioned Blacker.

Just the same, the call was curious, and she was not one to turn down a prospective sponsor. Not when they were short for the BOR.

"All right, let's give it a shot," she said with a shrug. "A couple hundred thousand euros"—the amount they needed to round out the BOR funding—"are probably less than his company's monthly coffee fund."

There had been eight people in Blacker's waiting room. Louella recognized the three sailors immediately: Georges Franchard, Pascal Dumay, and Randy Holiday. Two of them had raced with her occasionally during the past five years, and the other was a frequent rival. All were fiercely competitive, all were world-class racers, and she knew that all of them were still struggling to get their BOR entries funded.

"Looks like Blacker's going to listen to us all and pick which one he sponsors for the BOR," Scott whispered. "I'm sorry. I didn't realize our appointment was going to be a shoot-out."

Louella shrugged. "Part of the game, Scott. Listen, you go talk to the other suits. I'll see what I can find out from the sailors." She went over to exchange greetings with Randy, Georges, and Pascal.

An outsider would have seen certain hard-to-define similarities in the group of four sailors; but other sailors would have recognized them immediately. Randy and Pascal were burned brown by the sun, but Georges and Louella had started out brown by virtue of their ancestry.

Louella was tall, tough, and heavy boned; Pascal slender; Georges muscular, with a wrestler's build; and Randy was of only average stature and appearance. Each had their own style: Randy with his languorous drawl and deliberate movements; mercurial Pascal, who spoke in quick bursts; and phlegmatic Georges, who said little and seldom gestured.

She'd sailed with and against them all, but knew Pascal best. He'd been a navigator on her first Whitbread and, over the years had been navigator, tactician, winch crank, or sail master on her boats. They'd once drifted demasted for days with only a bottle of water to share between them, broached a hundred thousand dollar racer in 'Frisco Bay, lost a two-million-dollar racer in the South Pacific, and survived a storm to win the Bermuda.

She quickly learned that none of them had previously contacted JBI, nor had even considered doing so, for much the same reasons that Louella had outlined to Scott over dinner in Brisbane. All had been called around the same time as Scott.

"Mr. Blacker will see you now," an attractive young woman announced. Georges and Randy gave her trim figure a not-too-subtle appraisal and smiled at her. Too damn sophisticated for their tastes, Louella guessed, when the woman didn't acknowledge their smiles.

The man behind the massive desk was a shrunken caricature of a senior executive whose buzzard's neck stuck out of a collar several sizes too large. Louella had expected someone younger, more dynamic and forceful-looking. Then she got it. This wasn't Jerome Blacker; it had to be his father, the founder himself.

Blacker's hands were too large for his body, with swollen knuckles and mottled skin so thin you could see every vein and tendon beneath the many liver spots—a worker's hands, she noted. They were folded in front with blunt thumbs touching and fingers interlaced. She saw the slight trembling and realized he was holding them that way to steady them.

"My family's built JBI from the ground up," he began before they got settled. No handshakes here. His voice was surprisingly forceful, not at all the cracking, age-damaged squeak of a doddering oldster. "We financed the ships, constructed the stations, and started mining the moons. Made JBI a name to be reckoned with on Jupiter, by God."

Blacker paused and let his watery blue eyes scan the group. His mouth was set, daring anyone to disagree with his declaration. "Now my dear son has failed to convince the powers that be that we should reap the rewards of our efforts. The pissants will only let us take a fraction of my investment out of the complex. They want us to spend the rest out there, as if I was some damned economic tooth fairy."

Louella had been following the JBI news ever since they got the appointment. There was some sort of independence movement out at Jupiter, an attempt to develop their own economy and government. It had something to do with money and dependency on Earth, mutual trade and the like. It got hazy after that. She was a sailor, not an economist.

Blacker continued speaking. "Our goddamned weak-kneed politicos won't help me despite my contributions. Too unpopular, they say. That's why you're here. I want them to appreciate what we've done, and throw popular support my way. I've decided to appeal to the public. I want people to equate JBI with the grand traditions—risk taking, fighting at the edge of disaster, pushing the limits of possibility."

Scott cleared his throat. "Pardon me, sir, but the BOR isn't exactly a risky race. Granted that it might be exciting, but there's very little risk involved. The boats are hardly ever out of sight of each other."

The old man gave him a baleful stare. "Who the hell is talking about some trivial warm-water race? Waste of your talent, time, and money if you ask me."

There was a collective intake of breath. Louella and Scott were not the only ones to feel that they had been misled. Louella was the first one on her feet, followed quickly by the mercurial Pascal Dumay.

"You've just cost us two day's travel and God knows how many broken appointments," she said, glaring at the old man. "If you're not going to put up any money for the BOR, then why the hell did you invite us here?"

"*Je suis d'accord. Vous être a—*" Pascal stopped abruptly and continued in accented English. "This is imposition upon us at this stage of the game. I must launch in two weeks, and still have not the money for provisions."

Blacker raised his hand. "I'll pay whatever expenses you've incurred. Even throw in a few euros for decals on your ass if you want. Now shut up, sit down, and listen."

Louella and Pascal sat.

"I want you for another race. One where you'll carry the JBI name on your boats. I want to show the world what sort of company JBI represents. I want everyone to realize that we can achieve greatness only through great risk. I want to sponsor each of you in the next Super Grand Vendee."

Louella felt as if the ground had dropped away beneath her. The Super was a single-handed race around the world, 24,000 nautical miles of sailing across every line of longitude, through the absolute worst weather and water on the Earth, and returning. It was a single-hand race, so each boat, each sailor, had to be self-sufficient. There would be no landfalls, no supply ships, and no refreshing layovers allowed, save for repairs. The Super was a headlong race from start to finish, eighty-plus days and nights of continuous sailing.

It was more than just grueling. Fifty lives had been lost over the years in the Super, most in the depths of the Southern Ocean where rescue was nearly impossible. Others had fallen victim to the open ocean's mountainous waves, sudden storms, icebergs, and even to the ever-present danger of being run down by a freighter.

To win the Super you had to race around the clock with little sleep, live with a constant fear of failure, put up with extreme loneliness, and endure the unrelenting physical stress of sailing a high-performance boat twenty-four hours, day after day through the baking heat of the tropics, through the bitter Antarctic weather, and back again. It was the most punishing, backbreaking test of human endurance in sailing.

It was also an offer Louella had never dreamed of getting. The cost of outfitting one of the Vendee-class boats was way out of her reach. She'd never dreamed anyone would trust her with a boat costing that much.

"I'll do it," she said at once. Pascal added his assent only a moment before Randy's agreement.

"I'm no damned hero," Georges said as he stalked out of the room. "You'll get my expense sheet tomorrow," he shot back over his shoulder.

"What exactly do you mean by sponsor?" Scott asked quickly. "What sort of stake are we talking about?" The usual corporate share was ten to twenty percent, and that contingent on finding enough other sponsors to foot the rest of the bill.

Blacker scowled. "Whatever you need, just don't get greedy. You four are the best sailors money can buy, and your skills will mean more than any fancy boat."

"Three," Randy corrected, pointing at Georges's empty chair.

"Four," Blacker said with a smile. "I'm certain Franchard will come to his senses in the morning."

Louella knew he was right. Despite his parting declaration, Georges wouldn't back down from an opportunity to race the Super, not with the rest of them in the fleet.

"That's a very generous offer, sir," Scott said carefully, "But I hope you realize how much—"

"Do you know how much those stations on Jupiter cost?" Blacker demanded. "Thirty billion each—and that doesn't include the upkeep, staffing, or insurance. Want to know the price of launch facilities, the shipment costs, and the hourly rates those damn pirates manning the supply elevators charge? The price of your silly little racing toys can't compare. Tell me what you'll need for the Super and I'll write the checks. Just make certain that you four cross the finish line, and at least one of you gets there first."

A younger version of the old man entered the room. "Dad, I heard you'd come in today and—" he stopped speaking when he noticed the others, managed a smile. "Hello. I'm Jerome Blacker. Nobody told me you'd arrived."

The older Blacker chortled. "I told your damn fancy secretary not to bother you, Jerry. Figured you were having too much fun negotiating with those damned government sharks." Then he turned to Louella and the others. "You all get out of here now. I want a set of your campaign plans and budget estimates on my desk by the end of the week. Find some decent boats, too. Good day."

He waved his hand in dismissal. His son looked as if he were going to explode.

Which he did. Louella heard his raised voice as the door began closing. "I don't care if you are the chairman, Dad. You can't just promise these people—" The rest of his words were silenced by the closing door.

"I think we'd better hurry if we want to get that check," Scott said softly as he took his briefcase and coat from the slender secretary.

Randy lingered a moment longer to get his own coat, but still got no smile from Blacker's fancy assistant.

Old Blacker and a much younger man had shown up at the race party two nights before the start of the British Ocean Race, and joined Louella at her table. Things were going well. The aptly named Randy was alternating attentions between his wife and his mistress. Georges was in deep conversation with his fiancé. Scott was giving a German groupie some serious attention. As for Louella, she was flirting outrageously with a muscular pair from the Australian crew. Pascal, arm around one of his buddies, was singing what she supposed were bawdy ballads in a dialect of French that no one else seemed to understand.

"Damn, wish I were eighty years younger." The old man sighed with a nod toward Randy. "Course, back then I was more interested in making money than chasing tail. Good thing, too: JBI would never have grown the way it has if I'd been distracted."

"What brings you here," Scott asked as he peeled himself away from the German groupie's tight embrace and joined the conversation.

"Not that we aren't glad to see you, of course." Louella added tactfully.

"Decided you all needed a little help with the real race. This is Alex Humei, one of our engineers," he nodded toward the dark young man beside him.

"Sdras, at du." The youngster's accent was thick enough to cut with a knife. Louella guessed it wasn't French, Indian, or Russian, nor one of the Germanic tongues.

"He's down from Jupiter," Blacker said with a put-upon expression, "And talks like it."

"I am… engineer of ships," Alex said carefully. She could tell he was straining hard to keep the Jupiter patois, a mixture of English, French, German, Russian, and Hindi, out of his speech. "I build Jupiter boats."

"He means our atmospheric floaters," Blacker said, and a wistful expression crossed his face. "Damn, I wish I were young enough to sail on one." He let out a mordant laugh. "The launch would probably kill me, though. Not that my damn son would even let me try."

The mention of sailing was all Louella needed to hear. "Is sailing on Jupiter dangerous," she asked.

The old man didn't give Alex a chance to answer. "If you ask me, everything out there is too damn civilized now. Elevators from orbit to the stations, settlements on all of the moons, regular transport from the inner system—I tell you, Jupiter's turned into another damn suburb of Earth now. Hardly a frontier any more."

"Still, is dangerous," Alex said quietly. "Lose dozens peoples a year. Mistake can destroy floater in instant. To sail there, is not for those who can't live with fear."

Louella found herself taking a sudden liking to this husky lad. "What's it like to be on one of those deep atmosphere ships?" She was curious about the vessels he built. They were a cross between a submarine and a dirigible and floated on the interface between sharply divided pressure gradients within Jupiter's deep atmosphere. At that level of the atmosphere there were only two gravities, a load that most humans could bear, unlike the massive gravity well at the bottom. That is, if there were a bottom at all.

She'd seen a picture of one with its long, diamond-fiber keel that balanced the pressure on the massive sails. The sails were tough metal atop a structure that appeared to be a submarine the size of a blimp. The sailors rode inside and piloted blind across the windy vastness to reach their destinations. Despite their differences, they were still recognizably sailboats.

To a blue-water sailor like her, the idea of sailing across the surface of the largest planet in the solar system was intriguing.

"Sailing there a challenge," Alex answered. "You don't feel the wind or see outside—too much static for radar and not much light. Sail by feel, mostly."

She also knew they constantly faced death from the cold, the vacuum, all under the relentless pull of Jupiter. It took more than courage to sail across the huge planet's face. Craziness maybe? Like the sort needed for the big race to come?

"We use an inertial, our main navigation instrument, to guide us, and use heat sensors to find stations. Risky business, but it works. That what JBI want me to help you with—make race boats sail better, maybe."

Louella hoped there was some JBI technology that might give her a bit of advantage over the competition. But maybe not. The differences in the environment might just be too extreme. "I'm all for better," she replied.

Blacker interrupted again. "We have a warehouse full of equipment Alex can draw on. Soon as you all get your boats, you give him a call." He turned to the young engineer. "Run along now, and see if you can find your crewmates in the mess."

"Are you sailing in the race," Louella asked Alex, surprised by Blacker's unexpected announcement.

"But not skipper," Alex grinned. "Am crew. Do you think I miss a chance on race boat? Want to feel the wind and see the water big time." Alex smiled and bowed. "Fair winds and following seas."

Louella was pleased to hear the ancient sailor's blessing. "It's going to be interesting to hear what someone who sailed on Jupiter thinks about a blue-water race," she remarked as he left.

"He'll do just fine." Blacker said. "Now, I have some questions about this boat you said you didn't like. I thought the price was about right."

Business: the sure-fire party killer. She turned back to Blacker. "Listen, I didn't want a goddamned plastic bathtub of a boat that would probably bring me in dead last—if it somehow managed to hang together that long. The design was over ten years old, too old for this race. I need a fast boat that will get me back alive, and in first place. If you don't want to pony up the cash for that, then leave me out of the fucking race." Brave words for someone who was spending someone else's millions.

She regretted the words the moment they left her mouth. What if he took her up on it? God in heaven, she hoped he wouldn't. He just stared, waiting her out.

"There's one that ran the Volvo-Honda," she added quickly. "Belgian-built and available. I'm flying over there after the race to take a look. It'll cost you just a little bit more than that other scow."

"You're running out of time," Blacker said sharply. "The others have theirs lined up already. If this one doesn't meet your high standards," he put sarcastic emphasis on the last words, "you'll be off the team."

She just stared back at him and, after a while, he started to laugh.

The BOR went as expected. Louella and her crew came in second, a heart-breaking fifty-two second deficit that shouldn't have happened, but, when she ran into a hole in the wind a dozen kilometers from the finish, there was absolutely nothing she could do except drift on her momentum.

Pascal's *Soliel du Sud* had wafted past her on a cell of fresh air just a few hundred meters off her port side, forcing her to hear the boom of the finish line cannon as he passed the officials' boat.

The post-race celebrations were brief and predictable. Pascal got tossed into the chilly New England water by his cheering, all-French crew, everyone doused themselves with bottles of cheap champagne, and the losers were allowed to loudly complain of mischance and the foibles of the wind gods to anyone who would listen as they drank and bragged about overcoming the problems with their boats. Each tale sounded more outrageous than the previous, until the Portuguese skipper swore he'd had to lasso two dolphins to give him a tow out of a wind hole off Newfoundland.

After that, the details of the party got increasingly hazy. Louella recalled flirting outrageously with the Australians while Pascal and Jupiter's Alex had been deeply engrossed in conversation. Georges had been his usual dour self, and Randy and Ann Wilkerson, the English skipper, had been laughing at some private joke while his Canadian girlfriend fumed at the bar. Ann already had her boat entered for the Super. There was some sort of incident, one of the skippers threw up, a fight started, and she vaguely remembered kissing a lot of people.

Louella woke up the next morning in her hotel room between the two charming grinders from the Australian entry. She kissed them both soundly, threw her stuff in a bag, checked out, and took a taxi to the airport to catch her plane for Belgium. Sergio Pontclario was anxious to sell *Mistrial*, an older Open 80 design, so he could buy a new boat.

Pascal arrived at Logan around the same time in the company of his friends and barely nodded at her. They'd been competitors for years and, on occasion, crewmates—skipper and navigator/tactician usually. He was the best man on the plotting table she'd ever seen, but all his damn scientific approach couldn't beat the feel she had for the wind, water, and weather. Woman's intuition, he'd sneered dismissively during the revival Volvo-Honda Open 60 race. Well, that intuition or whatever it was had saved their butts from the hurricane during the Bermuda leg, just as his piloting skill had gotten them home with only a rag of a mainsail and the spare jib.

It had been a thrill the whole way.

Louella's feet were going numb from the constant wash of frigid water across the hull. The waves were only three- or four-meter swells, and at a frequency that let the overturned *Mistrial* ride up and down their gentle slopes. Each crest exposed her to the biting roar of the wind blowing at Beaufort scale five or six, at least twenty knots or more, and let her see the distant line of storm clouds heading her way. Black clouds growing visibly closer with each successive glimpse.

Odds of surviving a storm were not good. A storm-wind's force could push the waves to twenty meters or more, and whip freezing foam off the waves' crashing crests. Waves like that would carry her upside-down boat aloft, only to fall down their steep sides into the troughs. Each time tons of frigid water would crash down, making it impossible for her to maintain her already tenuous hold.

In the chill waters her survival time would be measured in mere minutes. Even through the insulation of her survival suit she'd lose too much heat. The driving sea foam, the froth of wind-whipped water, would infiltrate her nose and mouth, choking and drowning her. Which would come first, she wondered, suffocating or freezing?

Despite the absolute certainty of her approaching death Louella felt a strange calm. Everything that had happened had been a result of her deliberate choice. No one had forced her to enter the race. No one had held a gun to her head and made her sail this fragile shell of fiberglass and electronics into the misery of the Southern Ocean. All that had happened had been of her own choosing, her own decisions. The only regret she had was that she had let Pascal down, and ruined his chances of experiencing the fierce winds of Jupiter.

"Another question, I have," the Orca shouted again. For some reason he had suddenly acquired a Spanish accent. This was quite confusing, but she was in no condition to answer him. She just wanted to sleep—not that she dared. "Why would you ever sail in these dangerous waters?"

Sergio's Open 80, *Mistrial*, was totally unlike the Open 60s she'd raced in other around-the-world races. The Open-class boats all had broad hulls and smooth, slim contours; boats that were as much works of art as sailing machines—and many times more expensive than anything in the Louvre.

The Open 80-class were radically different, and not only because of their intense use of electronics and computers to manage every aspect of boat handling. She could handle the twenty-one-meter Open 60s by herself, but not one of these twenty-five meter splinters where they had sacrificed a lot of stability for speed.

"Isn't she beautiful," Sergio asked proudly.

Not to her. Louella tried to get her mind around *Mistrial*'s length. She was little more than an angular surfboard. A flat deck covered the entire length from bow to cockpit with an open transom at the stern. From the too-pointed bowsprit along the straight sides to the abrupt stern she was a thin wedge of a vessel.

The most striking aspect of *Mistrial* was the height of her aerodynamic, carbon-fiber mast. It stood forty and a fraction meters above the water line and held a fifteen-meter boom just above the deck. Four spreaders anchored the long, high-tensioned shrouds that kept the mast erect.

"*Mistrial*, she can carry over three hundred square meters of sail downwind," Sergio bragged. "Under full sail, she'll do nearly fifty knots close-hauled, and thirty on a reach."

That was far more sail than any boat of this length seemed capable of carrying. Louella knew she'd have to reduce sail on the upwind headings, of course. Too much power could easily drive the boat into the oncoming waves.

She dropped inside the cabin, three steps from the wheels, one from the motorized winches, and took two steps down into the body of the boat. Inside the cabin there was barely any headroom. The cabin was wider than it was deep. A spider-work chart table took up much of what little room there was.

The cabin's interior was all raw fiberglass with wooden floorboards. She saw exposed bolt heads, hull seams and rough glass surfaces everywhere. Only the overhead was padded—soundproofing, she wondered, or head protection from rough seas?

There was a fold-down canvas cot for the short naps she'd have to take. The walls were covered with mesh bags for clothes and the few things her restricted weight allowance would allow. There were no drawers, no cabinets, none of the fancy gear a cruising sailor might use to make life easier. This boat was all business, and her business was to sail as fast as possible.

The pilot's chair was just a mesh skeleton suspended from the thwarts, the galley a one-burner propane stove, useful mostly for heating water given that she'd have very little food to cook except soup and tea.

The chart table was nothing more than a frame with a spider-web of lightweight fiber threads that supported all of the communications, navigation, and other electronics she'd need.

"The cabin, she is watertight," Sergio had pointed proudly to the neoprene-rimmed hatch between the cabin and the cockpit during that introductory meeting. "In the cold seas you can be warm and dry inside."

As if I'd have time, Louella thought.

"The two swing keels," he continued, "are canted to either side to give her better stability on an extreme heel. They are married to the tilt of the mast by the computers."

"What if she overturns," Louella asked sharply. "Where are the hatches?" She well knew the history of the race, and how many lives had been lost from boats turning turtle. The problem was that this sort of boat was just as stable upside down, if not more so. Only the action of the ballast pumps, attention to sail set, and skillful piloting kept them from capsizing. Once flipped, with sails in the water, the Open-design boats stayed on their backs.

"Are access hatches there and here," Sergio pointed out two oval hatches; one on the foredeck accessed the sail locker, which doubled as a floatation chamber. The other hatch was amidships and provided access to all the electrical equipment. That was also accessible from inside the cabin through a crawl hole.

"Is there a hatch in the bottom of the boat," Louella asked. "I'd like some way out if she flips while I'm inside."

"*Mistrial* will not turn over," Sergio protested in a hurt voice. "The hydraulics and servos," he pointed mid-ships, where the complex of shroud servos, mast gimbals, and keel drivers were installed, "Will adjust the center of mass and angle of the mast if *Mistrial* heels more than twenty degrees. If she goes beyond that angle, they will compensate."

Sergio went on to explain at length the automated ballast pumps, the swinging keels that were coordinated with the mast, and the gyroscopic stabilization framework. He mentioned the triply redundant backup systems that controlled everything from winch motors to rudder. He spoke of angular momentum, of torque, of compensating forces. He explained about the boat's moment of inertia and her center of mass. He explained about rigorous testing, about modeling every possible contingency, and about all the past successes of *Mistrial* mastering the worst storms, all to prove the boat's stability.

Louella listened impatiently, only to break in and say. "I still wish there was a goddamned escape hatch in the hull." She had as much faith in his physics as she did in Georges's horoscope.

Sergio muttered something about women, sailing, and excessive caution, all of which Louella chose to ignore. Let him think what he would, he wouldn't be putting his ass on the line in the Southern Ocean.

L ouella left Scott to make the final financial arrangements while she prepared to have *Mistrial* hauled out for inspection. She wanted to make certain there were no hidden defects in the hull. After that, while the suits were passing papers and talking euros, she met with JBI's engineer to see what he could offer.

"We have a number of technologies we can use to outfit your boat." The JBI engineer handed her a list.

Louella saw that some shroud servos had an "F" beside them, and pointed at the entry. "What's this mean?"

"They are for shrouds, the lines that hold the mast," the young man replied absently as he looked over Mistrial's design sheets.

"I think I do know what a shroud is," Louella snapped. She didn't like being patronized by a damn engineer. "Do you use these to drive the cables on your floaters?"

The engineer appeared to be puzzled by the tone of her voice. "No. We use metal sails, so these motors could not drive the very strong chain that holds them. We can't use this thin sail fabric you use. That would be like using a spider web to harness a hurricane."

"So what the eff is the 'F' for?"

He laughed. "The 'F' means your teammate Franchard wanted them on his boat."

Putting extra strength servos on the shrouds would be just like Georges, ever mindful of caution and security. "I won't need them. I put brand-new, quarter-inch stainless shrouds and good Hercules servos on *Mistrial*."

"For Randy Holiday," the JBI engineer continued, pointing at an "H" farther down the page. "We're installing deck winches. They're the ones that can reel in the sails, even against Jupiter's hurricane-force winds."

Louella wondered why Randy wanted to that much power. The winches indicated were twice the weight of the Lewmar winches on *Mistrial*. Heavy-duty winches might come in handy during bad weather, but their additional weight meant he'd sacrifice speed. That was an option she could easily do without. She wanted *Mistrial* as light and agile as possible. "Any other suggestions?"

The engineer seemed intent on the design sheets. "How about your communications and navigation? Are they any good?"

Louella smiled. "She had a GPS on her already, but I'm installing a backup so I'll have two units. Also getting the best charting software I can buy with the money Blacker is giving me."

"I think we can give you some inertial tracking gear," Alex said. "It give you positive fix. Better than GPS, I think. Doesn't depend on anything but itself."

Louella hoped the unit would compensate for her less-than-stunning plotting skills. Maybe it would also make up for the GPS deficiencies. Down near the bottom of the world, the ocean surface deviated quite a bit from the smooth sphere of the theoretical GPS database. It would be best to have a positive position confirmation at all times.

"What does it weigh? I can't afford to add more than ten kilograms to my weight budget." She'd trimmed the list of her supplies to the bone already.

"Three kilos, she's thirty square and ten high," the JBI man replied, indicating the size of the box with his hands. "Most of that the case and fittings. She'll need to have a rigid base. The readout's a little case like that." He pointed to Louella's pocket computer.

"We'll put the box on the deck, in the cabin," Louella replied. Maybe they could put it under the nav table, where she'd use it for a footrest.

"We have some luxury food items," he continued. "Freeze-dried fruit, good soups. We ship stuff that don't weigh much. Saves money when we send to Jupiter."

That made sense. If she could reduce the weight of the food onboard she could add some more communications gear. Maybe even an extra set of cold weather gear. "Let's do it. Have you got a list of what's available?"

They spent rest of the evening going over the inventory and planning her menus. She was surprised at the number of gourmet items on the list, and selected the very best for her Christmas dinner.

She saved enough weight that she could afford to add a nice bottle of wine for her equatorial crossing celebration.

"**C**ome now, you must have more interesting things to talk about than sailing," said the Orca in an Irish brogue. "Did you sail here alone, or were you part of something else—a race, perhaps?"

She resented the question, especially now. The distant line of storm clouds looked more threatening with each successive glimpse. She wished he'd just go away. She was getting tired of his questions, questions, questions.

"Yes," she whispered. "There was a race."

Jerome Blacker sponsored a qualifying race to get around the rule that his entries had to race at least once on their boats. It wasn't illegal, just too difficult and expensive for most of the sponsors.

Louella was surprised he'd done so. Unlike the older Blacker, Jerome had paid attention to every peso they spent, cutting corners, making them get their multimillion euro boats as cheaply as possible, and being generally parsimonious with the sail inventory, as if you could even buy a used Kevlar-Tylvex mainsail for less that forty thousand and change. Despite the older Blacker's initial promises, the money actually flowing from the obscenely wealthy JBI was just barely enough to cover expenses.

As if getting qualified wasn't enough of a problem, there was the initial bitching and moaning by the race committee about Jupiter not really being a country, and that none of JBI's skippers were really citizens of Jupiter anyway, and—

The Blackers had quickly produced papers attesting to their employment at JBI in general and their contract to sail on Jupiter to offset the first objections. The others died quickly enough when Nigeria recognized the Jupiter Free Trade and Independence party's claim to nation status. France, hoping to steal the march on the rest of the European Union, quickly followed, and the committee had to accept the fait accompli.

The older Blacker and Jerome probably shit Jupiter-sized bricks when they realized that the devils who were causing them so much grief on Jupiter were the reason for their success in getting accepted for the Super.

Pascal cornered Jerome Blacker at the bar during a pre-race party. "Monsieur Blacker," he began. "I've a proposition," he began. "Actually, it was one that your Alex, the cute engineer, joked about earlier."

Jerome raised an eyebrow as he sipped his glass of wine and surveyed the boisterous crowd. "Really?" He wrinkled his nose as if Pascal wore an unpleasant scent. Pascal had seen this look before, many times. Usually it was the older crowd of Jerome's age and position. Perhaps the look was in response to his hair, the earrings, or the pale puce jacket he wore—all signs of his preferences.

"Would JBI be interested in sponsoring a race across Jupiter?" Pascal said, trying to convey the excitement he felt at the prospect and overcome the distaste Blacker obviously displayed. "I think you should sponsor a race from one station to the next, much the way the Volvo-Honda Around-the-World does here on Earth."

"And why would I be interested in doing something as foolish as that?" Blacker said. "The idea appears to me to be a great waste of resources with very little purpose." He started to turn away.

"It would be great publicity for JBI," Pascal replied loudly. "The race would demonstrate the work JBI is doing out there. It could show Jupiter as an interesting and exciting place instead of just a big ball of industrial raw materials. It would gather you more press than le Grand, I'm positive."

"We get quite enough publicity as it is," Jerome said with a sour look. "But most of it's bad, I'll will admit. That's one of the reasons Father insisted on sponsoring you in this race, despite its hideously expensive price. I just hope the return is worth the cost of your toys."

Louella walked up, arm in arm with the elder Blacker. "Did someone say toys," she asked.

"He means your boats," old Blacker growled. "Just like this one, Son. Had to shop around until she found one she liked best."

Louella squeezed his arm. "But *Mistrial* is so much faster than the other. She placed third in her last race and it only cost a little more."

"That's what my last wife said about the house I'm stuck with," the old man growled. "Well, never mind. We got a good price on the lease anyway."

"Ready to go, Dad?" Jerome asked, draining the last of his wine from the glass.

Pascal felt panic as the opportunity started to slip away. "Perhaps your father would be interested in my idea," he said in desperation.

Jerome's father cocked an eyebrow. "Tell me more, son." Jerome the younger looked as if he'd been struck.

Ignoring the dark looks he was getting from his sponsor, Pascal quickly outlined the concept of racing the Jupiter boats from station to station, boats that would be manned by professional sailors, such as himself.

"That's a great idea." Louella applauded. "Hey, it might even be fun."

When Pascal saw that the old man looked interested, he pressed his case. "It wouldn't cost JBI any real money like le Grand has. Weren't you complaining that you had funds out there that you couldn't put your hands on? Well, why don't you use that money to outfit the boats and supplies."

Old Blacker rubbed his chin. "Sounds like an interesting idea. The Board might go for something like this. Might even build on the race with some other projects."

Jerome Blacker started to take another sip of wine, but stopped with the empty glass halfway to his lips. "It's too risky. We don't know what sort of publicity we might get. What if something goes wrong? What if we lose a ship and crew. Those floaters aren't cheap, you know. Would you seriously consider letting someone risk their lives or one of our expensive ships?"

"Oh for God's sake, Jerome, forget your damn penny-pinching budgets," the older Blacker said. "The floaters aren't that expensive! Last year you pissed away more than they cost on those damn mining machines we've got on Io."

"But those machines will eventually produce a return," Jerome replied evenly. "I dislike dumping money into anything that won't show a decent return on investment. I think the whole idea is too chancy."

His father grinned. "Damn straight. Glad you learned that much from all that expensive schooling. The only thing you didn't learn was how to take risks with anything else. We've got to take chances, Son."

Jerome sighed. "We've been over this before, Dad. But we can't take on more risk than we're comfortable with.

"Humpf! Nobody learns a damn thing if they don't take a few risks."

Pascal saw an opening. "You could do this. The sailing world needs something more interesting than these around-the-world races. A Jupiter race will create excitement. It will gather more publicity for JBI than anything else. But only if you are the first to propose it."

"I like your spirit, boy," the old man said.

"The only trouble is," Jerome interrupted. "Is that you," he thrust a finger at Pascal's chest, "can't sail alone. Minimum crew, even for a deep atmospheric miner, is two on board. You'd need to find somebody else foolish enough to sail with you."

"I'll crew with him," Louella said boldly, and stepped forward to Pascal's side. "Crap, they're just sailboats, aren't they? What could be so hard about that?"

Pascal stared at her. Of all the people in the sailing community, Louella was the least likely in his mind to volunteer for this. Was she drunk and talking out of her head? Perhaps he should... But no, he had to take advantage of whatever wind shift came his way. "There we are," he said proudly, and put an arm across her broad shoulders. "We are a crew."

The old man slapped his son on the back. "There you go," he said with a laugh. "She called your bluff. You going to raise or fold?"

Jerome was clearly angered by his father's gibe. There was a red flush about his neck that was climbing toward his cheeks. "If I did such a foolish thing and went ahead with this crazy idea of yours," he began slowly and deliberately, "why wouldn't I choose one of my own pilots?"

"Damn it, man. We've both been sailing our whole lives," Louella said. "And, frankly, there isn't a damned sailor on the planet better than me and Pascal. I doubt some corporate monkey would do any better."

Pascal felt the probability of success, which only instants before had looked so promising, had suddenly plunged to negative numbers. Calling Blacker's pilots monkeys wasn't the most politic thing to say.

"So you want a challenge?" Jerome said, glaring defiantly at his father first, and then leaning toward Pascal. "Do you?"

"Yes. I want a race that will really put all the skills and knowledge I've gained to the test. I'll do it."

"And me, too," Louella said. "Let's see if these damned winds on Jupiter can beat me."

"Very well, I'll give you a challenge. JBI will put up one hundred and twenty million euros from our Jupiter holdings and let you use a floater from our fleet. It will be waiting for you on Jupiter. Think that would do it?"

"Jesus," Louella gasped, and threw her own drink back in one gulp.

Pascal would have done the same, had he a drink in hand. That was more money than he ever imagined JBI would offer. He'd gotten some idea of costs from Alex, but he thought much less would be enough.

Wait a moment. Blacker wasn't a man given to generosity, no matter how mad he was at *le pere*. "What do you mean about another challenge?"

Blacker grinned. "All right, sailor, here's the deal: First, you convince enough people to put at least three floaters in the race. Next, you both get in shape so you can walk around in two gees. And finally, one of you will have to be the first boat across the finish line in this race. If you can do all of that, I'll send you on the long trip out to Jupiter and back in two years."

"Two years?" Louella and Pascal said in concert.

Jerome smiled. "Yes, I don't want you wasting the time after you finish the Grand Vendee. I'll make certain you both get into prime physical condition and know every damn rivet on the ship you'll be sailing."

Pascal was the first to recover. Quickly, he scribbled on a napkin and pushed it across to Jerome. "Will you sign a contract on that?"

Blacker started at the words, aware that his challenge had suddenly crystallized. "I don't..." he began.

"Damn, I'd hate to play poker with you," the old man said admiringly to Pascal. "Come on, Jerry, sign the napkin. We can always have one of our obscenely expensive lawyers look at it later. Time to play your hand, Son. Call or fold."

Jerome scowled at his father and scribbled his signature on the napkin. He turned to face Louella and Pascal. "Personally, I doubt that you'll be able to find enough backers. What's more, I don't think you'll be able to find anyone insane enough to sail across Jupiter in a stupid race."

"If you think that will be difficult," Pascal smiled as he slipped the napkin into his pocket. "Then you don't understand sailors."

Louella's sea trials with *Mistrial* gave her few surprises. She'd expected the boat to handle well, even in the wilds of the North Sea's winter.

Nor was she surprised at the speeds *Mistrial* was able to achieve under full sail; she expected that with so much sail area pushing a long waterline. However, the sound her huge sails made astounded her. They sang a deep bass note, a steady thrum, thrum, thrum as wind whipped across their huge surface area. The mainsail's song was accompanied by the fluttering of the staysail's trailing edge, and only occasionally drowned by the drumming boom whenever the huge spinnaker filled with wind.

Mistrial was a thoroughbred. She was a fast and temperamental machine that demanded constant attention, even with all the automated systems supporting her. Louella quickly learned that it only took a moment's lapse of focus for the craft to go awry and turn to windward or heel dangerously.

But all of those problems were as nothing when balanced against the joyous exhilaration of flying across the sea, skimming the blue-green waves, feeling the wind in her face, and hearing the spray hissing off the rudders. The experience made every bit of stress worth it.

"But surely," the Orca asked in the patois of the Jupiter workers, "zey vould nay race allow so quick-quick."

Louella shook her head. The damned fish was really getting bothersome. Of course they wouldn't let a novice into the race. Not only did you need to be qualified for ocean racing, but you also had to prove you knew how to handle a highly automated Open 80 design.

The start of the Super was a watery riot. Nearly every boat in the North Sea had come to see the start, despite the chill November weather. They crowded so close to the course that Louella feared one of them might collide with the race boats. The race marshals' skimmers dashed back and forth to keep the starting lanes clear, but there were always a few sightseers who encroached. All it would take to ruin a couple millions-of-euro investment was for some damn weekend sailor's cruising crap boat to hit one of the racers.

Louella wished they'd had the foresight to arm the marshals' skimmers with cannon. Shooting the more egregious of the violators would make the rest more cautious. But she knew that would never happen. The weak-kneed officials would worry about the negative publicity and how it would diminish the tourist trade. She thought otherwise, thinking the crowds might enjoy a bit of blood sport to liven up a gray autumn day.

Georges waved at her from the deck of *Monte de Olimpo* as they danced back and forth near the starting line. He had bargained for one of the newer boats, about five years old. *Olimpo* had a shorter mast. That stub might give him greater stability, but at the sacrifice of total sail area, which equated to lower average speed. Georges had, as usual, been as conservative in his choice as he had in his heavy-duty shrouds. Speed was what would win the race, not security.

Randy was the odd man out. He was sailing *Io-Io*, an English boat as old as Louella's, but much broader and shallower. On a following wind, *Io-Io* would lift and surf the waves, which was an advantage, but she would do far worse on beating to windward. That would hurt him in the roaring forties, the lower latitudes where high and dangerously shifting winds roared across the open ocean. He, more than the others, would have to pay close attention to the weather charts and avoid the worst of the wind.

The rest of the boats varied only by degree from each other, differences that became more and more subtle with each generation of the boats as the architects converged on the ideal Open 80 design. Every race entry was an experiment in perfection. Everyone was also quite aware that any design failure would be punished with the loss of the race, the boat, or a life.

She looked past Georges's boat to see another of the team. The mast of Pascal's boat, *Mon Ami*, was as tall as her own, but on a Farr-designed hull. *Mon Ami* was narrower, longer, and sat higher in the water. Unlike *Mistrial*'s drake-back, his boat had an open transom.

Pascal made a sudden tack and switched to her windward side. She looked at the committee boat and estimated the amount of time it would take to clear it. She turned to port, forcing him upwind, and then straightened her line to aim directly at the committee boat.

"Starboard!" she yelled to let him know she demanded right-of-way.

There wasn't enough clearance for Pascal to go downwind without cutting off the Spanish entry, nor was there any way for him to pass her. He shouted something unintelligible and turned upwind, across the line and into a technical foul. Now he had to make a one-eighty around the committee's boat before he could cross again.

It hadn't been a nice thing to do, but the foul wouldn't hurt him much. The difference of a few minutes at the start was insignificant considering the eighty-odd days it would be before they reached the finish. Besides, she owed him one for getting her into that Jupiter race thing, not that she regretted the decision. Besides, she was still pissed because he had beat her to suggesting Alex's idea to Blacker.

The race's fleet stayed together along most of the coast, spreading out only after they cleared the English Channel. Louella engaged in a tacking duel with *Besta*, the American entry, most of the way.

After *Besta* and *Mistrial* cleared the channel, she turned south to hug the French coast, while *Besta* followed the rest into the Atlantic with a strategy to head south and west of the Canary Islands. That route would let them take advantage of the Azores high, a permanent clockwise flow in the North Atlantic winter.

The JBI team planned to split, with two of the boats shooting the gap between Africa and the Cape Verde islands. While Pascal and Georges went to the west with the fleet, she and Randy hoped to catch a boost from the weather blowing across Africa from the Indian Ocean. Both strategies had the objective of getting across the equator and through the doldrums as quickly as possible.

Once through the doldrums, most of the fleet would curve back east to gain whatever advantage they could of the South Atlantic high on the other side of the equator.

They'd know which was the better course by the time they reached the south twenty latitudes.

Louella's luck improved slightly. The storm appeared to be passing to the north, sending only some driving rain and bitter winds across the hull. Had she really talked to an Orca? It didn't seem possible, but the memory was so vivid. Why would an Orca hang around her anyway? Was it interested in her as a person, or simply looking for an easy meal?

She looked around, but there was nothing in sight but gray-blue water, a few clouds, and the EPIRB bobbing a few meters away from the hull.

Reaching the calm doldrums north of the equator presented no problems for Louella. She and Pascal had followed a western course that took advantage of the Azores high, a region of circulation that helped carry them farther south.

Three of the leading boats had caught the edge of an infant hurricane boiling out of Africa. *Jean Rachel*, her mainsail shredded, was limping toward the coast in hope of repairs so her skipper could continue the race, even though Louella doubted he would ever make up the lost time.

Another boat, *Aeguela*, one of the French entries, was also waiting for pickup, her rigging and sails too damaged to continue. Nobody had heard from *Europa Royale* since the storm passed. She hoped Eric, her skipper, was all right. Lack of communications was a bad sign.

Luckily, Louella and Pascal had run into a wind hole off the Canary Islands. At the time she had cursed loudly, as she limped along at less than ten knots. Even with full sails and with a two hundred square meter spinnaker flying, she'd felt as if she'd been barely moving. But then, if she'd been speedier, she'd have caught the storm as well.

She spent Christmas singing carols and stringing paper cutouts across the cabin. She popped the bottle of wine she'd been saving, ate *foie gras* from a can, and tossed the wine bottle with a note to the wind gods into the ocean.

The winds were so light that she'd slept a lot while letting the autopilot handle the navigation. At ten south, the weather download revealed a low forming behind her.

This time of year the warming climate was spinning small wind cells off the equator in quick succession. She steered westerly to get on a downwind edge of the low to drive her farther toward thirty degrees south, where she could pick up the trade winds.

Pascal was kilometers behind her, and ever-cautious Georges was farther east, but quite a bit north. She'd lost radio contact with Randy the night before, but figured that he was keeping at least a hundred klicks ahead of her, but keeping to the same course. They had gone over the race strategy together so many times that they each knew the course by heart.

Louella was constantly checking the inertial and the readouts from the GPS to make certain that she wasn't drifting off course. So far, the box from Jupiter was agreeing with everything the GPS said.

The loss of contact with Randy wasn't worrisome. In the relatively benign area of twenty degrees south there was little danger of him having serious problems. He'd probably just had an electrical failure, or maybe he just decided he needed a little solitude.

That was one of the drawbacks of modern communications—you were never really out of touch with friends and family, never beyond the reach of your corporate sponsors, never escaped the grasp of the news-hungry press. Just the same, every sailor, at one time or another regretted having that voracious, demanding, but sanity-saving link to civilization.

The low was good to her. From the reports she'd pulled another four hundred miles ahead of poor, cautious Georges. And, if he was to be believed, she still had a large lead on Pascal.

The race's first tragedy struck suddenly. *Robblier*, the Spanish entry skippered by Yves de Santo, was run down by a Liberian freighter shortly after New Year and sank immediately. The emergency beacon had beeped as soon as it hit the water, pinpointing the location and alerting the crew on the freighter to what had occurred. Despite an extensive search of the area by the freighter's crew and the South African navy, no trace of *Robblier* or Yves could be found.

The accident sent a chill of fear through Louella. She could not stay awake for the entire race. At some point in each day or night, she had to rest. That meant letting the boat sail under autopilot with the hope that the radar reflectors and lights would protect her from other ships at sea. But ships' crews did not always stand watch, nor did they pay much attention to small radar returns in the middle of the night ocean.

She hardly recalled what Yves looked like; was he the wiry one with all that hair, or the bald one with the big feet?

Once she reached thirty-five south latitude she'd be clear of the major shipping lanes and, in the roaring forties, she'd not encounter another vessel of any type. But then, considering the dangerous Southern Ocean, other ships would be less a concern than practically everything else.

Louella was startled by the Orca's flowered belly and bright orange back. He spoke in the singsong rhythm of southern India. "Forgive my informal attire," he apologized as his snout emerged from the sea. "Please, as I said before, I am curious as to why a woman would choose to die here."

Typical male question, she thought. Women were not unknown to the Super. Three of the early competitors had been Autissier, Chabaud, and Thompson, women who raced as well as, if not better than, the men. They proved that internal strength of character and gritty endurance mattered most in this ultimate test and not just brute strength, as everyone had contended before then.

The Southern Ocean tested all sailors to the limits of their ability. Despite the spread of civilization across the face of Earth, it remained the one place where the single-handed sailor was absolutely, totally alone. Was that why she'd come south of the fifty? Had accepting the risk been for no better reason than to prove herself worthy to test herself against a frigging giant planet? If so, it was a hell of a way to do it.

There were far easier ways to die.

Pascal thought that the new shroud seemed to be working well. *Ami* mounted the larger waves and plowed through the smaller ones. According to his charting program, they had just passed over the south fifty and entered the Southern Ocean.

The ocean was the same gray-blue expanse as before. There was no maker or other division. The only thing marking the occasion was a tick mark on mankind's artificial line across the bottom of the Earth.

Just the same, he was not deceived. Down in this region, sudden storms could arise in minutes, ice floes were possible, and there could even be rogue waves.

The cause of rogue waves was still a matter of conjecture. Some oceanographers contended that they built up as a harmonic synchronicity of wave action. Others favored the seismic theory; that they were caused by abrupt earthquake shifts in the seabed. Then there were the wind force advocates, the Atlantis nuts, and the calving iceberg group.

Pascal believed all of the theories and none of them. It all depended on the state of his inebriation at the time. Despite the theories, the huge waves were a serious threat to any boat that chanced to encounter one, and especially dangerous when the boat was a narrow splinter such as his.

Still, such monsters were far from his mind on this balmy day. He figured he was about four hundred kilometers away from the beacon, roughly a day's sail at the speed he was going. He hoped that the weather would remain benign.

A few hours later he cursed the wind gods. The skies had darkened and loosed a miserably cold drizzle that drenched everything. In addition, the wind was abruptly quartering from dead ahead to ninety degrees to his line of travel and varying in intensity.

The sudden shifts forced him to remain at the wheel, constantly adjusting *Ami*'s heading so as not to lose speed. The wind changes from heavy gusts to a complete loss of breeze was irritating, especially since the constant changes kept him from taking a break.

At one point he chanced a dash into the cabin for water and a snack, only to be rewarded when *Ami* abruptly broached. The deck tilted suddenly as she slid sideways, only to tilt abruptly in the other direction as *Ami* turned into the wind. The boom swung from side to side, the main sail luffed, and the boat rapidly lost momentum. He could hear the keep motors and shroud servos working to keep her upright as he fought the wheel. Even with their help it took him several minutes to get her back on course again, and longer still to regain his former speed.

And he'd dropped his snack.

"I assume you have no high hopes of rescue," the Orca mused as it munched on a squid that looked suspiciously like Jerome Blacker. "You know that you can't stay awake for much longer."

Stay awake? Hell, she couldn't even stay alive for much longer. She could feel herself weakening, her strength being leached away by the bitter cold, the angry wind, and the steady pounding of *Mistrial* by the towering waves.

It would have been nice to have had time to release the life raft before she had to scramble for her life. With that nifty little rig she'd be warm, dry, and have something to eat and drink as she waited for rescue, instead of sprawling on the slick, upside down bottom of Sergio's damn and prophetically named *Mistrial*.

Was this what her life's arc had become: to die alone and cold in the depths of the most remote spot on Earth? Had her whole life simply been preparation for this rather stupid end? Still, it hadn't been a bad life. She'd enjoyed the camaraderie of the sailing community, enjoyed being feted by the rich and famous, liked having her pick of handsome men, and, best of all, absolutely loved beating the pants off anyone who thought women had no place on a high-performance sailboat. It was a real pity that she wasn't going to be the first woman sailor on Jupiter, to show them what she could really do.

What would Scott do when she was gone? He was her executor, so she had no concerns about property or money. He'd get everything, of course. It was the least she could do for her partner. She just hoped he didn't take up with some airhead who didn't know a fairlead from a turnbuckle.

She regretted not being there to help Georges, Pascal, and Randy tie one on at the end of the race, nor seeing the joyous faces of their significant others as they returned safely to the port. Would that she could do likewise.

The Orca broached. "I must say, you are taking a rather long time to die, aren't you?"

She didn't respond.

She got the bad news about Phil and *Besta* when she was well south of the Cape of Good Hope, skirting the Atlantic high toward the bottom of her course, and approaching forty-five degrees, the closest she dared come to the Southern Ocean. Weather showed clear sailing for a couple of days, but down here that could change in an instant.

They'd lost communication with *Besta*, Phil Peter's boat, soon after she crossed forty-two, south. Then, after he hadn't been heard from for days, his EPIRB chirped momentarily. None of his other communication gear had signaled, which meant something catastrophic must have happened. Nothing else would silence so many backups at once.

A Brazilian navy training ship, the closest thing to him, was steaming toward his last known position, but there really wasn't much hope without some sort of radio contact. A raft is a tiny thing in a few million square kilometers of ocean, too tiny for even the sat-cams to image.

She cried over Phil's loss for a solid hour, remembering the good times they'd had, and how Phil had been laughing when they last parted.

Crying! Maybe the solitude was starting to get to her. She'd only been at sea for thirty-eight days, a little less than halfway through the race.

For a while she envied Randy and Ann, who had somehow managed to hook up in the doldrums—that is, if the radio chatter had been right. Neither would say whether the gossip was true or not, so speculation was rampant for at least a week. That's how boring were the early stages of the race.

These daily chats with the unseen skippers spread over hundreds of square kilometers helped dispel her loneliness, but those minutes of precious socialization were hardly enough to satisfy her. On those days when there wasn't enough sun to provide the surplus power she needed for the radio, the feeling grew worse. How would she ever face the rest of the trip? There were at least another forty-odd days to endure before she reached the finish line.

Was she going to be a total whimpering mess by the time she reached the finish? Gods, she had to pull herself together.

Of course, her runaway emotions could be from lack of sleep, a poor eating schedule, or the constant effort of keeping *Mistrial* on course. All those combined had to be taking a toll on her.

Then too, the lack of anything to look at save *Mistrial*'s deck and the undulating sea didn't stimulate the mind that much. It was not uncommon for single-hand skippers to have hallucinations. The other day she swore she watched trees going by on either side, as if she were back in Scott's SL500 on the cypress-lined roads of southern France, and not in the middle of the ocean.

What she needed was more excitement.

Excitement? The roaring forties gave her that and more. A front had brought gale-force winds of over fifty knots. The crests of the twenty-meter waves were blown off, and gave the sea a white cover of foam. The storm had turned the day gray and filled the air with pelting rain.

Louella had reefed down the main sail to half of its area, but left the foredeck staysail as it was. Even with reduced sail, *Mistrial* was still moving at a steady twenty-five knots, according to the GPS readout and the inertial. It was like riding a roller coaster, only wetter.

Rest had become impossible, since every pitch of *Mistrial* jerked Louella this way and that. The bunk was out of the question. There was no way she could risk a nap under these conditions.

One of the lead boats, *Chateau Legal de France*, was reporting that they were feeling the first effects of another bad storm coming from the northwest. Louella studied the Australian satellite images and decided that if she headed farther south she could pick up the edge winds and possibly gain on the leaders of the race.

Going south and closer to Antarctica this soon in the race was dangerous, especially in the face of a storm, even if it was slated to pass to your north side. Aside from the storm, the greater danger was encountering icebergs or, worse yet, growlers.

The Southern Ocean contained icebergs of all sizes. It was easy to avoid the larger ones, the giants that reared high above the water and spread dangerously much wider below; wide enough to snag a boat's keel. It would be the smaller bergs—growlers—that would be a constant concern. Growlers show little above the water's surface, but are massive enough to damage the hull of a boat moving at speed. A single sharp icy edge was all it would take to rip through *Mistrial*'s composite skin, tear through the Kevlar panels, and allow the ocean to fill the floatation chambers so that the boat sank ever lower into the sea.

Mistrial would never completely sink, so long as two of her four airtight compartments were sealed. Even with half of them flooded, she would sink only until the deck was awash. The masts would still project thirty-six meters into the air and allow her to continue sailing.

Flooded, *Mistrial* would move only at a snail's pace, a fraction of her normal speed, but perhaps that might be enough to make it to a place of rescue.

On the other hand, did her chances of hitting a growler offset the advantage she'd gain in time? Maybe, by going south of fifty degrees, she'd make up for those lazy, useless days she'd spent in the doldrums. She wondered if the possibility of gaining on the leader was worth the increased risk.

She wished Scott were here. He was the one who knew all about risk analysis, about weighing risk against benefits, about threats versus probability. All she had to go on was her gut, and it was telling her that the risk of a few icebergs, storms, heavy seas, and who knew what else, might be worth seeing the looks on the others' faces when she made up the time. The risk wasn't that great. She was a good sailor and had handled boats in rough weather before. She could handle this.

She turned *Mistrial* toward Antarctica.

The Orca had surfaced again and was back in his formal wear, all black and white. "Still here, I see. You must fear dying awfully much if you are fighting this hard. Wouldn't it be easier to just let go? It's inevitable, you know, and I'm getting hungry."

Louella wondered if he was right. Why was she struggling so much when the odds were clearly against her? Thirst, cold, weakness, lack of sleep, or the mechanical action of boat and wave could all do her in. All she had to do was close her eyes....

The storm-driven waves had been building for two days, and now towered over *Mistrial* like liquid mountains. Each was angry and powerful, a churning mass of frigid, gray-green water flecked with wind-driven foam. The succession of waves thundered along with all the force of nature, driven by winds unfettered by geographic features.

For the millionth time, Louella regretted her decision to come this far south so early in the circuit about Antarctica. The more southern route exposed her to the roughest seas in the Southern Ocean for longer than she had planned. Farther on, when she approached the Drake Passage between

South America and Antarctica, there was no choice. This route had been a calculated risk, she thought, and definitely a miscalculated one. Well, she'd made stupid decisions before, but none that looked to be as bad as this one. Even that hurricane she'd weathered with Pascal hadn't looked this bad. Of course, then they'd nine other crewmen to fight the sails.

The wind was northerly, which allowed her to cut across the waves at a thirty-degree angle. It was a difficult tack. On each climb up the face of an onrushing wave, *Mistrial* would heel dangerously to starboard just before cresting the wave. She could hear the whine of the ballast pumps as they filled the portside tanks to offset some of the heel. She heard the screams of the servos as they adjusted the mast to compensate for her attempts to correct. At times like this she felt *Mistrial* was alive, a living partner in the race, but even her help wasn't enough to make the ride comfortable. Louella had to keep the rudders hard over just to maintain her heading.

After a few hours the partnership of boat and sailor fell into a rhythm of maneuvers that kept *Mistrial* stable; falling away as she descended the backs of the waves and fighting to starboard as she climbed the next. But that rhythm deluded her into thinking that she had everything under control. It made her imagine that she could tame the seas.

Mistrial spun about as she fell off a breaking wave just as the wind slackened. The wheel twisted hard enough to rip from her numb hands as the boat turned broadside to the following wave. She spun the wheel to recover, but before she could get *Mistrial* turned back on course, the next wave drove her even more sideways. *Mistrial* fell into the next trough, wallowed, and let the next wave hit the mainsail with tons of water with such force that it knocked the boat onto her side.

Mistrial's computers struggled to compensate and right herself when she was hit with another wave. The next thing Louella knew, there was a cloud of stiff Kevlar-Tylvex and crap falling into the cockpit, water rushing over the port side, and a snake of stainless steel, probably one of the shroud cables, wrapped around her leg. The boom had fallen directly between the two wheels, and another long pole—the mast?—lay on top of it.

Mistrial continued to tip as she climbed another large wave. The deck became a forty-five degree slope, and the tilt was increasing toward the point where she could not right herself.

The servos were grinding, winch motors growling, and every alarm on the boat was demanding attention with their shrill cries.

She tried to pull her leg free of the line as she pushed aside the mass of stiff sail that covered her. She scrambled down the tilting deck, but something long and hard stopped her. Another part of the mast, probably. She had to get past it. She had to get to the release.

Louella fought to reach the emergency raft. She beat at the loose sail, pushing it aside as the slope increased. Freeing the raft would deploy both the NEARCOM satellite beacon and the BARAD long-range positioning unit, her two best hopes for rescue.

Only she didn't have time to reach the damn release. Gray-green water swirled around her waist as she struggled to free herself, but the tangle wouldn't give way. *Mistrial*'s deck became nearly vertical, and Louella found herself tangled in sail and lines. Even the swing keels' counterweights couldn't compensate for something this extreme.

Knife! Louella reached down, flipped her sling-back blade open, and hacked at the stiff Kevlar-Tylvex fabric. The embedded glass threads were tough, even for her diamond-edged blade. She twisted the knife and cut along the long dimension of the fabric, opened a long slit, and felt around for the handle of the release. If she didn't get free, the boat was going to roll on top of her.

Time ran out. She kicked herself toward the stern. It was too late to try to go in any other direction if she didn't want to be trapped under the boat. She'd have a better chance to swim out from the stern. The damn cable was still wrapped around her leg. She grabbed it and yanked. There seemed to be a lot of slack. She hauled again, took a loop in her hand, and kicked again as another wave hit and *Mistrial* finally turned turtle.

Louella struggled to reach the surface as *Mistrial* rolled gracefully over, the rudders and keels emerging like the fins of some international-orange sea monster. Her suit had inflated enough to maintain buoyancy, but it made her every move awkward. She fought the waves and her survival suit. She had to return to the stern where she could clamber onto the exposed hull. She grew frustrated as the wave action took the boat away whenever she was within a few strokes of reaching it.

There was only a limited amount of time that the suit could maintain her body heat. With so much contact with the frigid water, heat was draining away fast. She looked at the approaching wave, timed her next move, and, with a burst of swinging arms and a powerful kick of her one free leg, reached the stern.

The smooth hull was slippery under her as she crab crawled across it to reach the keel. That was the only place where she could brace herself. As another wave passed, she started to slide, and threw arms wide to create as much friction as possible and arrest her sidewise movement.

It seemed to take hours to reach the keel, but she was finally able to brace a boot against it. With great care she unwrapped the line from her leg, threw the end around the second keel, and held the temporary lifeline with her right hand in a death-defying grip. The position was uncomfortable, but the combination of cable and keel held her solidly on the wildly rolling boat.

Having four hundred square meters of sail and a few hundred kilos of hardware beneath the hull acted like a sea anchor and stabilized the upturned boat in the angry sea. Just the same, she had to hold tight to maintain her position. Back in the water she wouldn't stand a chance of survival, even with her cold-weather survival suit on.

For the first time she noticed that night was falling. "Just get me to morning," she whispered. "Just let me survive."

After the short night, dawn presented the same seascape as before— a vista of blue-gray water, a few clouds, and the occasional chunk of ice. The EPIRB was still bobbing ten meters away from the overturned boat, hopefully screaming for rescue. There was no sign of the other two buoys nor of the life raft. Even the automatic release hadn't worked. All of her fancy gear was probably trapped in that mess that had fallen across the cockpit and stern.

There was only a one-percent chance of the EPIRB failing, but it would just be her dumb luck to be a member of that demographic. She hoped not.

How long would she have to wait? Would it be hours or days? Her arm ached and one leg had gone to sleep. Very carefully, she adjusted her position so that her weight rested on the other side. She just wished that the cold-weather suit had a little more padding. Yeah, and a lot more insulation, too. A little food and water would be nice, as well. She'd rather have a little vodka. It wouldn't help anything, but it might make the waiting more bearable.

Damn, it was cold.

"Allo?" came the querulous cry once more.

Damn, couldn't that Orca keep quiet for a while longer? Louella tried to force her swollen eyes open. She'd almost fallen asleep. She felt so weak. She could no longer feel the line she'd been gripping. Her body felt as if it weighed a thousand tons. She tried to will herself awake. If she fell asleep she'd die for certain.

"Allo," the Orca said again, louder this time. She didn't respond. She was finally getting warm and able to forget her misery. Despite everything she could do, she felt herself sliding ever so slowly into a dark pit as the sounds of wind and wave disappeared.

She felt a tug on her leg, as if the Orca was trying to get a purchase and drag her from the boat the way it did a hapless sea lion. There was a second tug, her arm this time. She'd hoped he'd at least let her die before he ate her.

"Let me be, damn it," she croaked weakly through cracked and blistered lips.

Pascal was near exhaustion. He'd been catching fifteen-minute naps during this race to rescue la noir, the black woman, but nothing longer. Twice the wind and waves had knocked *Ami* over, the end of the boom dipping into the water, and once, at night and in a howling twenty-knot wind shift, when he'd had to clear the jib from the mast, he'd nearly slipped into the sea. Thankfully, his safety line had held for that critical few seconds it took for him to regain his footing.

The seas had calmed somewhat since then, but the waves were still monstrous. It was difficult to see beyond the trough he was in and, when *Ami* crested the waves, all he could see was other waves. It was hardly the environment for a successful search where the needle was tiny indeed, and the haystack a thousand square kilometers of nothing but frothing seascape.

On the good side, Louella's EPIRB was still sending out its mindless signal, broadcasting the GPS location to all and sundry. It would be a simple matter to get close to it, Pascal thought, but he didn't want to risk ramming Louella's *Mistrial*—if she was still afloat. It wouldn't be smart to put both of them in need of rescue.

Instead, he tried to maneuver *Ami* downwind of the EPIRB and slowly drift toward it. That meant going close-hauled with the wind beating the jib backward and the main hanging slack. He had no control in that situation, however *Ami* seemed to be stable as she slowly drifted EPIRB-ward.

Then, as he crested a wave, he spotted something orange in the water, like the belly of a very large Orca with a pair of bulb-tipped fins.

It was Louella's overturned boat.

On the next rise, he drew closer, and saw a body sprawled across the hull. Was she dead or alive? There was no indication of movement during the brief glance he'd gotten. Gods in heaven, three days exposed like that? How could she be anything but dead?

Time to make plans. How could he get to her? If by some miracle she was alive, most certainly she would be in no condition to swim across to his *Ami*, and it was sheer insanity for him to do likewise to bring her back. Could he lasso her, like one of her western cowboys? No, he had not the skill to cast a line with any accuracy.

Neither could he approach the wreck closely. He had no idea of what lay beneath the surface. It could be a tangle of lines and sails, all too willing to snag his keel or wrap around a rudder. Best to keep well clear of the wreck.

"Allo!" he shouted across the twenty meters now separating the two boats. "Allo!"

There was no response. Not a twitch, not a wave, not the slightest hint of life.

Ami was starting to drift past the wreck, so Pascal dropped sail, hoping that he could match drift with the wrecked *Mistrial*. For a moment, it looked as if they were continuing to drift apart and then, a moment later, together. Stable, he thought, and considered his options.

He could not leave the woman like this, even if it was only her dead body. Everyone deserved a proper funeral, a burial if at all possible. When he died, he wanted to be buried as far from the sea as possible, perhaps in the deserts of Arizona that he had once visited. Wouldn't she wish the same?

So, what to do? There seemed little option but to get across to the wreck and retrieve her.

A quick call to Georges brought less than the expected agreement. "No one will think less of you for letting her go. We're just glad we found out what happened."

"I understand," Pascal replied. "But I cannot do that, Georges. It would be a dishonor for me, for us, to not bring her back. I just want you here in case anything goes wrong."

There was a pause. "I'm about five hours away but I'm coming. Hey, I'll bet Blacker's worried how much the accident's going to cost him," Georges said.

"I care little for Monsieur Blacker's feelings in this matter," Pascal said. "He is not a sailor. He is not a racer. He would not understand."

"I do, Pascal. As will the rest. Do what you think best, and we'll all be behind you. See you in a bit."

Pascal dressed: Three layers of thermal underwear, cold weather gear, and a survival suit just might be enough to let him survive the frigid swim over to the wreck. Once there, he would wrap the body in plastic, tie a line to it, and haul it back to *Ami*. It sounded simple, but the confusion of lines, the pitching hull, and the restrictions the survival suit placed on his every movement made this a strenuous undertaking. Even with all the protection, he didn't want to be in the water any longer than necessary.

He clamped his facemask tight, checked to make sure the lines were secure, and waited for the boats to swing closer together.

There! He leapt from the transom into the freezing water, gasping as the cold penetrated the outer layer. Swinging his arms wildly, he paddled toward the wreck, and was pushed back twice by a wave. Finally, he reached the overturned boat, took hold of one swinging rudder, and dragged himself onto the ice-covered hull.

He grabbed hold of Louella's leg as he pulled himself to her side. It looked as if she'd donned her survival suit before *Mistrial* capsized. That had probably helped her survive for a while, although you could hardly call that a blessing in this weather.

"*Mon chere, c'est si mauvais, pauvre fille,*" he whispered as he pushed his dragline under her. Then he tied a bowline, the only knot he could make with his thick gloves, and tugged on it to make sure it would hold.

"Let me be, damn it," she croaked weakly and tried to push him away. "I don't want to answer any more of your fucking, stupid questions!"

Pascal was so startled he nearly fell overboard. "Louella! You are alive!" It was unbelievable. Alive, and after all this time! Georges would never believe it.

Her head lolled, and her body went slack.

Pascal knew there was no time to lose. Louella had to be in a fragile state after so much exposure. Would she survive the shock of being dragged through the freezing water? He had no alternative. Regardless of her condition, he had to get her to *Ami* quickly for whatever medical care he could give her. She needed fluids—maybe warm tea, hot soup, and pain killers? Yes, that would probably be the priorities once he got her safely to *Ami*.

Pascal made certain that her survival suit was completely sealed, threw the sheet of poly around her for extra flotation, and secured the line holding her to his own waist before cutting her from the thin safety cord.

Immediately, both of them slid off the icy deck and into the water. Pascal struggled to get out from under Louella. He had to keep from getting their lines tangled.

Once on the surface, he pulled himself and his burden hand-over-hand to *Ami*. When he reached her low transom, he tried to lift Louella from the water, but could not. She was too heavy, and he was too tired.

He hauled himself aboard and, teeth chattering, staggered to the rearmost winch, threw her line around it, and, with agonizing slowness, hand-cranked the winch to lift her aboard. Then he pushed, pulled, rolled, and otherwise manhandled her body into the cabin and out of the weather.

"Georges, she is alive!" he broadcast on the emergency channel as he gathered medical supplies. "She is alive!"

This had been a race within the race, and he had won. Despite everything the Southern Ocean had thrown at them, she was still alive!

L ouella sat in the pilot's seat and stared at Pascal as he stood at the wheel. It had been two days since she woke, and she still felt weak as a newborn kitten. She barely had enough energy to warm tea or fix soup. How many days had she been asleep, and how had Pascal managed to take care of her and the boat in that time?

The navigation equipment told her that Pascal was now pushing *Ami* through the worst part of the race, out of the Ross and into the Bellingshausen Sea. This was where the icebergs were thickest as the current and the wind pushed them toward the Drake Passage.

Thankfully the seas were calmer here; possibly because of the tremendous amount of slush that moderated the waves. Ever since the warming had accelerated abruptly in the late fifties, the Antarctic shelf was sending ever more ice into the sea. The imminent danger of the Ross shelf completely detaching itself and seriously raising the water levels around the world was a grave concern.

She knew her presence on the boat was making a serious dent in Pascal's food and, worse yet, his water. To save weight he carried only enough to last the ninety days afloat. With the output of the desalinization unit it could last him a hundred days. With two of them on board, and more than half the race over, there was enough for perhaps thirty more days, and that only if they were sparing in their intake.

Limiting water was a dangerous option. Once they got above the south thirties, they'd need more water to offset that lost to perspiration, an effect that would only grow more acute as they crossed the equator once again.

The bad news was that she had to hang off the stern to snag small chunks of berg they could melt to extend their water supply. The forward hold made a decent ice storage unit.

The good news was that there were lots of chunks.

Midday the wind had died to nothing more than a stiff breeze with only a mild chop to the water. Earlier in the day they had passed a jagged iceberg that reared at least one hundred meters above the water, and surely spread at least that far on either side. From the foredeck Louella marveled at the way the iceberg's colors changed from white through green to deep blue as its depth increased in the clear water. She watched for any underwater green ahead, which would indicate a submerged berg, but Pascal managed to keep the boat well clear.

The growlers were more numerous in this area. Small chunks of ice floated everywhere. There was a constant rattle of ice along the hull, every hard clunk reminding them of the danger of a torn hull, a stove side, and the danger of losing a rudder or keel.

Pascal was picking his way carefully through the icy maze. Sailing like this was tedious, tiring, and took far too much time. They were barely moving, about five knots, a snail's pace compared to the thirty-six she'd made in the fifties.

"Growler," Louella shouted as they approached a dangerous floe. *Mon Ami* immediately canted to port, and nearly sent her into the water.

"Watch what you're doing," she shouted. "I damn near spilled my tea!"

"Passengers, they should not be on deck," he scolded.

"I'll sit where I damn well please," she shot back. She'd be damned if she was going to let him boss her around just because he was skipper. Damn, why was he was going so slowly? "Take in the main," she yelled in aggravation. "You'll catch more air."

Pascal ignored her suggestion.

"You'll never catch up with the leaders this way. You're worse than Georges with his damn caution."

"*J'ai un plan,*" he replied confidently. "I have a plan."

"Right, and I have a million more euros of Blacker's money," she replied.

Once the race's leaders cleared the Drake, they'd shoot past the Falklands and up the coast of South America, taking advantage of the South Atlantic high as they raced through summer and into the early spring of the northern hemisphere.

"You'll never catch up," she growled. Or make up the time he'd lost coming to rescue her, she added, but only to herself.

As they were approaching the South Shetlands, they decided to have a big meal. Once in the passage where so many ships had perished, there would be little time for such diversions. The meeting of Atlantic and Pacific in the narrow passage, and all below sixty south, made for horrific sailing conditions.

"Perhaps we will have to break open the wine cellar," Pascal joked during his dreadful dinner of Jupiter crew kibble and slop. "I think I have a few bottles of good vintage."

By God, she wished he did. She could use a strong drink about now, even if it was only French wine instead of her favorite New Zealand red. "I'll settle for melted bergs," she replied, hoisting her cup.

The melt water wasn't enough to wash down the dry pellets that had so much nutritive value. Alex had sworn that a steady diet of the kibble would extend her life, but Louella suspected that it would only make it seem that way.

Shooting the Drake Passage was as hair-raising as any of the storms she'd seen in the south fifties; the conflicting currents created swirling, choppy seas, while the winds were blowing almost directly north, toward Cape Horn. Adding to their danger was a storm that drove bullets of rain horizontally across the boat.

Mon Ami was running at extreme heel, her deck tipped at nearly twenty degrees as she plowed at a steady forty-five knots, leaping from wave top to wave top with a steady pitching motion. She tried to study the set of the sails to see how he managed to get so much speed, but all she could see without sticking her head outside was the mainsail.

Louella braced herself in the cabin, checking the weather maps and satellite images, trying to figure out how they could best get clear of the storm. One option was to swing to the east, but that would mean beating back west later so that idea was immediately discarded.

"Keep her on a steady thirty degrees," she shouted, then looked up from the maps to make certain Pascal had heard her.

But there was no Pascal at the wheel.

"Son of a bitch!" she shouted as she clambered from the cabin to reach the wheel. His safety line was slack and detached from his harness. Had he been washed overboard? How the hell could she hope to find him in this weather? Could she even turn the boat around in this wind?

All this flashed through her mind in the seconds it took for her to stand and take control of the wheel. She was suddenly aware of the biting cold and her own vulnerability. She had neither harness nor gloves. She should have been wearing her survival gear, not the ill-fitting clothing she'd snagged from Pascal's bag.

"What are you doing?" Pascal exclaimed as he appeared at her side. "Get below!" He put one hand in the middle of her back and shoved as he regained control of the wheel. "At once!"

"I was afraid you'd been swept overboard," she shouted.

"*Et je t'aime,*" he replied with a laugh. "I love you, too."

"What the hell were you thinking, leaving the wheel like that?" she demanded. She was still seething over his apparent disappearance.

Pascal shrugged. "I had to walk the spinnaker around the mast."

"The freaking spinnaker!" Louella looked forward, and was shocked that he had put that much sail up. "You're a damned idiot," she said and glanced at the tachometer. Fifty-five knots! To get that kind of speed, she might have put up the big rag herself. Nevertheless, it took nerve to fly such a huge sail in these conditions. She doubted there were many who'd have the skills to handle it. Or who, like her and Pascal, would be foolish enough to do so.

"Just the same," he shrugged, "I appreciate that you were concerned for my safety."

"Crap, with you gone I had to take control of the boat. She sure wasn't going to sail herself, was she?"

"Perhaps not," he said and smiled. He had a nice smile, which was a pity. Leave it to her luck that the man who'd rescued her was the one guy in the entire freaking race who wouldn't be willing to jump her bones.

"A fucking pity," she laughed, and laughed again at his puzzled expression as she stumbled back into the cabin.

A few nights later, the storm was past, and *Ami* raced along under clear skies.

"I think we will not be able to fulfill our part of the contract," Pascal said regretfully. "We will not be first."

"Not the way you're sailing," she replied. "Hate to tell you this, friend, but you sail like an old woman. Tighten your line, damn it. If we keep moving at this prudent speed we'll run out of drinking water long before we reach France."

Pascal nodded. "*Oui*, we must put in for water or have someone bring it to us." He shrugged. "Of course, that would disqualify us."

"We'll never be first across the line anyhow, so taking on water would hardly hurt our chances."

Wait a minute! Had she just said "First?" She leaped up and began to dance around. "I've got it. Pascal, we don't have to win the race. And maybe we don't have to take on water."

Pascal glanced around, as if to see if there were something nearby with which he could restrain the mad woman dancing in the cockpit.

"Your napkin," she shouted. "The one Blacker signed. The contract his lawyers tried to replace with their two-hundred-page monstrosity."

Pascal shook his head. "It is the moon, perhaps, that has made you mad?"

"Listen to me, you damn snail eater. He wrote that we had to be the first boat across the line. He didn't say we had to win. He didn't say we had to have one skipper. He didn't say anything but that one of our boats had to be first."

"But we are so far behind," Pascal said.

Louella put one hand on the wheel and the other on her hip. "Listen, if the two of us work together we can tighten the sail more, hold a better line, and plot a strategy that will make up the time. If we work together we can sail a lot better than any single skipper working alone."

Pascal hesitated. "If I had more time to study the weather..." He screwed his face into a wicked grin. "We are three hundred kilometers behind the leader. Do you really think we can make that up in time?"

"We have twenty-six days of water left," she said. "That's one day over the record for this race. If we work our asses off we just might be able to pull it off."

Pascal paused to make a minor adjustment of the wheel, squinted into the distance, and then, very carefully, took his hand away. "Could you take over while I study the charts? There is much we have to do."

Louella took the wheel in both hands and moved *Ami* slightly closer to the wind. She looked at the first stars of the evening, smelled the clean ocean scent, felt the wind in her hair, and tasted the salt spray on her lips. This was what she lived for, what she almost died for: the exhilaration of wind and water, of mastering the most magnificent machines crafted by man. This was sailing. This was her life.

All doubt had left her mind, there was no longer any fear of failure. "We're going to do it," she shouted defiantly to the heavens as the motorized winches took in the boom and *Ami* heeled toward Jupiter.

Chapter Two—Jupiter

Away from the station the wind was free. Out there, in the vastness that was Jupiter's atmosphere, the wind hummed sweetly, bragging of its freedom to move. But when it encountered the sharp prow of the station it screamed as if angered by this barrier, this obstacle to its travels.

Jake Sands listened to the voice of the wind through the thick plating of the E-2 station. He could sense the power of the five-hundred-knot wind as it was split on either side by the station's sharp prow. He could feel the raw force of the fierce wind that, were the station to become separated from the tether that held it to the synchronous station far overhead, would toss it—and all of its fragile contents—as if it were no more than a child's beach ball. Jake listened as the wind spoke to him, listened to the voice of Jupiter.

"You've got that look again," Marie said. She was nursing a precious cup of coffee in her hands, sipping the liquid gold slowly, as if it were the nectar of the gods.

Jake snapped the cap on his own cup of tea, the only drink he could afford. He carefully measured a spoonful of sweetener into the dark brown brew, and added a dollop of ersatz cream to lighten it. That done, he sat back and sipped it slowly, so as not to burn his tongue.

"I heard weather reporting a storm heading this way," Marie continued. "Figured that you'd be heading out, but wasn't sure until I saw your face."

"Am I that transparent?" Jake grinned as he took another sip. "And here I thought I was being old stone face."

Marie grimaced. "Don't kid around, Jake. Mining these storms is dangerous business. You should leave it to the kids."

Jake snorted. "I'm a lot better than most of them. Hell, by the time I was their age, I'd already worked the wind all the way around Jupiter three times. Isn't a thing me and *Pumpkin* can't do better than them; not a single damn thing!" He took another sip. "Besides, you know how much we need to mine the storms."

Marie didn't respond immediately. Everyone who worked in the stations knew how expensive it was to bring goods, especially raw materials, down the elevator from geo-synch. Every gram they could mine was one less they had to bring down. It was also one gram less dependence on JBI's mining operations on Europa, Io, and Callisto.

Jake leaned forward. "Now, don't get upset again, Marie. You know I wouldn't do this if I didn't have to. Shoot, one day I'll get lucky and find a big one. Then I'll pay off my debts and get shy of Jupiter faster than the wind could carry me. Take you with me, I will. You can bet on it."

"You keep saying that," Marie replied sadly. "But every time you get a little ahead, you find some change you want to make on that ship of yours. Tell me, have you made any progress on repaying the loan in the last few years? Or have you kept rolling over the loan to pay for the modifications?"

Jake hesitated. "I'll admit that *Pumpkin* needs quite a bit of upkeep." Then he grinned widely. "But then, she's not a lot different from any other woman!"

Marie slammed her soft plastic cup down, which lacked the effect she wanted, and slopped the expensive coffee over the side besides. "Don't make a joke about it, Jake! I nearly have a heart attack every time you say you're going into one of these storms. I never know if you are going to come back." She clenched her hands before her. "I don't think I can take it much longer."

Jake took her hands in his own. "Listen honey, *Pumpkin*'s a good ship, and I know what I'm doing. There's no need for you to worry. Shoot, there isn't a storm the old man can throw at us that *Pumpkin* and me can't beat. Haven't I always come back to you?" He squeezed her hands when she nodded. "And I always will come back, Marie. To you, darling. To you! You've got to believe that!"

Marie sniffed and pulled her hands free. "The problem is, Jake, that I don't think I can really and truly believe that any more. I worry about you. I'm always afraid that something will happen, that I will lose you. I'm sorry, but I just can't help the way I feel."

"Man's got to go where he can make some money," Jake said. "Storm's the only way *Pumpkin* and me can get the high payoffs. Hey, don't I make enough to live on from what I find?"

"You could make a lot more if you'd run shipments or take passengers. You could even get a good station job with JBI."

Jake paused, but only for a second. "JBI won't give an independent like me any shipping contracts, not while they have their own huge fleet of transports. And you know as well as I that *Pumpkin* isn't set up to handle passengers. Shoot, there's hardly enough room for me and crew!"

"You could let the bank have *Pumpkin* and take a position on one of JBI's stations," she said quickly, not willing to concede.

"Huh, I'd sooner cut off my arm than let them turn me into one of their popinjays. Besides, they don't like us old guys—want them young and pliant, they do. Shoot, can you picture me in one of them fancy uniforms, strutting around like I was somebody?"

"You'd look great in JBI blues." Marie shot back. "And you aren't that old; you're only forty-five!"

"Yeah, forty-five and nearly broke. Which is why, with the payment on *Pumpkin* due next week, I've got to go after this storm. Now come on, give me a kiss for luck and let me go. I've got to check on that lazy crewman of mine."

Rams, Jake's sole crew member, was talking to the refit boss when Jake arrived at the shipyard bay. Both of them were wearing their pressure suits, which meant that they had either just come back in or were preparing to go out.

"Costing me time and money to let you two jawbone all day," he grumbled as he approached them. "How's the inspection going?"

Rams snapped to attention as if he were some damn JBI staffer. No matter how much Jake protested, Rams would not stop this silly routine. Jake half-expected him to salute.

"Checks t'damn 'all right!" Rams chimed in a singsong Jupe accent so thick that you could cut it with a laser torch.

The boss nodded agreement and shoved the clipboard into Jake's hands. "Signed and certified by your crew, Cap'n. Double checked every item m'self, I did."

Jake scanned the sheet. All the checklist items were neatly marked off. Apparently everything he'd requested had been done, or at least Rams had signed that they had. The evening before he'd personally inspected the internal systems work for himself, just to be absolutely certain it had been done correctly. "I'd like to put my own eyeballs on the deck fittings," he remarked, and pointed to three items in the middle of the list. "Wait here until I suit up."

The boss blustered. "Look here, I have other things that…"

Jake turned and glared at him. "If I remember my rights, a ship's not certified until her Captain signs off, no matter how many crewmen think she might be." He glared at Rams and the boss, defying them to contradict him. When neither replied, Jake stamped to the fitting room.

*P*umpkin floated high in her berth. Her keel was fully retracted, leaving only the enormous bulb of her counterweight hanging beneath the smoothly rounded hull. Jake noted the deep scars on the surface of the bulb, each one a mark from the storms they'd weathered over the years. Similar scars on the nose of the ship itself had been erased as part of the refit. Jake nodded when the boss pointed out the fresh welds where the scars had been.

The boss wore one of the new suits, lightweight and flexible, in stark contrast to Jake's bulky, heavy, second-hand suit.

"You did a good job, there," Jake admitted, and pointed at the ladder ahead of them. "Now, let's take a look at the topside fittings."

Even at this altitude, still within Jupiter's atmosphere, the effective gravity was just a bit more than two gees. Adding that to the weight of the heavy pressure suit made climbing the ladder a major undertaking, even for someone in good shape. Jake, long accustomed to working under Jupiter's heavy gravity, didn't mind. Besides, the climb gave him an opportunity to inspect the hull's sides.

The shiny new deck fittings stood out from the rest of the deck gear. Jake bent over one of the new blocks and checked to make certain that it had been fastened per spec. He carefully read the serial number off the block and checked it against his own manifest to be certain that the numbers matched. He'd ordered those blocks from the best fabricators in high orbit, and was damn sure that these shipwrights weren't going to foist some substitute off on him.

"Look here," he said as he pointed at the mains'l shroud, the covering that protected the sails until they were deployed. "That looks like a cold weld—see how rough it is! I want that corrected before we leave. Smooth it out and show me the deep scans afterwards!" Nobody was going to abuse *Pumpkin* while he was around!

"You don't need scans of that weld. It isn't load bearing," the boss protested. "That weld's just decorative—to make the installation look smoother."

"It might be," Jake bit out. "But if a worker gets sloppy on something trivial, then he's probably sloppy where it matters. If I were you, I'd fire the slob who did this," he advised.

E arly the next morning, after another detailed inspection of the shroud, Jake made himself comfortable in the captain's chair. The tell-tales on the status board all read green.

"Rams, is everything in order down below?" he shouted down the short corridor to the forecastle.

"Aye, Cap'n," Rams responded. "I even tied down the fine china and put away your best crystal."

"Very funny," Jake replied dryly. Four plastic cups and two bowls constituted their entire dinnerware.

He turned to the console and toggled the intercom. "*Pumpkin* is ready to go, Echo Two. Can you grant me clearance?"

"*Pumpkin*, this is Echo-2 control. Ready to accept the report, Jake?" It was Marie's voice. He'd forgotten that this was her shift.

"Sure, Marie," he responded laconically. He'd already gotten all of the weather information he needed before boarding, so this last bit of official folderol was pretty irrelevant.

"Weather reports the wind at one-twenty meters per second and falling," Marie recited in a sing-song rhythm. "The storm's about one hundred and twenty thousand kilometers away and moving south by southeast at about two hundred meters per second. Weather predicts that the center will pass about eighteen thousand kilometers to the north of the station."

"Excellent. That will give me plenty of time to get into position to make at least a double pass as it goes by."

Marie hesitated, and then resumed her report. "Laminar wind flow of the Kilo Kilo and Lima Lima bands will be somewhat disrupted by the storm, but weather predicts no lasting effects beyond the double Kay bands. We do not advise—"

"You don't have to say it," Jake interrupted.

"We do not advise the northerly course you have filed," Marie continued as if she hadn't heard. "Please record your acknowledgment that you will not hold the station responsible for loss or damage as a consequence of your sail plan. Do you so acknowledge?" There was a barely concealed crack in her voice, as if she were hoping that he would not do so.

"I understand and acknowledge," Jake said dryly, and then added; "Don't worry, Marie. I'll be all right. Done this plenty of times. Don't worry."

"I have recorded your acknowledgment," Marie continued in her official voice. "You are cleared to depart."

The huge clamshell hatches behind *Pumpkin* groaned ponderously open, exposing the ship to the whipping winds that howled around the station. *Pumpkin* bobbed and strained at the clamps that held her fast to the berth as the wind sucked at her stern.

"*Pumpkin* ready to depart," Jake said as the little ship strained toward the opened hatch. "Goodbye, Marie."

"Fair winds and good passage, Cap'n." she replied with the standard sign off, and then added in a rush. "Watch yourself, Jake. Come back to me."

With those words, she released the station's clamps. Jake could hear them clang through the pressure hull as they released. Now, the only thing holding *Pumpkin* to the station was her own tie-downs.

"Ready for release," he warned Rams as he tightened his own seat belt another notch. As soon as Rams acknowledged that he was secure, Jake hit the release button. The retraction motor in the bow whined as it pulled the docking lines aboard.

Pumpkin drifted quickly backward. The closer she came to the opening, the faster she moved. In a matter of seconds, the ship had accelerated so that the walls of the station whipped past in a blur.

Then *Pumpkin* was free. She slipped into the air stream and was tossed backward, rocking and tumbling until her speed equaled that of the surrounding wind. The radar image of the station disappeared in the white hash from Jupiter's constant electrical activity.

"I'm setting our course for sixty-five degrees," Jake shouted over the rattle of the gear as Rams lowered the keel to stabilize them. "I figure that we've got three days to get ourselves into position."

After Jake checked Rams's work to make certain that the keel had been set properly, he activated the winch that pulled the mainsail out of the shroud and into the wind. The sail luffed for a moment until Jake forced *Pumpkin*'s nose into the wind and tightened the main sheet. The ship heeled dramatically as the breeze caught and filled the sail, tilting them to a precipitous thirty-degree angle. As the ship leveled, she drove forward, cutting across the prevailing wind at a steep angle.

A few minutes later, after he was satisfied with the set of the main, Jake deployed the small foresail and winched her as tight as she'd go, forcing the wind through the venturi formed by the tight angle between main and jib. With the additional sail area unfurled, *Pumpkin* increased her speed. On this course, he needed to run as close to the wind as possible. *Pumpkin* ran smooth and true, as if she was grateful to be finally free.

"The barrier layer feels a mite rough today," Jake said casually as he fought the wheel. The little craft was being tossed about in the turbulence at the boundary between the dense atmosphere beneath them and the relatively light air above them. There was continual turbulence between the layers, causing them to mix and tumble and make the boundary layer resemble the rolling, tempestuous seas of Earth.

*P*umpkin raced toward the oncoming storm with hardly a hairsbreadth deviation from Jake's carefully plotted course. When the inertial navigation system indicated that they were in position, Jake hauled the jib back, turned *Pumpkin* head to wind, and let the main fly free. *Pumpkin* rocked precipitously for a moment.

"This heave-to trick of yours always scares me," Rams said nervously as *Pumpkin* began swinging wildly.

Jake laughed as the ship's oscillations damped with each swing. "Don't worry, Rams. Done this lots of times. She'll run slow into the wind this way. All we have to do now is wait for the storm to come to us. Keep an eye on the manometer. Soon's it starts to fall we'll need to make ready." That last instruction was just to give Rams something to concentrate on while they waited. He'd set the automatics to alert them long before the pressure gauge showed any sign of movement of the storm's approach.

He was surprised at Rams's reaction. In their few years together, he'd taught Rams how to balance keel and ballast and how to adjust the buoyancy of the ship. He told him the secrets of playing the winds of

Jupiter's storms to capture its treasures. He had tried to teach Rams to love the wild winds of Jupiter's wine-red seas. He wondered if his efforts had been wasted.

"I wish we could see what is happening out there," Rams said wistfully.

"Sure, and I wish that I had a ship that was ten times the size of tiny *Pumpkin*, but wishes won't make it so," Jake said. "It's black as pitch outside." He didn't need to add that the radar was useless; there was so much electrical energy around Jupiter that returns from more than a few tens of meters away were pure hash, impossible to decipher.

The echophones was more useful, although not in any way the designers of those systems intended. Jake had learned over the years that he could use the echophones to listen to the approaching storms. He'd learned that Jupiter's winds had their own voice.

Sometimes the winds sang soft songs of the vast distances they travelled as they swept the vast planet, as if they were boasting of the millions of kilometers that had passed beneath their fleet feet. When *Pumpkin* was moving, he felt that the winds sang a slow song, one of gentle passages across the vast uncharted distances, of ports hundreds of thousands of miles apart, of long voyages where only the wind and the ship mattered.

When a storm approached, the wind whispered hymns of power and majesty. There was a deepening to Jupiter's eolian voice, a deep basso that seemed to say, "I am coming. I am coming to duel with you, pitiful little humans. I can crush your tiny craft, rip your very atoms apart, and spread the pieces over a billion square kilometers. I could kill you in an instant!"

Jake knew that he and *Pumpkin* could best any storm. He'd acquired the skills needed to ride the updrafts and beat to weather in a hundred voyages. The ship might just be a tiny bulb of metal and plastic, but—unlike the storms—he could use his knowledge and skills to show *Pumpkin* how to ride the pressure waves and dance on the cyclonic winds.

"Come ahead," Jake whispered to himself as he listened to the storm's challenge. "Come and get me if you dare!"

Alarms shrilled within the cabin. Jake was off the bunk and onto his feet instantly. All traces of sleep vanished as he tightened his truss and worked his way back to the helm. Jake's heart was pounding furiously. He could feel the rush of adrenaline, the nervous sinking in his stomach, the tingling of his entire body as the excitement of the storm's arrival washed through him. This was what he lived for, the challenge of beating Jupiter's furious storms, of the anticipation of great wealth that they would find, of the excitement of the moment. Nothing else equaled it. He was grinning broadly by the time he reached the helm.

Rams was already fighting the sails and the wheel. Jake noted that Rams had already lowered the keel to maximum length. Good. The blinking red light on the console told him that Rams had also started pumping ballast to give *Pumpkin* some more weight.

Their kilometer-long diamond fiber keel contained pipes and pumps to pull denser material into the keel to balance the force of the wind on the sail. Since it was always easier to lose ballast than bring more aboard it was wise to enter the storm with a full load. According to the indicators, it wouldn't take long for the ballast pumps to finish.

"You're showing her too much of our beam," Jake shouted as *Pumpkin* heeled to port. "Let me take the helm!"

Jake slid into the seat and twisted the wheel. As *Pumpkin* turned, he quickly adjusted the main, pulling it in as much as possible. He then tightened the jib. *Pumpkin* responded to the adjustments and slewed into her new heading, cutting into the storm and accelerating quickly.

Rams lowered the gain on the radar in preparation for their mining run. If the storm was carrying anything from down below, it would show up on the short range radar display far brighter than the static.

Jake jibbed the ship from side to side, favoring always the side of greatest pressure and bearing into the teeth of the storm. *Pumpkin*'s relative speed increased with each maneuver as Jake worked their way to the center of the raging arms that guarded the periphery of the storm.

"Down on Earth they'd call this a million-year storm!" Jake shouted as *Pumpkin* rocked ahead. "Just a tiny little turbulence out here, eh?" He laughed as *Pumpkin* tilted from a sudden gust.

"I'd rather not be on Earth in a storm like this," Rams admitted. "Too much open down there, I'm told. No protection against the wind at all." He shivered visibly. Like most native Jovians, he was most comfortable in the close confines of ship and station.

Jake laughed. "Grew up down on Earth. Didn't come to work the old man until I was in my teens. You'd like Earth, Rams. Lots of pretty girls, plenty of fresh food, and air that doesn't smell like damned ammonia all the time."

"Nothing wrong with our food," Rams protested. "Besides, what good are pretty girls to me? I am already married."

Jake grunted. He'd hardly call Rams's arrangement with a woman back on Earth a marriage. As far as he knew, Rams had only seen his bride in photos, and never touched or spoken to her. Such were the ways of his people. He wondered wryly how they would ever have children; would Rams mail her a frozen specimen?

Pumpkin heeled suddenly as another gust hit. Instead of steady westerlies, the fierce winds were now blowing the ship directly south. One look at the new heading told Jake that the storm was to their north, and passing them by. He had misjudged the track and sent them too far below the storm's path.

Jake quickly released the wheel and spun *Pumpkin* about. He let the jib balloon wide and let the main swing to the opposite side. For a moment he could picture the titanium-strengthened sails whipping like soft silk in the intense breeze as they flew across the deck and then filled with the wind that was now to their back. Pumpkin tipped forward as the sails filled.

The wind drove the ship downward for a few seconds until *Pumpkin* found her balance, steadied, then accelerated as she raced northward along the face of the storm. As they passed closer to the center of the turbulence, the pressure decreased, and they dropped lower and lower.

"Have to stay clear," Jake said as a caution to Rams, but mostly as a reminder to himself. "If we fall into the low pressure at the center, we'll lose to much altitude. Be a bitch to fight our way back." He said it calmly, knowing full well that if they fell too far into the low-pressure center they could die. Without the supporting P12 layer, they would fall forever until Jupiter crushed the ship as if she were made of foil.

But the risks of falling were worth taking. Close to the center was where the strongest updrafts could be found. Nearest the center were the vertical winds that brought the riches of the deep up to his level.

Metallic, ice, and stony meteorites dropped through Jupiter's atmosphere until they reached a point where their density equaled their surroundings. At that point they floated, a sargasso of astronomical history. Any storm whose center reached down to that level wrenched them upward and tossed them about. And, occasionally, the storm brought them up to where Jake could mine them.

There was a sound like raindrops on a metal roof. "That's gravel hitting us!" Rams exclaimed excitedly. "Should I drag the scoop?"

"Wait a bit," Jake replied with one eye on the radar. He didn't want to waste his time on this early, tiny dross. Further along, closer to the storm's mouth, the gravel would be larger, the riches would be more plentiful. He made a slight adjustment to turn *Pumpkin* more toward the center, and felt her drop noticeably.

The clatter of the gravel's impact grew louder. A field of bright sparks glowed in the display; a decent radar return that meant that they were at least half a meter across. The rocks were prime size!

"Hit it!" Jake shouted, and jinked the ship sideways as Rams kicked the release on the scoop. *Pumpkin* bucked as the wind hit the deployed netting. Jake fought to keep her on course, fought to keep her from falling into the center as he steered the sharp division between safety and certain death.

The stream of gravel didn't seem to have an end. There was a continuous pounding on the hull. In a matter of moments, their net was loaded to capacity, and began to drag on the ship, slowing her speed.

Rams reeled the scoop's harvest into the hold as Jake fought to work *Pumpkin* outward and upward. He had to make use of the updrafts, skipping from one to the next, while avoiding the even more fierce downdrafts.

The proximity alarm sounded a shrill alarm. Jake glanced at the display and saw an enormous radar return. It was so large that it had to be nearly three meters across!

Jake spun *Pumpkin*'s wheel, hoping to keep the fleeting phantasm in view. But the huge nugget disappeared from the display, leaving only the occasional sparks from gravel. "Did you see that," he asked. "Did you see that big mother?"

"See what?" Rams said in puzzlement, looking up from the scoop controls. Apparently he had not been distracted from pulling the scoop aboard when the alarm sounded.

"We almost hit a big rock. From the way it reflected the radar it had to be pure metal, I'll bet—a solid nickel iron meteorite! Damn, if we'd caught that one it would have paid off a big hunk of *Pumpkin*'s debt."

"Next time, for sure," Rams said, repeating the standard prayer of the storm miners. He really didn't sound as if he believed Jake at all. "But for now, let's get out of here. I want to see what we've caught this time."

Jake turned *Pumpkin* outward, away from the storm's center, away from the tantalizing riches that he had just missed. The winds dropped, and *Pumpkin* rocked along on a course to the nearest station.

Jake was upset. Not only had they barely made a profit from their catch from the storm, but, worst of all, none of the other miners believed him about the huge nugget he'd seen.

"Probably another miner's craft," one of them said. "Better get your recognition coder checked, Jake—else you might think a station's one of them there Jovian whales!" The room had erupted in gales of laughter at that.

Their amusement was his own fault, he thought miserably, reflecting on the fact that he had exaggerated slightly on a few occasions in the past. He rose, took a bottle by the neck, and stepped toward the joker. "You calling me a liar, Brian?" he muttered.

"I think it is time that we found ourselves something to eat," Rams said loudly as he put himself between the two miners. "Captain, let us go."

"You'll see," Jake shouted, as Rams steered him away from his glowering adversary. "I'll come back with the biggest damn hunk of rock anybody's ever seen down here. Just you wait!"

"What shall we have to eat this evening," Rams asked once they were away.

"Steak and gravy," Jake replied grimly. "Best meal we can afford on what we made. Yes, station steak and gravy would be just the thing."

You the captain who brought that little ketch in last night?" a harried-looking man demanded as he approached their table. Jake looked up from his plate of station steak and gravy —the cafeteria's nightly special. A single glance took in the man's expensive clothing, his neat haircut, and the pair of new, unblemished boots he wore.

"*Pumpkin*'s a barque, not a ketch," Jake said slowly, indicating by tone that he thought the man's education sadly lacking. "And who the hell are you?"

"Pavel Grobbka," the man introduced himself. He sounded as if he had other things on his mind. "Listen, I need someone to run me back to station E-2. I understand that's your home port."

Jake scooped another big spoonful of beans and chewed them slowly, as if they were pieces of the real steak he couldn't afford. He swallowed his too-dry beans, and then took a drink of cheap beer to wash them down. "I think you've got me confused with the JBI liner desk. They can sell you a ticket on the next packet ship out of here."

"I can't wait until next week," Grobbka protested. "I have to get back to E-2 as quickly as possible. Listen, I'll pay if you'll take me right away."

"Me and Rams here figured to spend a day or two resting up," Jake drawled. "Might sail back the day after tomorrow."

Pavel placed his hands on the table to bring his face level with Jake's. "Tomorrow or the next day is too late, captain! I really need to leave immediately! Tell me what you want to take me as a passenger, and I'll pay it."

Jake pushed some beans and rice together with his spoon, moving them into a tiny puddle of thin pseudo-gravy. "Money's not the point. Like I said, *Pumpkin*'s not outfitted for passengers and, just in case you didn't hear me the first time, I'm in no hurry to leave. Need my rest, you know."

Pavel slumped into the extra chair and put his head in his hands. "But you've the only ship available. All the rest either have to be refitted before they can sail, or are already cleared for someplace else. You've got to take me!"

Jake slowly savored a mouthful of the highly spiced rice that was mixed with his beans. "Life's too short to be rushing about. What's so all-fired important that you can't wait another week?"

"I have to get up the elevator to my wife," Grobbka explained. "I was supposed to be back last week, but was delayed by... well, no reason to go into that." He stopped for a moment and then said, almost too low to be heard; "I guess I'll miss the delivery."

Jake's ears perked up. "Delivery? What, some big deal cargo coming in that you have to handle?"

The man smiled sadly, "In a manner of speaking. It's my first child. My wife's up in geosynch right now, waiting for her time. I... I was supposed to be with her."

Jake wiped his mouth and finished the last of the beer. "C'mon, Rams, we got to empty out the equipment hold."

Rams choked on his beans. "Why? You told me to pack all the spare gear in there just this morning."

Jake stood up. "Well, things change. Come on. We can't expect our new crewman here to sleep on that pile of crap, can we?"

"Crewman?" Grobbka and Rams exclaimed.

"Well, sure," Jake smiled. "I said that *Pumpkin* don't carry passengers, and she doesn't. Crew's another matter entirely." He looked at their startled expressions. "Well, come on! We got a delivery schedule to meet!"

There was a celebration in progress at the Rat's Nest when Jake and Rams wandered in. Surprise of surprises was that Marie seemed to be in the middle of the festivities.

"I passed my finals!" she shouted as she threw her arms around Jake and planted a huge kiss on his lips. "God, I missed you!" she added when they came up for air. "I was so afraid."

"Didn't I promise you that I'd be back," Jake replied. "And I missed you, too," he added.

Marie danced away and pulled him into the circle of fellow celebrants —all station people, Jake noted.

"Great news, isn't it?" remarked a tall black man. "Master Marie Monarimi. Has a certain ring to it."

"She'll have a station of her own within a month or two, you can count on it," said another—Jake thought his name was Toma, a guy who shared watches with her.

Marie sneered. "Not likely. I'm tenth on the list, which puts my station a year or more away."

Toma shook his head. "I heard that fabrication is launching two new stations a year, Marie. You might move up that list faster than you think."

"Yeah," the black man said. "I think a few of the old hands are ready to rotate back to Earth. Cross your fingers for luck!"

Jake wondered if it were true. Was it possible that Marie would be leaving E-2 to manage one of the floating stations that circled Jupiter with the winds?

"Y ou'll come with me, won't you?" Marie said, when they reached the privacy of her quarters. "I can support the both of us on a Master's salary. You wouldn't have to mine the storms any more. You wouldn't have to put yourself at risk so much."

"Still have to make the payments on *Pumpkin*," he said slowly, as if pointing out the obvious. "No sense letting the ship go when I put so much into her."

"You could get a station job—I could authorize that."

Jake shook his head. "Don't know much about station tending. Besides, what would happen to *Pumpkin* if I had some kind of job?"

"Well, for starters, you could stop thinking about that damned ship of yours and start thinking about us for a change. Jake, I want you with me when I get my station. I need you with me when I go."

"*Pumpkin* has to be moored at one of the tethered stations, you know that," Jake continued, oblivious to her protests. "Can't mine the storms without adequate weather data, and the tethered stations are the only place I can do that."

"Forget mining the fucking storms!" Marie screamed. "You won't have to do that once I start drawing a Master's pay. You won't have to sail that stupid barque of yours. You won't have to do anything but be there for me!"

Jake stood up abruptly. "So you want me to be a damn lap dog? I've always paid my own way, and always will. Spend your Master's pay to buy a cat or something if you want a pet. I'll have no part of it!" With that, he stomped out and made his way to where *Pumpkin* was berthed.

The ship's bunk was especially cold, hard, and lonely that night.

R ams woke him the next morning. "I saw another captain having breakfast with Master Marie in the dock cafeteria," he reported. "Did you two have an argument again?"

"Keep your nose out of other people's business," Jake bit back as he rubbed sleep from his eyes. "Marie's a grown woman. She can eat with whoever she wants."

Rams looked thoughtful. "Ah, I see. You did have an argument, didn't you?"

"I think you need to repack the sails, Rams. Wouldn't be surprised if it took you all day to do that."

Rams was taken aback. "You will not be helping me." It was a statement of fact, not a question.

"No, I think I need a bit of breakfast myself. Guess I'll wander over to the cafeteria and see what they have that might interest me."

Rams smiled as he pulled on his work gloves.

Marie was sitting in a corner of the cafeteria when Jake arrived. She was freshly showered and wore a clean uniform that was in stark contrast to Jake's rumpled bearing. There was a half-empty cup of tea before her. His competition was nowhere in sight.

Jake sat down. "Good morning."

Marie stared at him. "Do you think that you can just walk in here and act as if nothing happened last night?"

"Missed you terrible," Jake said, and gently stroked her cheek with the back of his fingers. "Maybe we both need to forget about the future for a little bit and let things settle themselves out."

Marie pulled away. "No, that's what we do every damn time! I can't just let things drift any more, Jake. I want to know what sort of future we are going to have. I want to feel confident about what we can build together, and that means that I can depend on you next week, next month, next year."

"Sorry you feel that way," Jake said slowly. "After you been down here in the old man as long as I have, you'll realize how little control we really have over the future. Storm could blow that station of yours off of its track so's you could never find your way back. Ships go out and get lost, broken, destroyed by a storm, or maybe have some other mischance. You plan too far in advance and you're bound to be disappointed. Future's a chance happening here on Jupiter, not something you can depend on."

Marie chewed her lip. "I can't live that way, Jake. I need someone I can depend on. I want somebody stable—someone willing to invest time and energy in a relationship. Damn it, Jake; I want to know that my man is going to try to stay alive for me and not rush off into every damn storm that comes along!"

"Now, you don't really mean that, do you, darling?" Jake smiled widely as he drawled out the words. "Nobody puts as much time and energy into a relationship as old Jake. Come on, let's go home and make up."

Marie stiffened. "Don't try to wheedle me into bed, Jake. Stop that," she pushed his exploring hand away, but gently. "I really shouldn't let you touch me. Ouch! That pinched!" She aimed a slow swing at his chin, which he easily deflected and pulled her closer. "Damn you, Jake. Damn you to hell and back!" Marie said as she returned his kisses with increasing fervor. "But first, let's get you a shower and a shave."

Rams had the entire sail set repacked by the time a smiling Jake returned.

Marie was excited when she got off shift and burst into their quarters. She shook a flimsy in Jake's face. "Why didn't you download the mail today?" she demanded. "Look! Look what came! This is important!"

Jake snatched the flimsy from her waving hand and tried to read it in the dim cabin light.

"It's an offer of a contract with JBI!" Marie exclaimed before he could finish reading the tiny text. "Someone over at corporate has actually offered to give you a long-term contract! They want you to make speed runs between stations for high priority shipments."

Jake scanned the address block and recognized the name at the top. It was that Grobbka fellow, the one with the pregnant wife. Apparently this must be his way of repaying the favor.

"Looks like tight schedules, constant demand, but the pay could be good," Marie said excitedly as she danced around the room.

"Pay's not good, but adequate," Jake said slowly. "You know that JBI won't give a small shipper like me top rates. I'd probably get all the shit jobs they don't want."

Marie sat in his lap and threw her arms around his neck. "Don't you see? You can do this. No more storms. No more putting yourself at risk. It's a good, safe way to keep *Pumpkin*."

"Maybe," Jake admitted slowly. "But before I reply, I think I need to talk this over with Rams and see what we'd have to do to the ship. Might need some more modifications, you know. Could be costly. Cargo take different equipment."

"Then get another loan," Marie laughed. "Hell, I'll even pay part of it. Oh, Jake. I do love you. Now we can be together. Now we can have a future!"

"Together don't come with making freight runs," Jake corrected her.

"But you will always come back, won't you," she said smugly. "I'll know that you'll always come back to me!"

A month later, *Pumpkin* had been refitted. Jake had them widen the hatch to the scoop bay, which was now the cargo hold, and replace the heavy-weather sails with a set of standard issue. The new sails would allow *Pumpkin* to make speedier passages, provided they stayed out of the heavier winds.

The contract required a number of safety modifications that would make the barque less agile. Jake had protested, but let Marie and Rams overcome his objections. He might be able to carry higher value cargo, they argued, if he complied with JBI's safety regulations.

"First shipment's due in two days," Rams announced breathlessly as soon as he returned from the Factor's Office.

Jake looked up from the satellite shots and rubbed his chin. "Look here," he pointed at a spot of turbulence at the edge of the KK band. "There's a big storm due around that time. Supposed to pass real close, just northeast of us."

"Not a problem," Rams replied quickly with a flashing smile. "According to the manifest, we are to be heading southwest, in the opposite direction, completely out of the path of the storm. We are so lucky!"

"Just the same, I'm going over to weather to take a look at the raw data myself. Never did trust those pointy-headed weather people to make a decent prediction. Want to get a good look at this monster for myself."

Jake knew how to read the signs of Jupiter's weather, having figured long before the scientists had put an equation to it that the depth of a storm was a function of its radius and its angular speed. The higher the product of the two numbers, the deeper it would pull up the stuff that floated below, where even the five hundred million tons of meteorites that rained onto Jupiter each year were light enough to float. Jake could look at the first satellite pictures of a forming turbulence and decide whether it was worth the trouble to mine its depths. This gave him a clear advantage over the others, who waited until weather confirmed Jake's instincts, and therefore arrived too late or found themselves in the wrong position.

Rams came back from dinner to find Jake arguing with the yard boss. The heavy canisters of their new sail sets were lined side by side on the dock floor. Four of the stevedores were swinging *Pumpkin*'s old heavy-duty sails into the sail locker.

"What is happening," he asked as he ran to Jake's side. "Why are you changing the sails?"

Jake finished giving the boss instructions, then turned to face Rams. "It's the storm!" he said with rising excitement in his voice. "Rams, I've never seen a storm this deep. It's the biggest, widest damn thing that the old man has ever boiled up! From the satellite pictures, I figure that it must go at least two thousand kilometers deep. This one is going to bring up stuff that we've never seen before—it's going to be the richest haul we'll ever make!"

"But what about the cargo?" Rams cried. "We must make the run tomorrow, when the shipment arrives down the elevator! Whatever shall we tell the JBI?"

"Screw JBI and its stinking cargo!" Jake shouted. "Didn't you hear me? This storm is the big one! This storm is going to make us rich beyond belief! Now, come on, get a move on. We have a lot to do if we're going to set sail this evening." He turned to shout more instructions at the stevedores as Rams stood with his mouth agape.

"What the hell do you think you are doing?" Marie screamed when she arrived at the dock, oblivious to the dock hands that she left scattered in her wake. "Are you out of your mind? What about the contract? What about the cargo you promised to carry? How can you think of going after some stupid storm at a time like this?"

"Rams shouldn't have called you," Jake said. "I knew you wouldn't understand."

"What's to understand, you fucking idiot! You have obviously lost whatever brains you had. Weather is screaming that we should think about evacuating the station because of the size of this storm. Everybody with an ounce of sense is sailing away from the path of the storm, and here you are, rigging that miserable excuse for a ship of yours so you can go right into the monster's mouth! Lord, Jake, you must be out of your freaking mind!"

"Like a fox," Jake said with a smile. "Storm this deep's got to pull tons of stuff up from below! I just wish I could convince more miners to go with me—this one is going to make us so much money...." His voice trailed off as he caught Marie's expression.

"Come on! Think of it, Marie; you won't have to be a station Master. I won't have to worry about paying off *Pumpkin*. We can live a life of ease on what I'll mine from this one. When I get back, we'll be free and clear for life!"

"So you won't stop this foolishness," Marie asked in cold, measured tones. "You really are going to go through with it?"

Jake took her by the shoulders. "Why aren't you listening to me, woman? This is my big chance. This is the storm that will let us get away from Jupiter once and for all! One final run, Marie, let me take this one last grab at the golden ring. Let me show everyone what *Pumpkin* and I can do!"

Marie looked at Jake, stared into his eyes for a long time, and then turned away without saying another word. She walked slowly off of the dock.

"Aren't you going to wish me luck?" Jake shouted after her.

Rams was easier to convince than Marie, but still, it had taken a promise of one quarter of whatever they found to get him to stay as crew.

"*Pumpkin* out at 1545," he radioed as they exited the dock.

"Fair winds, Cap'n," was the Master's automatic reply as he released the clamps. The station was nearly deserted, save for a caretaker staff working at triple overtime rates. Even with a reduced crew, the Master hadn't deviated one iota from the standard departure checklist. Jake had fumed as he ran into block after block until, finally, he had filed a fictitious sail plan just to get out before the storm passed them by.

Whatever else the Master had to say was lost in the hash of white noise as Jupiter blanked any hope of electronic contact with the station. The radar display lost the station a few moments later as the wind ripped *Pumpkin* from the station.

"Course set for 280 degrees," Jake said aloud as he made further adjustments to *Pumpkin*'s sails, trimming the small ship to race ahead of the prevailing winds on a broad reach. With luck, he could get far enough ahead of the approaching storm to tack northward into direct line with the storm's predicted track.

Then they just had to wait until the monster came to them.

For the past six hours, *Pumpkin* had been drifting along, cutting back and forth from 350 north to 160 south. Rams noted the difference in headings and remarked, "*Pumpkin*'s got a slight inclination to weather, Cap'n."

Jake snorted. "Yeah, thanks to those damned JBI safety changes. Glad we have our old sails back, though. Couldn't work out the storm with those flimsy ones they wanted us to use."

The leading edge of the hurricane touched Pumpkin with a gentle kiss of a breeze—an abrupt wind change to the southeast. Jake turned *Pumpkin* eastward and ran for another hour, and then tacked back. This time the heading was 320, which meant that something was seriously altering the prevailing wind.

"Get the weather sail ready to hoist," Jake instructed. "And get a second set of lines ready to deploy. If we lose the sail, we'll have to get another one out there in a hurry!"

"Aye, Cap'n," Rams replied.

Pumpkin was being buffeted by even heavier breezes, if 200 mps winds could be called breezes. Still, it was light wind compared to the ones they would feel farther in.

Jupiter's swirling hurricanes were fed by thermal disturbances deep within the atmosphere, far below the relatively thin atmosphere surrounding *Pumpkin*. Within the storm were thick bands where the heated air ascended to the cool crown of the storm before sinking into the depths. Pushing the rising and falling air masses were the rotating winds. The rapid rotation of the planet gave these hurricanes a sideways thrust that drove them onward.

Jake knew the structure of the storms, could tell where he was in the stack by listening to the roar of her winds through the sonar, through the echophones, through the strumming tone of the rigging as it strained against the wind.

Pumpkin's tendency to weather grew more pronounced as they encountered heavier winds, forcing Jake to fight the jib and main against the natural pull of the wheel. She wanted to turn into the center, to head right for the most dangerous part of the storm, where they would be carried down to depths. But Jake held her back. He steered a course that took them gradually down as they progressed inward. He wanted to get far enough in that he could ride the heavy upwellings closest to the center—that was where they were most likely to find the flotsam from the depths.

The first pass yielded little. They detected lots of small gravel, objects that ordinarily would represent a lucky find, but which Jake insisted were just a teaser. Jake maneuvered *Pumpkin* within the upwelling, steering in a tight circle that brought them to the outside edge of a thermal just as it crested.

Jake swung the main and pitched *Pumpkin* on a steep heel as they raced away from the center, cutting the oncoming wind at a twenty-degree angle. They ran on this course for an hour before Jake jibbed and beat his way back inward, downward, into the storm.

The third pass was the lucky one. Rams nearly screamed as the radar display flashed with a brilliant spark. "Damn, she's nearly as big as a house!" he yelled as he fumbled for the net release. Jake swung the ship to track the find, spilling the wind to hold his speed down to that of the nugget.

The alarm rang again as a second spark appeared to their stern. Rams nearly had the scoop deployed, which made *Pumpkin* steer like she had a sea anchor out. Jake pulled in more sail to hold their speed.

"Hate to ignore that one," he yelled. "Ping them with the sonar to see what we have." If the rock they were trailing was metallic then it would ring when the sonar hit it. Rock and water meteors usually absorbed the ping.

"Listen to that!" Rams yelled, and turned the loudspeaker up as far as it would go. The return sounded like a huge church bell.

"The nugget must be pure iron!" Jake screamed, dreaming of wealth beyond imagining. "Try the other one!" The response was the same.

Jake thought quickly. If he could back wind just enough to get behind the second rock, then they might be able to close and capture both of them. The hold would just have enough room for the one, but they could sail home with the rock hanging below them in the scoop. It would be hard sailing, but well worth it.

The maneuver worked perfectly. Rams was able to winch the first one aboard and deploy the net a second time in the time it took to catch up with the original target.

Pumpkin bucked as they drew nearer to the rock. Jake fought the wheel. The additional weight of their find made the ship wallow like a whale. He couldn't get nearly the speed he wanted from the sails, it seemed. It was those damned safety features that restricted the set of the sail, he knew.

"Something is wrong," Rams reported from his station at the radar display. "The rock appears to be dropping."

Jake stole a glance at the display and grunted. "Maybe the wind is subsiding. Does that sometimes." But at that moment, *Pumpkin* pitched forward. He had been concentrating so much on capturing the rock that he hadn't realized they'd reached the top of the stack. The sudden drop meant they were now pitching down into the mouth of the storm. If they didn't act quickly, *Pumpkin* would be lost forever!

Jake pulled the sail in and turned the ship to weather, hoping to catch a breeze that would provide enough power to pull them out of hazard. But *Pumpkin* lumbered in the wind, scarcely increasing her speed.

"This does not look good, Cap'n," Rams said quietly, which meant he was seriously worried.

Jake ignored his pessimistic crewman. "We'll have to work our way outward, toward the downdraft's wall. Then we can transition to the updraft, if we're lucky, and start making our way out of here."

"I fear we are already too deep, Rams replied, pointing at the inertial. "I doubt anyone has recovered from this depth."

Jake smiled. "Well, even Jupiter can't produce a storm that me and *Pumpkin* can't beat. Hang on, Rams. This is going to be a hell of a ride!"

The next ten hours were a maddening fight of wind and sail. *Pumpkin* rocked from side to side as Jake tacked ferociously to take advantage of every shift in the winds. At one point they rode upward so swiftly that they could actually feel the acceleration. But their hopes were dashed minutes later as *Pumpkin* dropped precipitously to her original depth.

Rams and Jake took two on and two off at the wheel, trying to get a little rest in the rocking ship. It was during one of these rest periods that Jake felt the keel rock violently, which made the hull ring like a gong.

"What the hell?" he exclaimed, as the ship slewed around in a complete circle. The radar alarm rang shrill in his ear as the display lit up in a shower of sparks.

Jake couldn't believe his eyes. They were floating in a field of rocks as large as or larger than the one in their hold. He had been right; this storm was bringing material from the depths like none before. These were riches beyond measure.

Pumpkin continued to ring. "The keel's hitting the damn rocks," he yelled. "Take us to port. No, don't do that! Luff the sails instead—we need to get out of this mess!"

Rams spilled wind as best he could, and Jake watched the sparks disappear from the display. *Pumpkin* regained her balance, and the vibrations from impacts on the keel damped.

They continued working their way outward.

They were on the port tack of a circular course when they encountered the outer edge of the downdraft. The first indication was the hammering and buffeting of *Pumpkin*'s sails, which made the rigging clang against the hull.

Jake was prepared, had been prepared for this for hours. He hauled the sail close, tightened the jib, and threw the wheel hard over. *Pumpkin* pitched and heeled, nearly lying on her side as she was whipped around by the turbulent winds of the barrier layer. Every loose piece of gear rattled around the ship, smashing from side to side, bow to stern. Jake watched a cup roll toward the stern as *Pumpkin* tipped bow upward, and go in the opposite direction a few seconds later to smash against the navigation.

The circular course they were sailing was of an opposite sense to the one on the other side of the barrier layer. This meant that they'd reached the periphery of the rising stack. Jake tried to steer *Pumpkin* to where he hoped the strongest updrafts would be.

The radar alarm was sounding so constantly that they had to shut it off to concentrate. Never had Jake seen such an accumulation of junk in a storm. He tried to imagine the devastation that the base of the storm was causing at the bottom of its funnel. Huge pieces of junk pulled up and tossed about as if they were nothing, rocks the size of a ship flying about. It was incredible to think of the forces involved.

Yet here he was, he and *Pumpkin*, fighting the wind, fighting the storm, drawing on its strength to survive. Instead of controlling them, it was they who controlled the forces of the storm. The feeling of power, of winning, was overwhelming. It made him feel so alive!

With a laugh that drew a sharp look from Rams, he cut the wheel and turned *Pumpkin* closer to the wind. Yes, they could even dare the center of the tornadic updraft.

Then *Pumpkin* rocked as if she had run aground, and bucked like a rodeo horse. "We lost our main," Jake screamed as his tell-tales blinked red. "Let the jib go!"

But it was too late. The jib tore loose, and her leads rattled against the hull, beating a fierce tattoo. *Pumpkin* pitched and yawed as if she were nothing more than another bit of flotsam on the winds of chance.

"We are sinking again!" screamed Rams. "We have to dump that load."

"No!" Jake shouted. "There has to be some other way out of this!" But he could not think of anything as Rams stared at him, expectation written on his face. Did the boy think he could create miracles? What the hell did he think he was, anyway?

"Drop the load," Jake said with resignation. "And pray."

With the ship lightened, she bobbed higher and higher, until she finally reached some relatively calm air. As soon as the violent pitching stopped, Jake and Rams squeezed into the sail locker and shifted a new sail set into the shroud housing, attached the control lines, and made their way back to the helm.

Pumpkin tilted with the wind as the sails emerged, then rolled slightly and cut across the face of the wind. Jake sullenly maneuvered them across the storm's tearing arms, fighting always against being sucked into the downdrafts, and avoiding the buffeting winds between the arms.

The storm had carried them so far that it was a fourteen-day voyage back to the station. A fourteen-day trip during which Jake could think only of the riches he had seen, and those he had lost.

Marie was standing at the hatch to the docking bay when Jake emerged. One look at the dark expression on her face was enough to tell Jake that he was not going to get a hero's welcome.

"Your shipping contract has been canceled," she said. There was an angry undercurrent clearly evident in her voice. "Pavel went way out of bounds to help me, and you threw it right back in his face."

"Don't you want to know what happened?" Jake asked, amazed that she expected him to be thinking about some stupid shipping contract after what he had gone through. "We barely escaped with our lives!"

Marie continued as if she had not heard him. "The contract was canceled because you decided to make one more run at this stupid, risky storm mining. They found someone else to do it."

"What did you mean about Grobbka doing this for you?" Jake said. "I thought he was repaying the favor, not—"

But Marie didn't let him finish. "What the hell were you thinking about, Jake? How the hell could you throw our future away like that?"

"I was thinking about our future," Jake shot back. "If we hadn't had a string of bad luck, I would have been far richer than a hundred stupid, dull JBI contracts. Anyhow, I can always make those runs between storms once I get *Pumpkin* fixed up right."

Marie snapped. "You stupid fuck-up! You'll never get another chance like the one you threw away. Nobody wants to deal with someone they can't depend on!" She kicked at the deck in anger. "Damn it, Jake. You'll never get that stupid ship of yours paid for, never be out of debt, never be anything except a flat-broke sailor until the day you die, which will probably be in one of those storms of yours." There was a catch in her voice. Tears were streaming down her face. "Jake, this was your chance to be somebody."

"Marie," Jake said, as he moved to give her a hug.

Marie stepped backward. "No! You're not going to sweet talk your way out of this, Jake Sands! I've let you slide by a hundred times, and every time I think I can trust you, you slip away and risk your freaking scrawny neck. I can't do it any more. I can't go through my life wondering if the next storm will be the one that kills you. I can't live with that kind of uncertainty. I just can't," she finished in a weak whisper. "Oh, Jake. I just can't."

"But this was the big one," Jake tried to explain. "We snagged a huge metallic hunk that must have massed at least two tons! And there were other pieces just as big—bigger! If we hadn't lost the sail, we would have brought it back. Think of what that nugget would have brought us, Marie. Think of how much money that would have produced! Lord, it would be enough to pay off my debts, buy my way out of Jupiter, buy our way out of Jupiter for good and all!" He held his hands out as if impeaching her belief.

"They assigned me to a new station while you were gone," Marie replied flatly. "I ship out to commission it next week. I've already packed my stuff to go. You can come or not, but not as a miner—never as a miner! I won't have it any other way."

Jake chewed his lip. "*Pumpkin* needs repairs, and weather says there's probably another storm behind this one. Maybe, if we can get refitted in time, Rams and me can snag those nuggets we lost. The next storm will probably bring them up again. Yeah, once we catch those, we'll have our ticket out of here."

"Don't you see what is going to happen, Jake?" Marie said, shaking her head and backing away from him. "You aren't ever going to get rich."

"But I know that I can do it this time," Jake protested. "I know that *Pumpkin* and me can do it!"

Marie stood stock still for a moment more, tears streaming down her face. She took half a step toward Jake, stopped, hesitated a moment more, and then took a deep breath. She wiped her eyes with the back of her hand before speaking.

"You'll never learn, Jake. I don't know why I've believed you all those years. I guess I've been a fool for a long while, too long, perhaps. But no more. This is goodbye, Jake. Goodbye!" With that, she turned on her heel, and stomped away without looking back.

Jake stood where he was as she walked away. He knew that all he had to do was shout and she would come back. All he had to do was call her name and she would come back. He knew that all he had to say was "All right," and they could stay together.

But he said nothing as she disappeared through a hatchway.

A few days later, Jake stood in the vee formed by the prow of the E-2 station, listening to the voice of the wind through the thick plating. The power of the five-hundred-knot wind was a palpable presence here in the prow. He could sense the wind's energy despite the thick armor that separated him from the outside. He could hear the wind calling to him. He could hear the voice of the storm as she called him to her bosom.

Marie will get over her mad, he thought, as the sound of the howling wind washed over him. She would come to him once he got *Pumpkin*'s loans paid off. All he had to do was get the big one that was out there, waiting for him. That's all he had to do.

Meanwhile, *Pumpkin* was waiting. She was eager to dive into the storms once again. She was waiting for his hand on her helm. She was waiting for him to fulfill her destiny. The storm was calling.

Rams found him a few hours later. "Marie just left," he said slowly. "We all wondered why you weren't there." He hesitated. "She cried," he added simply.

"Just a short separation," Jake replied. "Couple of months. After I grab the big one, we'll get together again."

Rams shook his head. "I don't know, Cap'n. She said some really bitter things when I brought your name up—words I do not like to use."

"Don't worry about it, boy. Now, forget Marie. Weather tells me there's a nice storm coming. If we're lucky, maybe we can catch those rocks we dropped. That'll show them that old Jake isn't full of gas—that the big stones are really out there for the taking!"

Rams hesitated. "You are not going to go after those shipping contracts?"

Jake spit on the deck. "Hell no! We can make more with one rock than we could with a hundred years of JBI's best shipping contracts. *Pumpkin*'s made for the storms, boy, not hauling canapes and toilet tissue."

"There are some ships on the block," Rams said. "JBI is decommissioning some of the smaller craft—uneconomic to operate, they say. Grobbka says if I had one he might reconsider that contract."

"Waste of time and effort," Jake said, wondering why Rams had taken it upon himself to intrude in his affairs, and why he'd thought he'd even consider partnership in some low-ball shipping contract. "I know those ships—not worth a damn in heavy weathers. Good for the blue-suit boys, not for people like us."

"I looked at one of them—the *Primrose*," Rams said. "Maybe I could…"

Jake exploded. "Listen you fool; what are you going to use for money? Doubt if JBI will let one go on credit, especially to some miner's crewman. Look all you want, Rams, but don't get your hopes up. Ship's expensive, even at salvage prices."

"I have saved some funds," Rams countered. "Then there is the share you promised me. Perhaps that will be enough for a down payment."

"Sure it will, and I'll sell you a barrel of Jovian whale blubber for what is left over. Now, come along—we have to get *Pumpkin* ready. We have to push off by evening tomorrow."

They were sixteen thousand kilometers out of the station when they detected the edge of the storm. Jake pulled them into position, and let the storm's arm pull them toward the center.

"*Primrose* is a fine ship," Rams said as they fought the jib into position. "And for only three million down, I can have her."

"Where are you going to get that much? Even if you saved every centime I ever paid you, you'd still be short two million and a hell of a lot more!"

The alarm shrilled moments before the patter of incoming gravel rang through the hull. Jake cut across the scattering of stars on the radar display until they had fought clear.

"First Bank of Jupe will advance me one and a quarter against earnings on the contract," Rams continued. "And the Hespera Group promised the same. Watch it!"

The bright spot on the display grew quickly as it raced by the ship. "Big sucker," Jake observed. "Nearly as big as that one we lost. Let's get in deeper and see if there are any more like that one." *Pumpkin* heeled over as he tightened the main.

"This is not a good idea," Rams said worriedly. "We are already further down than we should be. We do not want to repeat the last time, do we?"

"Got to go where the big ones are," Jake replied. "So, how did you manage to get two banks to cooperate on a loan? Most bankers are tighter than a storm jib."

Rams blushed. "They do not know of each other," he admitted. "I did not think it important that they should be bothered by all the petty details."

Jake guffawed. "Kiting a loan! Well, there is promise for you yet. Hell, you might even make it, providing you stay out of jail. Here we go!" He pointed at the radar display, where several sparks were emerging from the hash of white noise. "There they are. Ready the scoop."

"Aye, sir!" Rams replied, as Jake steered the ship to intercept. "They ping metallic," Rams exclaimed with rising excitement. "We will be rich!"

Jake jounced *Pumpkin* to the side, bringing the scoop directly in line with the largest rock. As they made contact, *Pumpkin* shuddered violently. "Must mass a couple of tons," Jake remarked, as he held the ship steady and Rams drew their treasure into the bay.

"I'll call this one Marie," Jake said quietly. "For luck. Now, where's the next one?"

Rams looked around with an alarmed look on his face. "Another one? Isn't this enough? Let's take what we have and get out of here before we get into trouble."

Jake laughed. "No problem. Got us out of worse than this, just in case you don't remember. Come on, Rams, let's run with the luck while she's with us." He steered toward a second spark.

Rams disengaged the scoop and deployed it again, casting their net in Jupiter's seas. He watched the display with fascination as Jake closed on the second target.

Contact! This time *Pumpkin* shook and tipped downward. Something in the forward compartment broke loose and crashed against the deck. Rams felt the ship sinking.

"What the hell?" Jake said, as he fought with the helm. He threw the switches that released the ballast in an attempt to stop their descent. *Pumpkin*'s descent slowed, but did not stop.

"Dump the rock!" Rams screamed. "It's too heavy. It's pulling us down."

"Can't imagine what it could be to mass so much," Jake swore. "Probably worth a fortune—enough for you to buy *Primrose* and have enough left over for a barque with your share!"

"I don't give a damn about that," Rams replied. "I want to live! Forget the money. Just get us out of here."

"Wait a bit," Jake said. "I know I can get us back. These two rocks will give me enough to fix *Pumpkin* up proper!"

"So you can spend more time out here in the storms? That's not much to look forward to. But then, I guess that's all you've got." Rams said bitterly.

Jake started to reply, and then stopped. What else did he have to live for? *Pumpkin* gave him a lot of pleasure, and fighting the storms for their treasures was a rush like nothing else.

But he was, as Marie had said, getting up there in years and, to be perfectly honest, the storms weren't nearly so exciting as they were frightening. If it hadn't been for the promise of these huge rocks, he probably would have gone with her. Somehow, right now, dying in the depths with a fortune in tow didn't seem quite so satisfying as he'd expected. Maybe Rams was right—he didn't have much of a life now that Marie was gone.

He jiggled the ballast switches. "Damn, we're empty!"

Rams reached over and put his hand on the release. "I'm going to drop the rock, Cap'n—it isn't worth our lives."

"Do that, and you'll never sail with me again," Jake threatened. "You'll never get another mining berth, so help me."

"Sorry," Rams said, and threw the release. "But I no longer wish to pursue a mining career."

Jake cried out as Rams fired the releases that dropped the net. "I'm taking the cost of that scoop out of your share," he declared angrily. Rams had no right to throw away those riches.

Pumpkin rocked suddenly, heeling hard to port, turning completely around, and coming to a dead stop. The tell-tales indicated that the sails were filled with wind, but when Jake tried to turn the craft, the sails stayed in the same position.

"Check to see what's jammed the rigging," Jake said. "I can't move the sails."

Rams turned on the deck camera, which was ordinarily used only for docking, and scanned the deck. Something was wrapped around the winches and tangled the boom. "I don't know…" he began, and then stopped. There was something familiar about those lines. "It's the scoop! The damn scoop's blown back into the rigging, Cap'n!"

Jake swore. *Pumpkin* was continuing to sink in the downdraft, but slower than before. He had to get the rigging clear if they expected to get out of this.

"Should I dump the other rock?" Rams asked. "Maybe lightening the ship will help us."

"Are you crazy? That rock has to be the biggest nugget anyone has ever found! Solid metal, Rams, think about that—it's worth a fortune. Maybe enough to help you get that ship."

Rams hesitated. "Fortune is not good to us down where we are heading. Come on, Cap'n; let me dump the load."

Jake locked the wheel in position, and made certain that the sail winches were as well. Then he stood up, leaning against the slope of the steeply inclined deck. "Watch the ship. I'm going out."

Rams blanched at the thought. "You can't do that! The winds out there—"

Jake didn't let him finish. "I have to cut the sail loose. Even if we dropped the rock, we still couldn't steer worth a damn. Now, come and help me suit up. We're wasting time jawing like this."

Jake checked the safety line twice before he climbed out of the hatch onto the deck. One slip on the steep cant of the deck and he'd plunge several thousand kilometers while simultaneously cooking from the heat. His suit would become a pressure cooker, basting him in his own juices as he was slowly being crushed.

But he didn't dare think about that right now. He had to get that damned netting off the rigging. He struggled to the stern, where the net had snagged on the aft winch housing. With every second step, he hooked one of the safety lines to a tie-down and released the trailing one, until he finally reached the winch.

He fired up the cutting torch, which threw a harsh blue-white light into the darkness surrounding him. The hard, armored strands of the netting resisted the torch for a moment, glowing through red to orange, then white, and finally parting in a shower of sparks as the portion of the net flew into the void.

Jake carefully worked his way forward, staggering as an occasionally strong gust hit the locked sails and tilted the ship. He fell once, but the safety lines held so he was able to recover his footing.

The next tangle was wrapped around the end of the boom and the main sheets. From the way they ran, he wasn't sure if cutting them at the closest point would clear the sail. Once he severed the net near the deck, he would have no way of getting to the parts that hung on the end of the boom, which hung over the side of the ship, well beyond his reach.

At the limits of his light he could just barely make out some netting stretching forward. Perhaps it was tangled somewhere toward the bow. He began to make his slow way forward.

Sure enough, the net was caught on the short docking boom just below deck level. The problem was that, with the ship canted over so far, the boom was pointing nearly straight down, under the ship.

Jake thought fast, calculating the configuration of the net and ship. If he could loosen the portion on the docking boom and then sever the part on the sheet, perhaps the wind would pull the net away from the boom. Sure, and all he had to do was dangle on his safety line, swing under the ship, cut the netting loose, and climb back up—doing all of this under two gravities and wearing a pressure suit that weighed more than he did!

It was impossible.

No! Wait a minute, Jake thought. What if he cut the rear line first? Then he could come forward and work on the docking boom. Once the net was free, the ship would right herself, and he could walk up the deck. Sure, it wouldn't be that hard. Piece of cake, as Rams would say.

The struggle back was even more difficult than before. Must be getting tired, he thought as he clicked the safety line in place. The only good thing was that he didn't slip.

The tangle of net was more complex than the one at the stern. It took him nearly an hour to sever the last strand.

"Try to haul the main in," he told Rams through the intercom. A moment later, he saw the main sheet tighten. It began to vibrate visibly.

"Hold it there," he yelled. "I don't want to be up here if that line parts." With that much strain on the main sheet, it would whip around like a scythe, clearing the deck of anything that got in its way. He'd once seen a breaking line cut right through a man, back in his construction days. The man's torso went flying off into the black while his legs stood there, held in place by the safety lines.

Jake worked his way forward. He was getting awfully tired, moving around in the heavy suit. His arms and legs felt as if they weighed a ton. All he wanted to do was rest. But rest was impossible: They had to save themselves from sinking further, and Rams wouldn't know what to do. He had to keep working on the problem. Damn, was his age finally starting to tell on him?

When he reached a point just above the docking boom, he began rigging his safety lines. The jib was stretched tight, so he had to go under the jib sheet, over the fairleads track, and then down the side. He estimated the length of line he needed to play out, gave himself a little slack, and then started to crawl slowly backward down the sloping deck. The torch clanged against his side with every move.

Jake placed his feet on the fairleads track and grabbed the jib sheet with both hands. Beneath his feet was the empty void, a black pit to forever. From this point on, the only thing that would hold him to the ship were the two safety lines. It didn't matter that they were tested for one hundred times the load they had to bear, they still looked awfully thin and insubstantial.

Jake took a deep breath, removed one foot from the track, and leaned backward, over the deep dark. With a brief prayer, he let go of the sheet and felt himself fall, swinging out and down, falling into the night.

Snap! His fall was arrested with a suddenness that snapped his teeth together. Then the side of the ship was swinging toward him as he reached the top of his swing.

Jake reached desperately for a handhold, grabbing a double strand of the netting to prevent himself from swinging back. The weight of the suit pulled on him, trying to rip his grip loose. Jake pulled himself upward with all of his remaining strength, thrusting an arm into the netting to hold himself in place.

He rested for just a moment, dangling from the netting with his legs swinging free. Then he grabbed another handful of net and swung his legs to propel himself toward the boom where the net was anchored.

His arms felt as if they were on fire by the time he reached his objective. His fingers were starting to cramp and his forearms shook with the effort. He clamped himself to the boom and let himself hang for a moment, letting the blood rush back into his hands, letting his muscles rest.

But only for a moment. He unhooked the torch, prayed that there was enough gas left, and fired it up. The flickering light played tricks on his eyes as he cut though the multiple strands of netting. He was careful that none of them would entangle him when they came free.

He was working on the final strand when something hard hit him on the side. He glanced down and saw a glittering scar on his suit where the impact had scraped the paint away. Damn, just his luck to run into a pile of gravel at this point! If that piece had hit his helmet, it would all be over —for him, for *Pumpkin*, and for poor Rams. He applied the fierce flame of the torch with sudden urgency.

As the final strand glowed orange Jake braced himself. When it let go, the ship was going to swing violently and, even though he was belayed to the boom, he was going to suffer the consequences. Well, nothing to be done but ride it out, he thought and continued cutting.

The net let go with explosive force, disappearing instantly. *Pumpkin* dipped further for a moment and then rocked back upright, twisting forward and to starboard.

Jake, at the end of the short boom, was tossed over and up, swinging in a complete circle before he slammed against the boom and blacked out.

When he came to, *Pumpkin* was riding level, and he was lying atop the boom. He grabbed his safety lines and managed to pull himself erect. He stood on the boom to bring his head level with the deck. He tried to pull himself up, but didn't have the strength. He'd spent all of his energy getting *Pumpkin* free of the netting.

He looked up at the edge of the deck illuminated by his helmet lamp. So near and so impossibly far. Was this how it was going to end—with him lashed to *Pumpkin*, like some latter-day Ahab, plunging into the depths with his obsession? Well, he couldn't think of a better way to go.

Still, he had a few regrets. One, he'd be taking Rams with him, which was a shame, because the kid had a lot of good years ahead of him. Then, he'd not be seeing Marie again, and he really owed her an apology for being such an idiot. She was right, and he'd known that. He was too old for this business. He'd pushed his luck too far, one time too many. Well, for what it was worth, she'd probably be happy knowing she was right.

He toyed with the idea of releasing his line and opening his suit. It would be a certain death, messy, but quick. Better that than slowly roasting as they descended. He reached for the clamp.

Then something happened. Perhaps Rams had somehow perceived his plight. Perhaps some vagrant wind had taken *Pumpkin*. Or maybe *Pumpkin* had decided to take matters into her own hands, and heeled to starboard.

Suddenly, the side of the ship became a gentle slope, one that he could easily climb. He took a double handful of safety line and worked his way up to the deck, then crawled back to the hatch, carefully alternating his attachments as he went. He wasn't so tired that he ignored common-sense precautions.

Rams was waiting inside the hatch, and helped him remove the heavy suit. Jake lost no time in taking the wheel to bring the ship into the wind. He noted that Rams had already done so, which made him reevaluate his opinion. Maybe the boy had learned a thing or two.

Yeah, and that wasn't the only thing he'd learned.

Marie was curious when she got the call from the docks that Jake had arrived. There had been no storms nearby in the past month, nor had weather predicted any new disturbances. What, then, could have brought Jake this far away from his home station? And on board a packet ship, at that.

As she headed down below, she hoped that he hadn't come seeking some sort of reconciliation. That he hadn't come with hopes of sweet-talking her into bed, worming his way back into their old relationship. All that was behind her—she had mourned him for weeks, and waking up in the morning without him was finally becoming bearable. She would not allow him to open that door again. No, she was stronger now. She would make her position clear, just as she had when she told him goodbye.

But all that certitude vanished when she saw him step out of the hatch and walk across the deck. She felt the cold icicles of her resolve melt in the heat of his smile, the snowbank of her supposed indifference disappear to reveal buried memories of the good times they'd had. So help me, she thought, if he so much as touches me I will start to cry. She bit her lip and tried to strengthen her resolve. There would be no contact, no excuse for letting him steal her heart again.

Jake stopped two paces away from her and smiled. He fumbled in his jacket and pulled out a pink sheet. He handed it to her without a word of explanation.

Marie took the pink sheet and stared at it without comprehension. There were some words on the paper—standard bill of sale—complicated words that didn't make sense. There was Jake's name and *Pumpkin*'s in big letters. Down at the bottom was a big stamp that said "Paid in full."

"Sold her," Jake said, keeping that idiotic smile on his face. "Figured you'd like a honeymoon trip to celebrate."

"I don't understand," Marie said. "Trip?" She did a double take. "Did you say 'honeymoon'?"

"Yep, I finally got the big one. The rock we brought back assayed out as pure nickel—worth a bloody be damned fortune! Finally had enough to pay off the loan and a lot more. Now we can get back together and…"

"We don't have a future, Jake," Marie said slowly as she handed the sheet back. "I thought I made that perfectly clear: no storm mining, no *Pumpkin*."

"Now wait a minute, there. I'm offering to take you up the elevator for a nice zero gee honeymoon," he said as he held up two tickets. "Then we can come back down, set up housekeeping, and get back to normal. It'll be like old times, only without the arguments over *Pumpkin*." He stepped forward and held out his arms. "Come on, Marie," he said softly. "*Pumpkin*'s gone for good."

Marie hesitated, and felt her body moving forward, ready to surrender itself to those familiar, warm, embracing arms that she knew so well. It would be so easy to say nothing, to go along with Jake's plans, to enjoy the vacation from the heavy pull of Jupiter, and to have a man to share her bed once more.

But she stopped herself. "No," she said. "I'm not going back to that old relationship. And it wasn't just your ship. It was the stupid risk-taking, the storms, the uncertainty. I told you before, it's the storms or me, take your choice!"

Jake dropped his arms. "That's a hard choice, darling. But you mean more to me than any storm does." He hesitated for a moment, held out the pink sheet once more, and smiled again. "All right. *Pumpkin*'s gone, and my storm mining days are over. I figured that's the only way you'll have me." He reached for her.

Marie threw herself forward and embraced Jake. "Oh Jake, you have made me so happy. I know how much you loved that old ship. Oh, this is going to be so wonderful."

"Yeah, wonderful," Jake repeated as he kissed her again and again.

He just hoped that she would be as understanding about his new boat.

Chapter Three—Jupiter

Rams had stopped at the station in the hopes that there would be an opportunity for business. That, and a chance to restock his supplies. In order to keep his ship, *Primrose*, he had to take advantage of every opportunity that came his way.

Jake, an irritable old scamp who knew everything there was to know about sailing the winds of Jupiter, had taught Rams how to sail. Rams learned that every ship had her own personality. He learned how to balance keel and ballast, how to adjust the ship's buoyancy to ride the turbulence.

After teaching him the basics of sail, rudder, keel, and line, Jake went on to show him how to heave-to in the hurricane-force winds so that they would ride easily, neither making way nor being blown back. They'd used that technique to mine the edges of Jupiter's storms. The updrafts in these dangerous hurricanes often pulled metal-rich meteorites and icebergs—worth their weight in gold to the floating stations—from the lower depths of the atmosphere. Jake showed him how to "cheat" the boat close to the edges of the turbulence, using jib and main to close on these bits of rock and harvest them.

Jake had shared all of his secrets of playing the winds of Jupiter's storms and winning its rewards. Jake taught Rams to love the winds on the wine-red seas.

Rams' transition from crewman to ship's captain hadn't been easy. He'd scrimped and saved every cent he could, and signed away nearly all of his future profits—all to buy a fast, outdated clipper at one of JBI's auctions. Clippers had been deemed too inefficient to achieve JBI's "acceptable" level of profitability.

Refitting the boat and replacing the instruments that *Primrose*'s former crew had stripped put him even further in debt. In addition, there had been the outlay for new sails and refitting the keel. Both cost more than he had expected and, suddenly, his debt for *Primrose* started to look like a financial black hole from which there was no hope of escape.

His first year had been a disaster. The cargo he'd hauled hadn't generated enough to pay the interest on his loans. To keep from losing her he borrowed even more. If he wasn't careful he could lose *Primrose* and be thrown him in jail: that was the penalty for simultaneously using her as collateral for multiple loans. Since then, it had been nip and tuck, keeping one financial step ahead of bankruptcy.

The second year of operations had taught him where the good money could be earned—carrying perishable goods on quick dashes. JBI's huge, lumbering cargo ships could move things cheaply, but they were neither speedy nor very maneuverable. Like the old square-riggers of Earth, they flew with the wind, stolid as the stations, and scarcely moving much faster. Sometimes their crews endured months between station-falls.

Rams usually got the best return when he had to make a darting emergency run from station to hub and back. Double charges both ways, and no hassle for it, either!

Best of all, the fees kept him out of prison.

"Wind one-thirty meters per second and rising, Cap'n. Satellite shows some deep turbulence spinning off the edge about twelve thousand klicks upwind and heading to intercept your destination. Weather advises you should try to stay within the central laminar flows of sub-bands MM and KK until you're almost to Charlie Sierra One. That should keep you out of the storm," the station master said.

"Put it down that I acknowledge the limits on bands double em and double kay," Rams replied as the 'master logged his ship out. "How much margin does Weather give me before that storm hits?"

"Best they can project is that you have about a sixteen-hour margin, give or take six hours. Of course, if it swings south of CS-42, the edge winds might give you a lift."

"When did I ever see one of those storms change course in a way that would help me?" Rams said rhetorically. "I'll plan on beating to weather the last leg of the trip. I just hope that Weather's prediction is right."

"I agree with that," the 'master replied. "You'd better keep a watch for any miners who might be prospecting on the periphery of the storm. Wouldn't want to run into one of those crazies, would you?"

Rams grinned, remembering when he had been one of those crazies. "I'll watch out for them," he promised.

"Well, it looks like you are all set to go, *Primrose*," the station master said as he popped the record from the computer and handed it to Rams. "Fair winds and good passage, Cap'n."

Rams checked the ballast tank when he returned to the ship. According to the leveling mark on the wall of *Primrose*'s berth, she was riding low—just a little too heavy, probably from the extra cargo he'd taken on. He switched on the heaters in the ballast tank. That would create enough steam pressure to drive the excess ballast out, lightening the ship. When *Primrose*'s bull's-eye was almost up to the mark, he turned the heater off. In a few moments more, she was floating level with the station.

"Ready to cast off!" Rams said over the intercom, and listened for the 'master to loose the clamps that held *Primrose* in the station's embrace. Four loud bangs resounded through the pressure hull as the clamps released. Rams immediately felt the ship list to starboard as she drifted backward into the fierce winds of Jupiter.

Primrose heeled as she caught the full force of the wind. Rams braced himself, checked the instruments, and then turned the ship downwind as she emerged from the lee of the station,

The station's infrared image quickly faded as they exceeded the viewer's range. A few seconds later, the sonar return vanished as well. Only a fuzzy radar image, quickly dissolving into a cloud of electronic noise, told him where the station rode. Even that image would fade once he got more than a kilometer away. After that, he'd be sailing blind.

Primrose ran with the wind as he lowered the keel. He pointedly ignored the keel meter as the diamond mesh ribbon uncoiled from its housing. The thousand-ton weight at the keel's end started its familiar swinging motion as the keel was unwrapped from its spindle. *Primrose* rocked in response to the motion. The pendulum's swing slowed as the ribbon paid out farther and farther into the thick soup of the atmosphere.

Finally, the rocking motion dampened, and Rams halted the winch, locking it in place. Only then did he check the keel meter. Although he relied more on the feel of the ship's trim when setting the keel depth, he liked to assure himself of the setting.

A single glance told him that his instincts had been correct. He'd halted the keel at 1,400 meters, one hundred meters shy of the theoretical setting the station master had calculated. He let an additional fifty meters of the mesh keel pay out; it wouldn't hurt to have *Primrose* a little bottom-heavy on an upwind run.

Rams reached for the sail controls. *Primrose* was being blown downwind at thirty meters per second, relative to the station. The station he'd just left plodded along slower than the wind, held back only by her massive drogues—a fancy word for sea anchors. The drogues that swung beneath the station's bulbous form created drag and provided a measure of control. It was sailing, but using anchors to steer instead of rudders.

Rams hit the switch to release his mainsail from its housing on the main mast, and braced himself. The ship tilted even further to starboard as the wind bit the suddenly increased surface area. He immediately played out the traveler, letting the main find the angle that would allow the fierce wind to flow across the sail's face. He kept a careful eye on the pressure gauges from both sides of the wishbone that constrained the sail, adjusting the sail's angle to maximize the front-to-back pressure differential. He wanted to get as much lift as possible from the airfoil effect.

Primrose finally stopped rocking and curved into the wind as Rams adjusted the line. *Primrose* was running at about sixty degrees to the wind when she finally balanced out, and was making an appreciable sixty meters per second.

"All right, girl, let's show old man Jupiter what we can really do," he said, and deployed the jib from its housing at the prow. There was a hellacious rattling from forward as the chain hoist protested the way the wind whipped at the small jib and smashed it against the pressure hull. Rams winched the line back until the jib sheets were taut and the small forward sail was funneling the wind along the back of the mainsail, forming a venturi between them.

Primrose heeled even more as the force on her increased from the additional sail surface exposed to the wind and turned tighter into the face of the wind. She was now running at about a forty degree angle. Rams grinned in satisfaction as her speed increased proportionally. He watched the knot meter rise past seventy, seventy-five, and settle at nearly eighty meters per second.

He checked his location on the inertial positioning display, and made a minor adjustment to the rudder, then adjusted both the mainsail and jib to account for the new angle of attack.

"Clipper Ship *Primrose* out at 1400 hours, under weigh and on course for Charlie Sierra Four Two." he said into the radio. The station master probably wouldn't be able to hear the formal sign-off, given the usual overwhelming amount of static in the atmosphere. Nevertheless, Rams was always careful to observe the formalities.

As *Primrose* pulled steadily away, Rams made a thorough examination of the ship. He wanted to ensure that everything on board was ship-shape. He double-checked the straps and buckles on all of the cargo crates, just to make sure they'd been properly secured.

Next he checked the topside sail locker, taking care to see that the spare sails were properly stored and ready for deployment when the need arose. If all went well, he wouldn't have to replace the sails on this trip, which would help his profit margin. Having them fabricated in orbit and brought down by elevator was bloody expensive.

He swung the power-lifters from their clamps and started working on the new sail. He strained against the resistance of the tough foil of the sail as he refolded it. Even so, he tried to keep from flexing the thin metal more than was necessary.

As soon as he had the sail properly folded and secured, he moved it into its canister. His arms ached as he struggled to get it into the correct position, cursing the financial situation that forced him to fire his crew three months before, and the expediency that kept him from having the time in dock to do this sort of housekeeping. One person could barely cope with the bulky sails against the drag of Jupiter's heavy gravity. Even with the one hundred-to-one ratio of the lifters, he still had to depend on his own muscle to force the cumbersome rig into the canister.

Finally, the sail was loaded. He stowed the lifters and rubbed his aching back before fastening the heavy chain lines at the head end of the sail; one line that would lift it into place on the mast and another to connect it to the traveler that limited a sail's movement across the top deck.

Whenever he had to blow the main, its lines would go with it. The lines were another expense he wished that he could avoid. But the only way to save them was to suit up, climb out onto deck, and try to disconnect them while fighting hurricane-force winds. Only a fool went outside without a backup crew, no matter how securely he was clamped to the deck! The lost money for lines wasn't as important to him as his life.

By the time Rams worked his way back to the cockpit, *Primrose* had moved far north of the station. From this position, he could start to tack without risking running into it. Just to make certain of his clearance, he peered at the screen, cranking the radar to maximum sensitivity to check.

The screen showed a uniform blur of undifferentiated noise; not even a shadow that could be suspected of being something other than the swirling electronic mist of atmosphere.

Rams and *Primrose* were now completely on their own and, in five days—more or less—he hoped to see the faint, white, heat signature of his destination. He hoped that the storm wouldn't spoil his plans—he needed the money to make the next payment!

"What a dump," Louella complained loudly, and threw her bag against the bare metal deck of the hub station, sheering as it lazily bounced back into the air. "Not even a bar on the place! To make matters worse, I have to share the damned cabin with you. I can't even have some Gods-be-damned decent privacy before the race!"

Pascal winced at the strident tone of her voice. He regretted accompanying her throughout the long voyage from Earth to the Jovian system. He should have come on another ship.

Louella's growing catalog of complaints had increased throughout the long transit from Earth. Thankfully, there'd been enough distractions on the transport to silence her complaints, once in the while. The transport had a bar to keep her amused, and enough willing young crew members to keep her bemused. But those diversions were short lived. Too soon, she came back to the fact that she wasn't racing, wasn't in control, wasn't at sea.

It made her bitchy.

"How the devil am I supposed to keep my sanity if they can't even provide civilized, basic amenities?" Louella continued in a rasping voice that cut across his nerves like fingernails on a piece of slate.

"Bad enough that I have to miss three seasons of the circuit for this fool race! Bad enough that we have to stay in this stupid can until the others get here! But that doesn't mean I have to live like some freaking Spartan in the meantime!"

She lifted the lid of the utilitarian toilet. "Jesus, we even have to share the damned can!"

"Perhaps you should complain to the hub master," Pascal said quietly, as he floated across the tiny cabin and anchored himself with one hand. "Maybe he can provide whatever it is that you need."

Louella spun gracefully around on her hold and frowned at him. "What is that supposed to mean?"

Pascal winced again. What had he said now? It didn't matter; she'd be hell to live with if he just let it be. "Nothing," he said. "I just thought that maybe the captain has resources we don't know about. It wouldn't hurt to ask."

"Humph," Louella huffed, as if unsure of the meaning of his answer. She kicked her floating bag into some netting to secure it. "You've got the bunk beside the door, asshole. And don't get any ideas about us sleeping together."

"I wouldn't dream of it," Pascal replied dryly, and turned to fiddle with the controls on the wall. Under his breath he added, "Nightmares perhaps, but not dreams." He pressed the switch to open the view port.

"What did you say," Louella asked sharply. "Something I wasn't supposed to… Oh my God! Would you look at that!" Pascal didn't answer. He was as awed by the sight as she.

Framed in the view port was the entirety of Jupiter, half orange, rose, and umber, and half in darkness. The rim of the planet filled the 'port from top to bottom, leaving only a narrow circle of stars at the edges to show that anything else existed in the heavens.

The bright line of the elevator cable extended from somewhere beneath the window and ran straight toward the planet's equator, far below, just as it extended thousands of kilometers out into space from this geosynchronous station. The cable's silvery line narrowed as it diminished into perfect perspective toward the giant planet.

Jupiter's great red spot wasn't visible. Pascal assumed that it was either on the other side of the planet, or somewhere within the semicircle of darkness that marked the night side of Jupiter. But there were enough other large features present to occupy the eye.

Wide bands of permanent lateral weather patterns ran across Jupiter's face. Each showed feathery turbulence whorls at the edges as they dragged on the slower bands toward the equator, or were accelerated by faster ones toward the poles. From here, he could easily see the separations between them.

In the center of one of the higher latitude bands was a dark smudge. Pascal thought they might be the persistent traces of the "string of pearls" comet, over a hundred years ago, but he wasn't sure. He couldn't remember if the marks would be on top or bottom from his viewpoint. He decided to ask the hub master about orientation.

"What a sight," Louella whispered as she moved beside him. "Gorgeous, just gorgeous," she said, with a touch of awe. "Where are the floating stations? Could we see them from here?" she said quickly, and pressed closer to the view port.

Pascal dismissed her inquiry with a shrug. "The stations are too small to see from here. You're still thinking in terms of Earth. We're over six-hundred times farther out than one of the orbiting stations would be at home. CS-6 would have to be the size of Australia for you to see it with your naked eye.

"You've got to remember that each one of those weather bands is several thousand miles across," Pascal continued as he backed away from the view port and the terrifying precipice it represented. "We could put the entire Pacific inside any one of them, and still have plenty of room left over."

Louella's face took on a rapt expression as she absorbed the scale of what she was observing. "You could sail forever in those seas," she breathed heavily. "Forever."

Rams encountered his first problem when he was thirty hours under weigh. *Primrose* had been beating steadily to windward since he left CS-15. By his projections, they should have been slightly north of the projected track of CS-42, the next station in line. This leg of his upwind trip would be two thousand kilometers long before he came about and headed south on the shorter lee leg. That was as far as he could travel and stay within the limits Weather had advised. He couldn't go beyond the MM sub-band without risking excessive turbulence. No, he thought, it was better to keep to the smooth and dependable jets of air in the middle of the band.

It was no small effort to steer *Primrose* between the two stations. CS-15 had been moving westward at a steady twenty-six kilometers per second under the slower westward winds of the KK sub-band.

The two stations had been about eight thousand kilometers apart when he had departed. He had planned to tack about eight times across the face of the wind; four two-thousand-kilometer legs to the north and four three-thousand-kilometer legs to the south. The southern tacks would gain him the least progress but give him good position to intercept the station as it raced toward him.

It was a good sail plan. The only problem was that it wasn't working out. The inertial guidance system indicated that, instead, he was steadily bearing west of his projected course. Rams checked the set of the sails and the pressure readings. Using these numbers, he calculated that *Primrose* was still bearing forty degrees to the wind, just as he had planned. What could be wrong? Was he was being blown off course by an unexpected head wind?

An hour later, he understood the situation. Something was disturbing the "smooth laminar flow" predictions of Weather. He was just encountering a more northerly wind than expected. He decided to adjust his tacking strategy to adapt to the shift. He'd have to take a longer line on the southern tack. But the slower passage would put him at risk from the storm, which could mean big trouble.

He plotted his course for the next ninety hours with great care.

As they sped down toward the seas of Jupiter, Pascal sat as far from the port of the tiny cab of the elevator as he could and tried to ignore the pit of blackness, a hole in the sky at the center of an enormous emptiness. The thought of all the distance they had to fall terrified him.

"I still don't understand how you guys do it," the pink-faced elevator pilot said from his perch at the bow. "I mean, I can see how a sailboat can go with the wind. The hot air balloons on Earth just go with the wind, right? Why wouldn't they do the same here?"

"It's the keel," John said. He and Al were their competitors from GeoGlobal. They'd arrived a few days before, along with the third crew that would participate in the race. "A sailboat would be just like a balloon if it didn't have a keel."

"Oh, I see. That's why the Jupiter ships have that long ribbon under them," the pilot remarked. "But how does that help them move against the wind? And isn't it impossible to go faster than the wind?"

"Good question," Pascal said, glad of the distraction. "A sailboat goes faster into the wind, not slower. The slowest speed of all is when you run with the wind directly behind you."

Pascal let the kid think about that for a moment before he continued. "A sail is an airfoil. One side forms a pocket of relatively dead air. The opposite side is bent out so that the wind has a longer distance to travel. The pressure differential pulls the sailboat along."

"A foresail funnels the air across the main and accentuates the effect," Al injected. "The closer you haul to the direction of the wind, the faster you go."

John spoke up. "It's just a matter of physics: the angle of force on the sail and the keel produces a vector of force that moves the boat forward. The steeper the angle, the greater the forward thrust. The trick is to balance the force of the wind and the sails, adjusting your angle of attack to obtain the greatest forward momentum possible, maximizing the transfer of static air pressure to dynamic motive force."

"Oh, I understand," the operator said, screwing his face up in concentration. "It's like continuously solving a set of differential equations." He smiled at them as if he were proud of learning the lesson so well.

"Don't bust a gut trying to do that if you're ever in a sailboat, kid," Louella said. "It's all scientific bullshit."

Louella glared at the three of them; a fierce set of her eyes and mouth that brooked no interruption. "These guys want you to think that sailing's a science—that it's all application of mathematical rules and physics. Listening to them, you'd think that you're constantly thinking, calculating, and plotting. Well, that's all a pile of crap; sailing isn't some branch of engineering."

She leaned forward to look straight into the operator's eyes, her expression softening as she did so. "Sailing's a love affair between you, the boat, the water, and the wind. Every one of them has to be balanced, held in check; let any one of them dominate, and you've lost it. A good sailor has to be conscious of wind and water and responsive to the boat's needs. You have to understand the language of wind and sea and ship— you have to feel that edge that means you're running a tight line with every nerve of your body. The boat'll tell you how she wants to behave; she'll fight you when you're wrong, and support you when you're right."

She brushed at her cheek, as if something had gotten in her eye before she continued. "The point I'm trying so damn hard to get across to you is that sailing is an art, not a bloody damn science. That means you have to sail with your heart, as well as your mind. When you're on the sea, managing the sails and the wheel, the rest of the universe could disappear, for all that you care. When everything works right, there's a rhythm, a reverie that transforms you, that makes you one with the universe. If you put everything you have into it, mind and body, your ego disappears—it's just you, the boat, the wind, and the water."

She turned back to stare out the view port at the advancing planet, and slumped into her seat. "If it was just science, JBI wouldn't be paying the big bucks to haul my ass all the way out here. No, they'd get some double-dome Pee Aitch and Dee to build a little machine to do it, and the hell with the beauty of a good line and a strong wind.

"But the fact that I am here to sail on Jupiter's orange seas says that there's still a human element to sailing that's better than the most refined engineering approach. It says that a human being can still stand on a ship's deck and dare the wind and the seas to do their worst. It tells me that even some damn overgrown pig of a planet can't tame the human spirit!"

The silence prevailed for long minutes. "Well," said Al, apropos of nothing. "Well."

Louella said nothing for the rest of the trip down into the thick atmosphere. Pascal tried to ignore the view as sunrise raced across Jupiter's face, too far below.

Rams's destination was floating along at twenty-odd meters per second to the east of his present position. Her track was so reliably managed that the station's precise location could be calculated to within a kilometer.

Somewhere on the other side of CS-42, a whirling hurricane was advancing. Given the right spin and direction, these storms could grow beyond reasonable bounds, turning into blows that made Earth's hurricanes look like a faint puff of air. Ninety-nine times out of one hundred, Jupiter's hurricanes dissipated quickly, within two or three of his ten-hour rotations. If Rams was lucky, this one would do the same.

Rams was dismayed to discover that *Primrose* fell even further westward off of her planned track whenever he turned to the north. That meant two things: the winds were continuing to shift, and the storm was deeper than expected. It looked like he'd hit the edges of a major storm.

For the thousandth time, he wished that Jupiter wasn't so electronically active. The ambient white noise on the radio bands was so intense that even pulse-code modulation couldn't punch a signal through. Just one crummy satellite picture, one quick radar image, one short broadcast was all he'd need to find out what was happening with the storm.

Instead, all he knew about the storm was its rough starting position, Weather's predicted track, and the data the station master provided about prevailing winds. He also had the data from his own inertial system. From those weak components, he had to navigate through a dark eight thousand kilometers, face unknown winds, and find the tiny station that was his destination.

"A little bit cramped, isn't it," Pascal remarked as they inspected *Thorn*, their tiny, nine-hundred ton, double-masted barque. He sat with one leg extended into the cockpit and the other in the "stateroom," which also served as kitchen, bath, and bedroom. A single bunk stretched for two meters across the overhead with a single, small seat below, which, when lifted, revealed the toilet. A tiny shelf with a built-in microwave oven and a recessed sink—hidden under the working surface—ran along the second bulkhead, to the right. Their food and medical supplies were stored in hanging bags, velcroed to the bulkhead above the microwave.

On the opposite bulkhead was a fold-down table whose opened edge would be in the lap of whoever was sitting on the seat. The navigation instruments, computer, and the storage for charts and instruments were revealed when the table was down. Rams could reach out with his left arm and just about touch the edge of the helmsman's seat, it was that close. For a big boat, *Thorn* had mightily small crew quarters.

"Maybe we shouldn't have picked a cargo hauler—it's a little cramped, isn't it?" Louella remarked as she ducked her head to peek into the compartment. "Place looked a lot roomier in the plans. I guess the crew wasn't supposed to stay aboard for more than a day or two."

Pascal looked around. "Why couldn't they convert some of that cargo hold—this is pretty tight. I don't relish spending a couple of weeks in here."

"Too much trouble just to give us a little bit of comfort. I don't think the expense would be worth it—might upset the boat's balance."

Pascal sighed, and wiggled in the tiny seat, trying to find a way to stretch his legs full length, and failed. "The navigator's station on the

Bermuda run was bigger than this," he complained, and tried to put his arms out. His right elbow hit the hanging bags. He sighed again—this was going to be damned uncomfortable.

"Yeah, but you weren't nearly as warm and dry," Louella reminded him. "I don't mind cramped spaces during a race. Hell, on most of our races, dry underwear's a luxury! Count your blessings, Pascal. Count your blessings."

While Pascal squeezed up the narrow tube to examine the sail locker, Louella sat in the helmsman's seat. She let her hands run over the controls. She loved the slightly sticky feel of the wrappings on the wheel. Here and there she noted the faint, oily marks *Thorn*'s captains' sweating hands had put there.

A bright, shining circle was worn into the dull metal beside the winch controls. She reached for a knob, as if to activate it, and noticed that the heel of her hand centered on the worn spot. How many hundreds of times had another hand briefly touched there to wear the finish like that, she wondered. How many captains had sat in this seat to guide the tiny craft across the dark seas of Jupiter? In her mind, those other captains were a palpable presence in the tiny cabin, a trace of the boat's memory.

Directly in front of the helmsman's seat were the screens that displayed the fore and aft camera views. Their controls were in easy reach, just below them. To her left were the inertial display unit, the pressure gauges, and various station-keeping controls. The house-keeping controls were mounted beneath the seat, where they could be reached from the stateroom.

On a swing arm above the wheel were the primary control readouts; sail pressure gauges, wind indicator, barometer, and dead reckoning display. Once they were under weigh, she'd be completely dependent on them.

There was a clatter as Pascal wormed his way out of the tube. "Sail sets look okay," he said as he slid across the deck and dropped into the stateroom's seat. "We've got spares for every sail, plus the extras that you ordered. All of them are marked and set for loading."

"Did you make sure that we have enough lines? I don't want to get caught short on tack once we get out of here."

Pascal snorted. "Of course I checked. My butt's going to be out there, too, you know."

Louella nodded, all business. "I double-checked the inspection reports. Just the same, we need to do a walk-around."

She'd said it so calmly that Pascal almost missed the implication of what she had said. When he did, he snapped erect, banging his head on the bottom of the bunk.

"Y… you mean… go… outside?" he blurted.

Louella sneered at him. "Sure. We can get some pressure suits and hand lights to work with. As long as you stay in the dock you won't have any problems. It will be just like going for our training stroll at geosynch. You didn't have any problems there, did you?"

Pascal stuttered. He'd been scared out of his wits the whole time, worrying whether his lines were securely attached, worrying about the ability of his boots to hold fast to the deck, worrying about slipping, about the vast distance that he would fall should he become detached from the station.

"N… no," he lied.

They didn't need the hand lights after all. *Thorn* was still parked in the repair bay, where there was plenty of external illumination. Louella held tight to her walker as she stumbled through the lock. The walker took most of the weight off of her legs, which was a blessing. Even though she didn't have too much of a problem with the two-gee's, the additional weight of the heavy pressure suit made movement difficult.

Pascal stumbled along behind her, clutching his own walker so tightly that it looked like he'd leave glove marks in the metal.

"What a pig," Louella remarked as she examined the bulbous skin of *Thorn*'s outer envelope. "Looks like a damned overgrown, pregnant guppy," she said as she walked along the side of the bulging hull, thinking of the sleek craft she had sailed in Earth's tame waters. Every few steps she stopped to examine a weld, a spot of suspicious discoloration, or one of the vents for the ballast hold.

"Let's take a look at her rigging," she demanded, and followed the crew chief to the boat's deck.

Two stubby masts projected up from the center line of *Thorn*'s upper surface. These were thick triangles of heavy metal, nearly six meters across at their thickest dimension. They certainly weren't the slender masts she'd known all her life.

The trailing edges of each mast were clamshells. These were double-locked doors that would open when they deployed the sails. A short track ran back from each mast, with a cross-wise track at the end. "We extended the travelers on both sides, like you asked," the crew chief said. "You're goin' to have a bit of trouble handling her. Keep a tight hand on the wheel and don't run close to the wind, is my advice." Disapproval was evident in his voice. "Don't think you should have done that, though; these little boats ain't built to take much heel, y'know."

Louella bristled as she checked the workmanship on the track modifications, looking for any indication that the repair crew had scrimped on her specifications. "Did you think about adjusting the traveler's winches to take the extra line?"

The crew chief bristled. "Of course I did," he said gruffly. "I don't appreciate you sayin' that I don't know how to do my job."

"Really? Well, I don't like you telling me how to sail a boat either, asshole!" she shot back, and moved to examine the other mast as the crew chief licked his wounds.

While Louella and the crew chief were above deck, Pascal examined the hull. The keel had already been retracted from the meter-by-meter safety inspection. The huge weights at the ends of the double keel swung slowly from side to side as *Thorn* bobbed up and down. *Thorn* was just a balloon when she wasn't under weigh. The keels' slender foils hardly seemed strong enough to support the three hundred tons of droplet-shaped weights. The blunt nose of the forward weight was smooth and bright, as if it had been polished. There were several long gouges along the sides.

"Impact scars," the crewman said, as she reached across the gap and shoved her glove inside one of the larger ones. "There's always some gravels being driven around the atmosphere, especially down deep, where the keel runs. Sometimes they're pretty big and movin' fast. That's what made these dings, y'see."

Pascal was still staring at the thin ribbons that supported the weights. Each was only a few centimeters thick, hardly the width of his hand. One rip from a rough piece of gravel, he thought, and the ribbon could be severed and the weight would be released, dropping down into the depths far, far below.

Suddenly, he realized that he was only one step away from the edge of the inspection platform. One step away from a fall that wouldn't stop until he reached a pressure level that would crush and kill him, compressing his suit and body into a tiny mass. He would still fall until it hit the layer of metallic hydrogen, hundreds and hundreds of kilometers below the station. No, that wasn't really true; he wouldn't fall that far. His body would come to rest somewhere where his density was equal to the surrounding atmosphere.

But he'd still be dead.

A wave of vertigo overcame him. He stumbled back from the dangerous precipice. "I... I need to get back inside," he told his escort, and clamped his hand on the safety line. "Now!" he shouted, when the crewman didn't respond at once. He had to get away from that horrid drop.

Twelve hours later, Rams realized that he was in serious trouble. Whenever he tried to head due north, he was forced farther west of his planned track. To be so affected at this distance meant that the storm was immense.

He prepared for the coming storm. The two things a sailor had to remember about surviving a storm, whether on Jupiter or on Earth, were to either be prepared, or be elsewhere. Rams began to go through *Primrose* and secure her. Even a small item flying about in a two-gee field could do substantial damage.

The galley and his own cabin were easy. Rams made it a practice to stow everything until needed. Just the same, he went through every locker to make sure that nothing would fall out and surprise him. He poured hot tea into a thermos and stowed that, along with some bread, in the cockpit.

Securing the cargo hold occupied him for an hour. He put double lashings on all of the containers, and tied them together, just to make sure. That done, he made certain that all loose lines were in the lockers, along with all of the deck gear. Nothing that could become a flying missile was left unsecured.

Since he wasn't carrying passengers this trip, the other four cabins were empty. Just the same, he checked them for loose gear or an open locker. He had to make absolutely certain they were secure.

Securing the sail locker presented a problem. Rams had to balance being able to hoist sail in a hurry—which meant he had to have one loose

—against the risk of it breaking free. He secured the larger sails and kept the two small ones ready to hoist as a compromise. If the blow was as heavy as he expected, the small ones were more likely to be used.

That done, Rams brought the ship about to begin another long, southerly tack. That way he could use the peripheral winds to stay on the outer fringes of the storm. With a little bit of luck, *Primrose* wouldn't be drawn into its roaring core. Then he settled down to see what the long night would bring.

Thorn was six days out from the start and making weigh at a steady one-fifty mps. Pascal had already grown sick of the close quarters, the five-hours-on, five-hours-off schedule that matched Jupiter's rotational rate, Louella's lousy cooking, even if it was better than his own, the dragging load from Jupiter's gravity, and the lingering, stinking ammonia smell from the boat's slight atmospheric leakage.

They'd added their own contribution to the atmosphere. After nearly a week of confined quarters, they had created a unique miasma. The cabin was redolent of recirculated air, collected flatulence, sweat, and the miscellaneous aromas that the human body produced. Only the ability of the human nose to filter out the worse of these protected him. Still, the smells remained, and, unfortunately, Pascal's nose sometimes forgot to ignore them.

He fidgeted at the wheel, keeping an wary eye on the instruments. It was important to maintain the sail's pressure differential right on the edge, in order to keep their speed up. All week, Louella had beaten his time. Somehow, she was able to wrest a few extra knots from the wind. No matter how much he pushed, Louella was always able to do better.

They'd been competing ever since he could remember, each trying to outdo the other. She dared him to become a better sailor, even as she relentlessly strove to beat him every time. He challenged her to become the better navigator, and laughed at her struggles with simple plotting problems. She's succeeded better than he, even if he never was able to offset her intuition with his science. Their teamwork had won numerous races over the years. Their success gained them prime berths in JBI's commercial racing fleet. Louella had worked her way from an Olympic dingy championship at age thirteen to finally being the helmsman on most of JBI's Cup winners, as well as the number one competitor in most of the other commercial classes.

Pascal had been a navigator on Louella's first Whitbread, and had saved her life on more than one occasion, most notably in *Le Grand Vendee*, for which she would be eternally grateful. Over the years, he'd sailed with her as navigator, tactician, winch crank, or sail master. He'd been helmsman when she was captain, and shared bunk with her on the Times' double-around-the-world. They'd weathered hurricanes and drifted demasted for days with only a bottle of water to share between them. They'd broached a hundred-thousand-dollar racer in 'Frisco Bay, lost a two-million-dollar racer in the South Pacific, and survived to win the Bermuda in spite of a hurricane that destroyed half the fleet and shredded their mainsail to ribbons. It had been a thrill the whole time.

He just wished that she wasn't such a pain in the ass.

Louella came awake in an instant, and checked her watch. She had managed to sleep for nearly five hours without being jarred awake. "Damn Pascal's eyes," she complained to herself as she fastened her truss. "He must be running safe again." That meant that she would have to make up for lost time during her watch, as usual.

She rolled out of the bunk, stepped cautiously to the deck, and used the toilet, splashing a little water from the sink up her nose to counteract the dryness from the ammonia fumes.

"Tea's hot," Pascal called down to her in a voice heavy with fatigue.

"Thanks," she replied, looking for the thermos. "How did you find time to make it?"

"You mean how much progress did that cost us, don't you," he replied sharply. "Not a bit, I'm sure."

"Do you think that the competition's doing better? Damn, but I wish we had some way of telling where the other boats are!"

A week before, everyone had set off from Charlie Sierra Six on the first leg of the Great Jupiter Race, as the press had been calling it. The first leg would take them around CS-15 and then back to CS-27, where they would come to windward and race downwind to CS-6, where they had begun.

Louella had watched the heat signature of their prime competitor fall to *Thorn*'s lee when they came out of the shelter of the starting station, indicating that they had caught the vortex off of *Thorn* and were spinning away to get good air. It was a trick most sailors learned before they left their cribs.

They had watched the diminishing white dot that represented the station fade into the background noise as *Thorn* pulled steadily westward, their speed climbing the whole time under Jupiter's fierce winds. It was therefore a little disturbing to discover a heat signature steadily increasing in definition on their aft screen. Somehow, one of the other boats had managed to catch a better wind cell than theirs.

Louella jibbed to port, hoping to create a pocket of dirty air behind *Thorn* that would interfere with the other's progress. The white dot responded by immediately moving to starboard, long before they could have felt the effects of Louella's maneuver.

"Obviously they can see us better than we can see them," Pascal cursed as he tried to crank up the gain. "It's probably the wind blowing our signature backward. Should we jib again?"

Louella dismissed the idea; *Thorn* lost some momentum each time they jibbed. "Let's concentrate on building up our speed," she replied, and made some tiny adjustments to the set of the sails.

The image of the other boat faded to port, and finally disappeared. They were six hours out from the start.

"What are they doing now?" Louella wondered aloud. "Could they have caught another favorable wind cell? Do you think they're starting their northward leg already?"

Pascal checked the inertial. *Thorn* was still a few hours from their planned turning point. "Let them go," he said. "Concentrate on our own course while I grab some sleep."

Pascal was having difficulty staying awake during his shift at the wheel. The days of five-hour sleep cycles, bland food, and lack of exercise were taking their toll. On most of the long races on Earth, he at least could stand on the deck, stretch, and get a breath of air to refresh himself. Down here, in Jupiter's atmosphere, he couldn't even stand upright, much less sniff the air blowing by outside the boat. Not that he'd want to, he hastily amended.

But it was dry, as Louella had said, and that was something. He recalled how he'd always hated the pervasive dampness, the clinging, sticky moisture that characterized every ocean race.

Thorn's trim felt wrong, as if she were lumbering in thick syrup, even though her speed was good. Perhaps, he thought, the boat would have a better feel if she rode a little higher, a little lighter.

He clicked on the heaters in the ballast hold. They had pumped nearly four tons of liquified gas from the bottom of the keel into the ballast tank to set their present trim. The heaters would expand the liquid and force the ballast out. He turned them off after an hour, when the trim felt better.

On the seventh day of their run, they rounded CS-15 on their port side, and watched the vivid image displayed on their radar screen until it faded back into the ambient noise. Pascal had dutifully recorded the close passage, to prove that they had indeed rounded the mark, while Louella concentrated on keeping *Thorn* a safe distance away. To do so, she maneuvered the winches to switch the sails from side to side, slipping a little to slew the craft about without losing momentum.

As much as they'd like to do so, there was no time to stop, and no way to find out if the station knew that they had passed. They'd tried the radio, but the deafening noise of atmospheric static masked any reply that might have been attempted.

"I wish we could find out which boats have already gone by," Pascal remarked as he stowed the log and climbed wearily into his bunk. He loosened the truss and breathed a sigh of relief.

"The hell with them," Louella answered weakly, in a voice that revealed that she, too, was getting tired. "We just have to do the best we can, and hope that the rest do worse. That's what racing is all about."

"Yeah, remember the last Whitbread? Didn't see another boat the whole race. It was like we had the whole ocean to ourselves."

"Not much fun there. What I remember is sitting dead in the water for three days while the sun baked us to a crisp; no wind, no progress. It was only luck that we caught the edge of that storm and got a boost."

"Won the race, didn't we? Luck falls to those with the most skill," Pascal said encouragingly.

"Let's just hope it works this time as well," she said dryly. "Now get some shuteye, so you can relieve me in two hours."

The rest of her watch passed without incident as she tacked at a twenty degree angle to the head wind. The new sails that they had deployed on day five were still serviceable, and were probably good for another two days at least. There was a minor fluctuation in the barometer, and Louella let the keel down a few hundred meters.

She nearly fell asleep at one point, she was so tired.

Louella was the first to notice how their track was consistently deviating to the south. On the last two tacks, they had strayed nearly fifty kilometers west of plan.

"Unless there are some different physics out there, we can't possibly be heading like the inertial shows," she remarked with a nod of her head at the instrument, when Pascal crawled up to relieve her.

Pascal looked at the readout. "This thing's supposed to be foolproof. Maybe you're misreading it?"

Louella snorted in reply. "You check it yourself. I'm getting something to eat and then some shuteye." She slid from the helmsman's perch, past Pascal, and into the stateroom. "See if you can figure out what's wrong."

Pascal kept an eye on the inertial throughout his shift. Sure enough, the southern legs showed the same deviation. If the machine were to be believed, then the winds were coming almost directly down from the north, instead of following the westerly course that they had been told to expect.

He wished that he was thinking a little more clearly. Something kept itching at the edges of thought. Something someone had warned them about. What was it? He looked at the curving southerly trace that the inertial was showing and wondered. It almost looked like a smooth curve... Then he had it! A turbulence eddy must have formed along the edge. If the readout was right, then they were already being drawn into its grasp. "Louella!" he shouted, "wake up! We have a bit of a problem."

Hours later, the winds rocked *Thorn* from side to side as Louella fought to make way. Unlike the smooth air they had encountered thus far, the winds on the edges of the storm were rough, uneven gusts that quartered with little warning. In one stomach-wrenching instance, *Thorn* had turned completely about, while pitching nearly sixty degrees to leeward, reversing as the wind switched and slammed them in the opposite direction.

She knew that they'd lost the foresail, and suspected that the aft was in tatters. There was no possibility of hoisting new ones in these rough seas. Something in the sail locker had torn loose and was smashing around. Pascal would be taking his life in his hands if he tried to go into the locker. For good or ill, they had to use whatever sail they had and hope that their skill, and no small amount of luck, would see them through.

"Can't even put out a damned sea anchor to steady her," she complained at one point. "How the hell do the sailors up here survive these storms, anyhow?"

"I think they are wise enough not to do something stupid like racing in small boats." Pascal said dryly from the bunk where he had secured himself. "How are we doing?"

Louella checked the instruments. "As far as I can see, we are straightening out our track somewhat. At least we aren't curving more."

"I hope that means we aren't getting sucked in. How big do you think this storm is?"

"No telling. I don't know how they scale these storms up here. Back home this would be called a one-million year storm, I'm certain. It's a monster!"

Another gust hit them on the side. Louella threw the switch to lower the keel, and their center of gravity, to give them some more stability. It was all that she could do.

The remnants of the aft sail blew away during Pascal's watch. The rocking of the boat stopped as she drifted with the wind. Since he now had no control over *Thorn*, he lashed the wheel in place and crawled into the sail locker. The only way they had of restoring some measure of control to the boat was to get another sail up.

The locker was a mess. The big specialty main that Louella had ordered for the finishing run had broken loose of its restraints and had swept the mountings clean off the deck. Bits of broken metal and plastic tie-downs were everywhere. A large dent on the bulkhead showed where the big sail had struck before it finally wedged itself behind the canisters.

Pascal stumbled over the wreckage and selected one of the smaller sails. He undid the lashings, trying to maintain his balance against the pitching motion of the boat. As he worked, he kept a wary eye on the huge mainsail, in case it began to roll his way.

Twice the boat moved unexpectedly and threw him against the stowed sails, smashing their blunt edges into his chest and back. He knew that he'd have massive bruises to show for it.

Finally, he secured the winch to the sail head, and locked the cables in place. He braced himself between the sail and the bulkhead, using the pressure of his legs to stay in place, and began the tortuous process of ratcheting the sail into place. It took all of his energy to move it the last few centimeters.

Louella was awake and in the helmsman's seat when he poked his head out of the tube. "Sail ready?" she asked calmly, as if nothing was amiss.

Pascal nodded. "Aft mast, small set," he said quickly, thankful that she had not made an issue of his reckless actions. She was all cool control and professional when the race was on.

"Brace yourself," she warned as she reached for the controls. "Release!" She threw the hoist switches to start the sail as Pascal tightened the straps to hold himself in the bunk.

Louella spun the wheel to bring the boat directly into the wind. The wind caught the edge of the new sail and pulled it the rest of the way out.

Louella adjusted the traveler. The wind filled the sail, throwing *Thorn* at a sharp angle. The boat heeled precariously, and then leaped forward with a force that snapped Louella's head back against the headrest. She managed the trim of the sail, a matter more of feel than science, until the boat was riding steadily downwind, making steady progress. *Thorn* rode safely and secure in the teeth of the storm.

"That's the right thing to do," she said softly to the exhausted Pascal. "Good going, partner."

The relative calm following the storm was a blessing. Rams had managed to be blown only a couple hundred kilometers south of his planned track through a combination of his skill and considerable luck. All he had to do now was intercept the CS-42 track and pray that the storm hadn't forced her too far from the projected track in his computer.

Rams checked the sail one more time, and then prepared to come about. It was time to head on a northerly leg. He buckled himself to the deck and released the hold-downs on the wheel. He felt a throb reverberate though the deck as the rudder cut into the dense soup, far below. He imagined it to be *Primrose*'s heart beat.

The hull began to sound a deep resonant note that echoed throughout the ship. "Damn harmonics," Rams swore, and retracted the keel until the sound disappeared. Left alone, the wind blowing across the keel would set up a destructive harmonic that could destroy the ship.

"Ready girl," he whispered, and turned the wheel ever so slightly to starboard. He put one hand on the port-side jib release and waited. *Primrose* rolled to the perpendicular, and then shook as her prow came through the eye of the wind.

Rams hit the port-side release and switched on the starboard-side jib winch. In his mind's eye, he could see the mainsail whipping across the deck, slamming the traveler to rest on the opposite side as it turned its port side to weather.

There was a clatter of chain against the pressure hull that stopped when the loose jib finally stretched taut. *Primrose* heeled and started to pick up speed on the downwind leg. Rams held the wheel loosely, searching for balance until he was confident that the ship had once more found her line. Only then did he lock the wheel into place and relax.

He unbuckled the restraints and started to pour the last cup of tea from his thermos when he stopped. Something was out of the ordinary, but he couldn't put his finger on it. Rams examined the instrument panel. Everything seemed to be in order; no red warning lights that would scream that the hull had been breached, no flashing indication that the rigging was damaged, no alarm telling him that some life-threatening life support system was malfunctioning. What could it have been?

Then the infrared display flashed again. Rams started in surprise. There, on the screen, was a white blob—a heat indication where there should be nothing but empty sky. A glance at the camera indicator told him that the blob was off his starboard bow, just at the edge of the imager's range.

Quickly, he released the wheel and spun *Primrose* about, pulling the jib tight and letting it backwind, just as Jake had taught him. The winds buffeted the ship for a few seconds, rocking it from side to side until, finally, the motion subsided. The ship was close-hauled into the wind, the pressure on the reversed jib equal to the pressure on the loose main, and both constrained by the kilometers of keel beneath him.

He carefully turned the aft camera around, trying to find another indication of that heat signature. Several times he thought that he had it, but was mistaken. Stare at a screen of random noise long enough and you are likely to see anything you want. He continued to search.

Then he had it. A definite heat source, and quite close, too. The object was moving at about the same velocity and direction as the wind.

They were so far off of their planned track by watch change that neither of them could see how they could make up the lost time. "I don't see how the other competitors could have avoided the storm," Pascal remarked as he examined the charts and the trace of the inertial. "Surely they're in as bad a shape as we are."

"Don't count on it," Louella snarled. "Most of them are tough sons of bitches. Somebody probably figured out how to use this storm's winds to their advantage. I wouldn't be surprised to find that at least two of them have a good day's advantage on us."

"Oh, when did you become such an optimist?" Pascal answered bitterly.

"When I got you as a partner," she snapped back.

Pascal checked the trim while Louella snored in her bunk. *Thorn* felt sluggish, probably Louella had taken on more ballast, he thought. He switched on the heater to vent some of it and lighten the boat.

A sudden gust blew *Thorn* to the side. She tilted nearly forty degrees as the wheel whipped from side to side.

"What the hell?" Louella yelled from her bunk.

"I think the sail's gone again," Pascal yelled down at her. "Take the wheel while I get another one ready."

Louella squirmed into the seat as Pascal dragged himself into the sail locker. *Thorn* was rocking steadily from side to side. She turned on the winch to let out more keel and steady the boat, letting out another hundred meters of mesh.

"Let's try the foresail this time," she yelled at Pascal's disappearing feet.

Pascal wiggled into the cramped space beside the sails and braced himself. He ached all over. No matter how he positioned himself, some bruised part of his body pressed painfully against something. He rigged the lines and gear until the red-tagged foresail was ready to be ratcheted into the loading compartment.

He carefully attached the pulley to the head end of the sail, and began to crank it into place. With every turn of the winch his muscles ached. He banged his elbow on the bulkhead with each long stroke of the winch handle. He ached all over.

With a twenty-to-one ratio, it took a long time to finally get the sail into place—long enough for the forgotten heater to turn the entire ballast load into steam.

Back in the cabin, Louella noticed the sideways motion of the boat. She immediately checked the pressure gauges, thinking the wind had switched unexpectedly. But that wasn't the problem; their heading was still good, and the wind had settled down. Why then were they slipping sideways? She tried to clear her head and reason it out. She wished that she wasn't so damn tired.

Then she noticed the blinking warning light above the heater switch. "Damn," she swore, "how did I miss that?" and turned it off.

Pascal stuck his head out of the end of the tube. "Sail's all ready to go."

"Right, brace yourself," she responded, and hit the winches to raise the sail.

Before she could react, the ship moved violently to one side, throwing her from the seat and smashing her against the bulkhead. She didn't even have time to scream.

Pascal came painfully to full consciousness. His head throbbed and his side was a mass of agony, as if his ribs had been crushed. The first thing that he saw was Louella slumped against the bulkhead of the cockpit, her arm at an awkward angle. "She must have forgotten to buckle herself in," he mumbled, and crawled to her. The pain in his side stabbed each time he moved.

Louella's pulse was all right, but her breathing was labored. He turned her to one side to relieve the front-to-back pressure from the two-gee gravity. She moaned as he shifted her.

He ran his hand down her arm, feeling for a break, a dislocated joint. The arm was all right, but there was a swelling at her wrist indicating a possible sprain or fracture. Since there was nothing more serious apparent, he climbed himself into the seat and buckled himself in. He could take care of Louella's medical problems later, after he found out what *Thorn*'s situation was: The boat always came first!

A quick glance at the instruments showed that there was no pressure differential on the sails. The wind speed indicator read a fat zero, which meant that *Thorn* must be moving at the same speed as the wind. He noted that the ballast was zip. In an obvious contradiction, the pressure gauge showed them to still be on the boundary layer. Nevertheless, *Thorn* was bobbing uncomfortably, as if she had lost some trim.

He clicked on the pumps that would bring more ballast up through the pipes. Once the boat had the proper trim, he could turn her back into the wind. As he was waiting for that, he looked at the inertial. According to the readout, they had lost most of their progress for the last day, at least. They were being blown back toward CS-15, but on a southward angle.

Since it would be a while until the pumps did their work, he got the first aid kit out of storage, and put a splint on Louella's arm. He prepared a dose of painkiller for when she woke. He'd only give it if she asked for it. Carefully, he turned her head, and waved a broken ampule under her nose.

"Wha… Where… Humph," she said, and tried to sit up. "Wha… what happened," she asked.

"Don't know. Was coming back down the tube when all hell broke loose. Threw me against the side and knocked me out. We're way off course now."

"Oh, your head," she said, and reached out with her good hand to touch his forehead. "You're bleeding!"

He brushed her hand away. "Just a bump, I think. Rotten headache, though. How do you feel? Do you need this?" He held up the dose he'd prepared.

"Can't take something that will knock me out. Help me get to the bunk so I can lay down. We need to figure out what we have to do. Maybe then I'll let you use it."

By the time he'd wrestled her into the bunk and fastened the straps to secure her in place, the pumps had been running for a good ten minutes. He dropped into the seat and checked the gauges. The stabbing pains in his side abated for a moment.

"That's strange," he remarked, as he flicked the pump switches on and off. "There doesn't seem to be any ballast."

"Yeah," Louella said. "You left the heaters on. I flipped them off while you were messing with the sail."

"Shit, I forgot about them when the sail blew. But that doesn't explain why the pumps aren't working."

"Maybe we're floating too high. Maybe the keel isn't deep enough to find anything to pump."

"Can't be. Pressure gauge says we're right where we're supposed to be." He glanced at the keel meter. "The keel's down as far as it will go, so we should be pumping ballast. Since we aren't, that means that either the pumps have stopped working, or something has damaged the lines leading to the ballast tanks."

"Either way, we can't trim the boat," Louella mused. "Well, let's try using the sails anyway, to see what sort of maneuverability we have. We have to be able to make one of the stations, or we're royally screwed."

Pascal threw the switches to pull the foresail back from its fully extended position. As the winches brought the sail tight, *Thorn* heeled to lee instead of turning into the wind. He let the sail out, hoping to run downwind instead. Perhaps on that setting, he'd be able to steer from side to side.

But the boat wouldn't turn that way, either.

"Unless you can think of any other things to try," he said, after an hour of experimenting various settings with sails and the immobile keel, "I think we're stuck. There aren't any rescue boats out here. It looks like you'll get your wish to 'sail Jupiter's seas forever.' According to my calculations, *Thorn* won't intersect a station's track for at least a thousand years."

"Well, Pascal," Louella said in a surprisingly soft voice, "If we're going to die, I can't think of anybody I'd rather do it with than you, and no better place than on a racing boat."

"I'm afraid that I can," he replied too quickly, and watched the gray nothingness of the infrared display as he contemplated his own death.

At least he'd be free of this damn headache, he thought.

Rams was puzzled as he approached the strangely warm object that had suddenly appeared. *Primrose* was now matched to the speed of the object. He carefully headed downwind and slowly closed the gap between them. Rams kept one hand on the winch controls as he maneuvered the ship closer and closer to the object, tightening and loosening the sail controls to creep forward.

At a few hundred meters, the infrared image resolved into a strange double blob. The large upper blob was a one or two hundred meters above *Primrose*. The smaller one was about the same distance below. A barely discernable thin line, apparently just a few degrees above the ambient temperature, connected the two blobs. He'd never seen anything so strange in all of the time he'd spent on Jupiter's seas.

As he drew closer, the upper blob resolved itself into the familiar heat signature of a small craft, possibly a cargo barque or maybe a miner. Maybe the connecting line was its keel, he thought. But what was the blob at the bottom? It was far too large and irregular to be keel weights.

He pumped a little more ballast into *Primrose*'s tanks and sank lower. He wasn't going to get any closer to the pair until he figured out what was going on. "Hate to mess up some science folks, wouldn't we," he remarked to *Primrose*.

The heat image resolved into two keel ribbons. They appeared to be tangled around some large shape that was below ambient temperature, as if it had come from deeper in the atmosphere. He flooded it with his sonar, watching as the display built up a ghostly image of the irregular shape.

On a hunch, he pinged it with the docking sonar frequency, and listened through the static for the reply: One, two, three pings came back, which indicated that he had made the lump ring. Either it was hollow, which made no sense, or it had a high metallic content. Somehow the other ship had been hit by a piece of rock brought up by the storm—a huge piece that could be worth a fortune.

He brought the ship back up until she was level with the other ship, carefully staying downwind to avoid smashing into her. With fine adjustments of the jib, he allowed the other ship to come closer and closer, until they almost kissed.

"Hello," he yelled over the radio link, hoping that they were close enough to overcome the static. "This is the clipper *Primrose*, four days out of CS-15. Do you need assistance?"

Louella started at the sudden and unexpected sound of a strange human voice coming over the static of the radio. Pascal tried to sit upright and looked around. Since the accident, he had slept in the helmsman's seat, letting Louella have the more comfortable bunk where she could sleep. She'd relented after the second day and let him administer the painkiller. "Just make sure it isn't a lethal dose," she'd jokingly remarked. "I don't want to miss the end of this race."

"Nor I," Pascal had replied slowly, and thought about what she had just said. He'd never considered that possibility. An "accidental" mistake in dosage would certainly be something to think about as the air grew closer.

To pass the time, they'd talked about things that they never seemed to have time to discuss earlier. Except for the long trip out from Earth, when she was still pissed after their big argument and wouldn't talk to him, the only time they'd had together was during the races, or while preparing for them. Under those circumstances, it had been all business: winning the race, discussing the set of the sails, the movement of the currents and the wind, talking about the positions and strategies of their competition, and the endless details of reconciling her art of sailing with his science. After every race, they went their separate ways until the next race, the next challenge that threw them together.

"Always wanted to have a place on Chesapeake Bay," Louella confided during one of the times they were both awake. Since the accident, they had abandoned their five-hours-on, five-hours-off schedule. "Some little marina where I could teach kids to race. Maybe have a dinghy school of my own. You know, take a shot at producing a batch of Olympic champions."

Pascal snorted at that: if he ever got out of this, he wanted to live as far from the ocean as possible, maybe in Arizona or New Mexico. Some place where wet clothing, must and mildew, and cold, sodden food were unheard of. Someplace where the damned footing was solid and the horizon always stayed level with your eyes. He yearned for some place that was dry, flat, and had no dangerous cliffs.

But neither could convince the other of the desirability of their dreams, even though the chances of achieving them were impossible. There was only a day or two left of the life support system. The water had gone the day before. Both knew that they were doomed. They would become a Jovian version of the Flying Dutchman.

"I repeat, do... **crackle**... hisssss... need assistance?" the voice rattled from the speaker. Pascal fumbled around under the instrument panel and found the microphone.

"I hear you loud and clear," he yelled. "Thank God you found us. I mean, yes, yes we need help badly!"

"Are... **crackle** pop**... under sail?" the voice said with what sounded like a tone of impatience.

"No," Pascal said in response. "We cannot maneuver. We are without ballast and cannot control our craft."

"**pop**... wish to abandon... ship?" came the hissing reply. "Do you... ****... rescued?"

"Of course we do, you fucking idiot," Louella screamed into the microphone. "Of course we want to be rescued!" Tears of happiness were steaming down her face even as she cursed the stupidity of the question.

"Tell him to give us instructions," Pascal said, wiping the moisture from his own face with one hand while he gently wiped at the tears on Louella's with the other as they hugged each other in the cramped cockpit.

Rams tried to understand what the woman was saying about the condition of their boat. The radio handled low frequencies better than high, and that made her voice difficult to understand. If only she'd stop and let the other guy talk!

" ****...can't maneuver...," she told him. "No food, no water... life support gone. We're afraid... **crackle** ...ship... complete loss.... abandon...** pop**..."

Rams wondered what sort of idiots they were to talk about abandoning their ship. Didn't they know the wealth that they'd discovered? Didn't they realize how valuable their own ship was? "I'll take her under tow if you want."

"Understand.... ***** ...need medical **tention."

"All right. I will bring you aboard and secure your ship. By the way," he said slyly, "Will you give me salvage rights if I do so?"

It took him several repeats before he could make them understand just what he was asking. He made sure that he had their request to abandon ship on file. It had to be clear that it was their idea, not a threat by him. He really had no choice but to help them—that was how you survived on Jupiter.

Rams struggled into the heavy pressure suit and, once inside, hooked its safety line to the ring near the hatch. Attached to his belt were lengths of high tensile strength line. He could use them to string the two craft together. Checking to make certain that everything was ready, he opened the hatch and stepped directly out into the howling winds of Jupiter.

Rams had brought the far larger *Primrose* to within fifty meters of the smaller ship's hull, letting the venturi effect of the winds in the narrow channel hold them close.

His exterior lights just barely illuminated the upper surface of the other ship. Rams watched as two figures struggled awkwardly out of the hatch and clamped their lines onto the deck rings.

The two ships bucked and lurched, the gap between them widening and closing. The decks rose and sank relative to each other as they bobbed, side by side. Rams prayed that he'd set the ship's sails properly to hold station with the drifting ship. He clicked his suit light four times to attract their attention.

When he got a wave of acknowledgment, he readied one of the lines, whirling the pulley at its end over his head in ever widening circles before releasing it upwind. The pulley sailed out and too quickly down, drawn by the higher acceleration of Jupiter's gravity. It clanked onto the near side of *Thorn*'s hull and slipped away.

Rams retrieved the line and tried again, and a third time. On the fourth toss, the pulley finally cleared the deck. The line whipped around to catch against the two figures, making the smaller of them stagger back from the impact.

The other figure secured the pulley to their deck with one arm and waited. Rams carefully pulled the light line back as he paid out a heavier one that was tied to its end. It took nearly half an hour before he had a slack double line rigged between the two rocking and bobbing craft. The line moved up and down, tightening and then loosening as the two ships lurched in the wind. He wrapped the line around a deck winch and locked it in place.

Finally, Rams attached a cradle of ropes and clamps he had rigged to a hook on the heavier line. Slowly he winched the cradle to the other ship, hoping that they would use it properly. The last thing he wanted was for someone to take a plunge.

"You first," Pascal said nervously as he caught hold of the rig. "Let me hook you up."

"No fucking way. I'm the captain of this boat and I leave last," Louella replied. "Turn around so I can hook the clamps to your suit."

"Yeah, and how are you going to hook yourself up with a broken arm?" he shot back. "Now turn around. For once, don't be such a bitch!"

"Why, Pascal," she said in surprise. "That sounds like you actually care about me."

"Well, it looks like we'll have the Whitbread next year after all," he said as he checked the rig's fastenings a second time to make certain they were secure. "I wouldn't want to be with anyone else in that race."

"It's a date, lover," Louella remarked.

Once he saw that Louella had been dipped, jerked, and lurched to the other ship, Pascal had to face what would happen next: In a few moments, the rig would return, and he would have to hook himself to it so that his rescuer could winch him across the bottomless chasm of Jupiter's atmosphere. Instead of a nice solid deck beneath his feet, there would be nothing but black nothingness that went down forever, down into the cold heart of this cruel planet. He'd be suspended by only a few thin filaments of braided cord and his trust in the skill of some unknown captain. For long minutes he would be swinging above the great void, helpless as the strong fingers of Jupiter drew him down, down, down.

He doubted that he really had the nerve. Could he really trust himself to that hopelessly thin cable? And even if he did, where would he then find the courage to step out, off of the solid deck, and place himself at risk?

The moment of decision had come. The rig was swinging out of the bright lights of the other ship and coming toward him. His stomach hurt. He was either going to die on this crippled ship, or drop to a certain death. He felt like crying, he was so afraid.

"What are you doing out here, anyway?" Rams asked as he unhooked the woman from the rig, confident that the suit radios would work at this close range. "You sure don't look like miners."

"We're one of the teams in the Great Race," Louella replied.

"A race? On Jupiter? What sort of foolishness is that?"

"Don't tell me that you haven't heard about the Race. Hell, it's been on every newscast for the last year. Crap, we're probably the biggest celebrities on the whole planet."

"Don't have much time for news," Rams replied. "Radio don't work down here. Have to depend on the media they send down the elevator to keep up with events. Besides, if it doesn't have to do with cargo or weather, I don't pay much attention to it."

"We're in a race with some other barkentines—it's the first Jupiter sailboat race," Louella explained. "JBI sponsored and financed our boat."

Rams cursed softly to himself, and then said aloud, "Must be nice to be able to waste money like that. I can think of guys who could use that boat for something worthwhile; something better than some fancy trophy!" he added vehemently.

"Well, I'm certain that JBI will be grateful. They'll probably reward you for rescuing us."

"Well, that might be nice, but I'm going to get more than a little reward out of JBI, you can depend on that. Salvage alone ought to pay off the debt on *Primrose*—that's my ship," he added, pointing at the deck with one glove. "The other thing might pay for something more."

"What other thing," Louella asked, but Rams ignored her.

"What's going on with your partner?" he wondered. "What the devil is he waiting for? Why isn't he hooking himself up to the rig?"

"I was afraid this would happen," Louella answered. "Pascal's afraid of heights. Probably shitting in his suit right now, just thinking about the drop in front of him." Louella waved her good arm vigorously over her head. "Come on, Pascal, you asshole; hook up and get the hell over here!" she shouted, forgetting that the object of her scorn couldn't possibly hear her.

After long minutes of waiting with no sign of action by the small figure on the deck of *Thorn*, Rams swore. "Do you think that you can operate that winch with one hand? Looks like I need to go over there and kick your buddy in the ass."

When Louella signaled the affirmative, Rams connected a pair of heavy lines to his belt. One of them was tied to the stern docking ring. He activated the winch to bring the rig back.

He grabbed the rig as it swung back, hooked it to the rings of his suit, and signaled Louella to start the winch. "Keep those lines from tangling," he warned her as he stepped off the deck and began to swing across the gap.

As soon as Rams's boots hit *Thorn*'s deck, he secured his safety line. He detached the rig and quickly clamped it to Pascal's suit, brushing aside the other man's arms when Pascal fought him. He secured the last clamp, unclipped Pascal's safety line, and waved his arm for Louella to start the winch.

Pascal protested, stiff-legged, against the pull of the winch. The resistance was putting an extra load on the line, so Rams stiff-armed him in the middle of the back, forcing him forward. At that moment, the two ships spread apart and pulled the line taut. With a scream, Pascal was yanked from the deck to hang above the inky blackness. As the ships bobbed and danced in the winds, he jerked on the line like a spastic marionette.

Rams headed aft to secure one of the heavy lines to the stern docking ring. The other end was tied to the docking winch on *Primrose* and could be used to pull *Thorn*.

After tying the line, Rams dropped through the hatch and recovered *Thorn*'s log. The owners would probably want it if they couldn't get the ship back. He stowed the log in his hip pouch, then emerged on deck just in time to catch the returning rig. He grabbed it and lashed it to the deck. It would stay until he was finished securing the other line to the bow.

Thorn lurched, dropping far below *Primrose*. She rocked violently from side to side, her motion the result of the enormous mass embedded in her keel. If that thin ribbon broke from the strain, it would release the weight, and *Thorn* would shoot up like a released cork, endangering both ships.

Quickly paying the safety line behind him, Rams struggled to the bow. Bracing himself against further moves of the deck, Rams clamped the second line to the ring. This way, after he connected the other end of this lead line to *Primrose*'s forward winch, he could adjust the two ships so they rode side by side.

Satisfied with his work, he took the free end and began his way back to the rig. When he managed a quick glance at *Primrose*, he noticed that her sails were shifting, which indicated that she might be drifting, changing her heading. He had to get back and trim her sails before she got out of control. He started walking faster.

He was halfway back when a sudden gust forced the two ships apart. The tow line he'd tied at the stern straightened and vibrated like a violin string. The safety line parted with a snap that whipped the rig out and back. In seconds it was flailing downwind, lashing the hide of *Thorn* like the whip of a deranged jockey.

Rams straightened as *Thorn*'s bow swung away and the ship came stern-wise to *Primrose*, where she jolted to a stop. He stumbled backward, trying to regain his balance, just as the wishbone switched sides and slammed to the end of the extended traveler.

And against Rams's right leg.

The intense pain in his leg was the first thing Rams felt when he recovered consciousness. Then he tried to make sense of the upside down view of the swaying side of the ship. He realized that he was hanging head down from his safety line, his left leg bent under him. First, he felt cold, and then hot as the pain from his leg shot through him. Waves of increasingly severe pain washed up from his leg until he could think of nothing else.

During a brief respite from the pain, he tried to move. Something was holding his arm immobile. He tried to reach across with the other arm, desperately seeking the safety line that lay somewhere out of sight. After a few fumbling tries he gave up. Hell, even if he could find it, he wouldn't be able to climb back to the deck, not in his condition.

He calmly assessed his situation before the pain returned. He obviously couldn't do anything for himself, and the only other help was a woman with a broken arm and a little fart who was too afraid to do anything. Neither one would be able to help him. He was going to die.

Without warning, he lost his dinner, fouling the inside of his helmet and filling his nose with sour, burning fluid.

Then he passed out.

Pascal picked himself off of the deck and looked toward *Thorn*. She was gone! In a panic he looked to the other side, saw nothing, and then looked to the stern.

Very faintly, he could see the dim reflection of the ship's lights off *Thorn*'s pointed stern. Glinting in the lights was the thin line that held the two together; it must be the line the captain had rigged before the wind hit them.

"Do you see him?" Louella's voice crackled in his ears. "I lost sight of him when the gust hit us."

"Was he blown away? I don't see the safety line he rigged."

"It broke when we separated. Do you think he fell?" Louella screamed.

A wave of nausea washed through Pascal; his worst nightmare: to fall endlessly into the heavy, empty blackness beneath them. That could have been him if the line had separated when he was coming across. Thank God he was safely tied to this deck when it happened, he thought.

Louella was pulling on his arm, pointing toward the hatch. He followed quickly, eager for the added security of the ship.

"I've got to bring the two ships alongside, so we can bring him back," were the first words he heard when he undid his helmet in the small air lock. "We've got to get the ships positioned like they were."

Pascal nodded his head in agreement. If they could turn this huge ship so that *Thorn* was once again flying alongside, they could toss another line across and pull the captain back to safety. He bit his lip; it would be hard, going out on deck again, but he felt that he could do it.

"I'll ready a new line," he said, screwing his helmet and his courage into place.

Louella couldn't possibly toss the line across with only one good arm. On the other hand, he had no doubt of her ability to handle this, or any other ship, even with one arm in a sling.

None whatsoever.

Through the most disconcerting lurches and jumps, Louella managed to bring *Thorn* back. *Primrose* was actually sailing backward, the wind on the reverse of her sails. This allowed her to drag *Thorn* by the single tow line back into the range of *Primrose*'s bright lights.

Pascal was dismayed when he saw the dangling figure of their rescuer. He waved furiously, hoping the captain would wave back. But his attempt was in vain—the far figure dangled lifelessly, swinging from side to side with every motion of the boat.

Pascal pondered his situation. How was he to get a safety line across if the other man couldn't secure it? He didn't know if the captain was dead or alive, awake or unconscious. But he couldn't just leave him there, alone in the dark, waiting to fall should that single, thin thread holding him in place break. What could he do?

He looked at the flapping remains of the former safety line whipping back and forth against the side of the boat, somehow hoping to find it restored.

Louella certainly wouldn't be able to help, not with her arm out of commission. He stood there for long minutes as he considered his options. First, Rams might recover and climb back up to where he could catch a line. That would allow him to winch the captain back.

If that didn't happen then he could, he could... what? Leap across the space between the ships, pick Rams up in his arms, and leap back? Pascal watched the motions of the two ships carefully as they rose and fell, closed and separated, shifted forward and back, the one with a little sideways motion and the other rolling precariously. Jumping would be impossible, not only because of the unpredictable movement of the ships, but for the distance as well. He'd barely clear the edge of the deck before plunging down... He let the thought stop there as he tightened his sphincters. He discarded that option quickly.

Maybe, he hoped, he could sort of catch the line on something over there and pull Rams back. Four futile tries showed him the stupidity of that idea. Which left only one option—going over to the other ship and bringing the slumped figure to safety. But how? He certainly couldn't get near the edge and risk that long, long fall beneath them.

He went back to the hatch, where he plugged into the intercom and explained the situation to Louella. Surely she would understand, he thought.

"You're wasting time thinking about it, damn it! Get your ass over there and get him back!" Louella screamed. "I don't give a rat's ass how you feel; if you don't get started in ten minutes, I'll make sure that it gets done, myself."

The thought of Louella with her arm in a cast trying to rescue Rams was so ludicrous that Pascal began to laugh. "You couldn't even get your suit on by yourself," he wheezed.

"Exactly, but one hand is all I need to lock the damn hatch so you can't get back in without him."

Pascal was horrified, doubting her at first, and then realizing that she was entirely capable of carrying out her threat. "You wouldn't," he said.

"Just try me," she shot back.

Pascal climbed back on deck and winched the stern tow line as close as was safe. He thought that he could slide down the line, but then realized that he couldn't chance it—one slip and he'd drop into the ten or fifteen meter gap between the ships and plunge into the forever, below. What if he froze halfway across? He'd probably hang there until he gave in to vertigo and then he'd fall, fall, fall into the black maw that thirsted, that called out to him. He shook his head and stepped back farther from the edge of the deck. How could he overcome this fear that left him incapable of action? There had to be some other way, some way to rescue Rams without having to risk a fall. There had to be!

He returned to the hatch and pleaded with Louella to think of something, some way that did not involve making him cross the deep chasm of his innermost fear. They reached the same conclusion as before; that he was the sole resource they had to save Rams.

"In case you think I was kidding, I've already locked the hatch," she muttered before cutting off the conversation.

Pascal debated testing the hatch to see if she had really carried out her threat, but decided against it. He really didn't care to find out.

He returned topside and worked his way carefully to the stern. He stood there and contemplated what he had to do; what he could not escape doing, no matter what his fear.

Louella had been doing a good job of keeping station. *Thorn* was still drifting off to the port side, slightly below *Primrose*'s level. Their positions gave the tow line a downward slope.

All that he had to do was tie himself to the line and slide down to *Thorn*'s deck. It sounded so easy, so terribly easy. But what if the line parted? No, he couldn't afford to think about that.

Pascal retreated to the winch amidships, tore the remnants of the safety line away, and wrapped a new line, fastening the other end to his suit. That would give him some added security, and could be used to drag Rams back aboard.

He fashioned a short loop around the tow rope with a short length of line, and tied both ends to his suit. After a moment's hesitation, he attached a second loop—and a third. Just for safety's sake, he detached the line that held him to the deck, and put that around the tow as well. Finally certain that he was quadruple redundantly safe, he lay under the tow and grasped the line with both hands.

Through the narrow visor of his helmet, he could only see the tow rope and the spider's web of lines he had attached. He concentrated on the line and his gloves around it, trying to suppress any thoughts of what he was about to do. He tried to drive away all thoughts of the depths below him, drawing him so deathly down, down, down....

Pascal shook himself. If he hesitated for one more second, thinking about it, he would be unable to move. Ignoring a shudder of stomach-wrenching fear that tore at his insides, he tugged at the tow with one hand, said a short prayer, and began to slide.

There was a snap, a millisecond of a fall, as the slack in his safety lines was taken up by his weight. The tow vibrated for a second more, and then Pascal was falling, sliding, hitting the deck of *Thorn* with a bone-jarring impact. He clutched the tow tightly through his gloves as he tested the solid reality of the deck beneath his feet. He had made it, he had not fallen. He had conquered the depths of his fear. Nothing was beyond him now. Nothing!

The smell inside of his suit told him that his body had not shared his courage.

Squirming around to pull himself upright, securing a new safety line to the rolling deck, untangling the many lines that held him to the tow line, and making his way forward to stand on the deck above Rams took only a few minutes. The captain was still hanging, just a few meters down the side. Pascal could see that he had the safety line wrapped around one arm, pinning it to his side.

"Captain?" he called when he thought he was within range of the other's radio. "Can you hear me?" Only silence answered him. He could expect no help from Rams.

But how was he to get Rams's unconscious body up on deck? It would be impossible to pull the man the short distance up the side with the safety line. At best, he couldn't lift his own weight under two gees. What chance did he have of pulling a larger man, and one enclosed in a heavy pressure suit, that far? It would be the equivalent of lifting three hundred and fifty kilos on Earth! Even professional weight-lifters had trouble with that kind of load. No, he couldn't do that.

Neither did he think he could maneuver the tangled safety line sideways to the winch and use that to pull him up. A lateral pull would be the same as lifting Rams a half a meter or more: out of the question.

There was no choice; he'd have to climb down and attach the safety line he'd brought with him. Easy to say—sure, just drop down and hang over the depths once again. Nothing to it, he told himself. After all, hadn't he come across the gap?

No, you can't, his mind replied, as the edges of his innermost fear crept back in. He tried not to listen to it as he rigged two lines to the deck; one to support him and one more for additional security. His empty stomach clenched in a knot of sour fear the whole time. He fervently wished that he didn't have to do this, that there was some other way. Tears stung his eyes. The fear of falling was too great to bear. Why did it have to be him?

The line he'd tied to the *Primrose*'s winch was attached to his belt, ready to clamp onto Rams's suit. Not incidentally, it provided another layer of security for himself.

Screwing up all of the resolve he could muster, he turned his back on *Primrose* and forced himself to take one small step backward, out and down, paying a few centimeters of line out behind him. He froze. He could move no farther no matter how hard he forced his legs to move. His fear had taken control. He couldn't put himself in danger.

Thorn suddenly started to roll to starboard, and Pascal watched the level deck in front of him start to tilt away. He rapidly stepped backward, trying to stay on the top of the rolling ship, letting out line as fast as he could.

Then, as *Thorn* heeled to a sixty degree list, Pascal found himself beside Rams. There was a solid deck directly beneath his feet. "Piece of cake," he remarked, and knelt to attach the safety line to Rams.

First, though, he had to disconnect the tangled line. The tension between that and the safety line to *Primrose* would break the captain's arm if he didn't. He freed the line and let the wind take it.

He disconnected the safety line from his suit to clip it to Rams's when *Thorn* began to roll the other way. Rams's body started to slide down the hull. Pascal extended the safety clamp, but was stopped short by the limits of the other line. The ship continued to roll. The captain was sliding. In seconds, he would plunge into the dark and fall.

Pascal fumbled to release his own line, trying to balance on the moving hull. His fingers didn't want to operate the clamp. He felt himself starting to slide on the steepening slope. With a final, desperate twist of his hand, Pascal released the restricting line, lunged forward, and clipped the clamp onto Rams's suit.

Both of them began to slide, faster and faster, down the increasingly steep side of the ship. In a panic, Pascal threw both arms and one leg around Rams's body, clinging to him in desperation, as the hull beneath him changed to a vertical wall.

Pascal screamed in pure terror as he felt them fall from the ship and down into the dark. He knew that the thin line he had put on Rams wouldn't hold the weight of both of them. He screamed louder as their

downward fall stopped and they swung to the top of their arc and began
to fall the other way.

"I am going to die. I am going to die," he repeated in an unending
string of fear-crazed babble. He could feel Jupiter pulling at him, trying to
pry his hands apart so he would fall, fall, fall. It was very dark, and the
manic strength of his arms were all that stood between him and certain
death. He clenched his eyes tight and prayed as he had never prayed
before.

There are moments in a man's life when he faces the core of his being;
a single defining moment when his true nature is revealed to him and all
pretense, all bluff and bluster, are stripped away. This was Pascal's
moment. He knew that he would never be able to conquer the fear that
rested in his innermost being. He knew that he was, at heart, a coward

Something clanged on the back of Pascal's suit as they slammed
against something, hard! He felt them start to swing out, and then
"*Clang!*"—he hit again. He opened his eyes and saw a vast gray
wall receding from him. In seconds, they reached the end of their arc and
the wall advanced to smash against him once more. He threw his legs out
to brace and absorbed the worst of the impact. Rams nearly twisted from
his grasp as they hit.

It took him a second to realize that the "wall" was actually the side of
Primrose. It took him another second to realize that it was moving steadily
downward beneath his feet.

He risked a glance up, and saw taut line disappear around the curve of
the ship. They were definitely being pulled up the side. He set his feet
against the ship's side and walked up the wall, clutching tightly to Rams
and frightfully aware of the depths behind him, beneath him.

As soon he came over the edge of the deck, he saw Louella standing
by the winch. Finally, he was to the point where he could walk more or
less upright. From Louella's perspective it must look as if he were holding
the unconscious form of Rams in his arms. He hoped that she wouldn't
realize that he was hanging on to the man for dear life. He hoped that she
had not heard him screaming in the dark.

"Secure the ship," Louella yelled as soon as the winch stopped. With
shaking hands, Pascal quickly clipped himself to a safety line. That done,
he struggled forward to secure the heavy line to the forward docking

winch. The slow progress forward and back gave him time to compose himself. Time for the acceptance of his true nature to sink in.

"**D**on't worry. Everything's under control," were the first words that Rams heard when he finally recovered consciousness. The pain in his leg had stopped, as had all other sensation below his waist. "We've got both ships secured, and we're out of the storm."

"My legs…" he began, and then stopped. A woman stood over him like a welcoming angel. One of her arms was in a sling.

"Gave you a nice little spinal to hold off the pain from your broken leg," the woman said with a chuckle. "But don't worry, you'll be functioning below the waist in a few days. At least I hope so."

"I don't understand. All I remember is getting hit from behind and…"

The woman smiled. It was a nice smile, he thought. "Pascal went after you and dragged your ass back here." She grinned. "I think he'll stop shaking by the time we make station."

"But how, where, what…" Rams mumbled in confusion, feeling himself start to slip back into unconsciousness. "I thought the he was too afraid."

Louella shrugged. "I guess the sea's got a way of getting the most extraordinary things out of you."

"The sea…?"

"Rest now. You've got JBI's most expensive and experienced captain and navigator looking after you. I would think we have a reasonable chance of finding a station with that combination."

"…station," Rams thought, as he succumbed to the call of the drugs. She'd said both ships were secure. He thought of the riches that awaited him.

The storms really did provide the most amazing things.

"**L**et her have her head! Stop fighting her," Rams raged at the big woman as she struggled with the wheel. He lifted himself on one elbow.

"What the hell do you think I'm doing," Louella shot back. "You try steering this damn overgrown tub with one arm and see how easy it is!" She lifted her sling to emphasize her words.

"Let me get over there..." Rams said weakly, as he tried to push himself up and failed. He flopped back onto the pallet Pascal, Louella's navigator, had rigged for him.

"Don't bother trying to get up. You'd fall right on your ugly face even if you ever did manage to get your ass in gear," Louella said nastily. "With that smashed leg you probably couldn't make it to the pilot's seat, even if you weren't so doped up. Now, be quiet and let me concentrate; I've gotten ships home in worse weathers than this. Trust me: I know what I'm doing!"

Primrose was a huge whale of a vessel, her crew quarters were nestled deep within a bulbous pressure hull. Beneath it hung a kilometer-long diamond fiber keel and on her upper deck were the enormously strong sails that harnessed the howling winds of Jupiter. Lashed securely to her side was a smaller ship, *Thorn*; a barque that, until recently, had been JBI's sole entry into the Great Jupiter Race. It was this tow that made handling *Primrose* so difficult.

Rams was still struggling weakly when Pascal arrived with three mugs of steaming tea. He placed one mug where Rams could reach it, and held out another cup out for Louella. "If you want to drink this, you'll have to let me take the wheel. You've only got one arm."

"Don't wreck my ship," Rams mumbled as he fumbled with the spill-proof cup, trying to put the nipple to his lips.

"Fifteen years of handling large sail, Captain. I think I can keep her on track while Louella sips her tea," Pascal replied affably. "Now drink your tea. It will make you feel better."

"Sure, long as she didn't make it," Rams grumbled. During Rams infrequent conscious periods, he always complained about the food. Of course, on that matter, Pascal could only agree. The one skill that neither of them had mastered in all of their years of ocean racing was cooking. On their two-person races, they'd usually eaten pre-packaged food, which required no cooking, and could be eaten wherever and whenever necessary. His own mastery of the culinary arts was limited strictly to a properly brewed "cuppa tea" and the boiled or microwaved pouch of whatevers when he had the time.

He couldn't understand this ship's advanced food preparation technology. No matter what he did, the best he could turn out were slabs of tasteless, tough, and practically indigestible generic foodstuffs (the package said it was meat, but he still wasn't sure about that—it tasted too much of wood pulp to come from an animal). Foolproof, that's what the instructions said; absolutely foolproof. Ha!

The only thing that was worse than his attempts at cooking were Louella's cinders of burned organic matter, offerings, no doubt, to her unknown teacher in the culinary arts.

Pascal had also been acting as the ship's medic, administering Rams's pain blockers for his smashed and broken leg. He had administered as much emergency treatment as he could with the limited medical supplies he found within *Primrose*, using medical skills that had been acquired in his years of ocean racing, when competent medical help for an emergency was, more often than not, hundreds of miles away.

He'd stabilized Rams, stanched the bleeding, evacuated the wound to prevent infection, and splinted the broken leg to prevent any further damage from inadvertent movement. More extensive treatment than that required a well-equipped medical center and trained staff who knew more than he, and that meant that they had to find their way to a station soon, before they ran out of pain killers.

Rams's ship, like every sailing vessel on Jupiter, held a complete database of every station. The data bank's information allowed the ships to venture into the fierce winds of the giant planet with assurance that they could reach their destination. The inertial continually calculated each station's relative bearing.

According to the inertial, they had been several hundred hours north and west of the nearest floating station when Rams had rescued them. Since they came on board, they had been steering as tight a course as they could to intercept that station's projected track.

Pascal knew that each station was stabilized to stay at a particular latitude. They maintained their track by manipulating huge drogues—bucket-like sea anchors—to maintain a constant and predictable velocity as they were blown along the belts by the winds of Jupiter. The floating and stationary hub stations were the only stability a sailor had in the maelstrom that raged at this level of the atmosphere.

For the first five days, they had hoped to intercept Charlie Sierra Twelve as she followed the steady fifteen-meter-per-second track in the data bank. Now it appeared that they would not intercept it as planned. They were falling further and further behind with each passing hour.

Primrose lumbered heavily with *Thorn* under tow: Louella could only bring her to within sixty degrees of the wind. What made it even more difficult to keep to the schedule they had set was that *Primrose* showed a definite tendency to try to turn downwind every time attention flagged. As a result, they were moving slower than planned. According to Rams's careful calculations, they would miss the station by two days, and possibly more. So close and yet so far. It was frustrating.

Pascal and Louella constantly fought the ship's desire to reach. If she did so, they would slow to wind speed. Such a turn could easily spell disaster. With *Thorn* tied to *Primrose*'s side, the force of the wind could easily smash the two ships against one another and cause extensive damage to both.

It wouldn't take much damage to an outer pressure envelope to send them to their doom in the endless drop below. A rupture of either ship would drag the other down.

So they had to fight the weather and their own ship. They had to hold to a line that held a possibility of finding refuge and aid. They had to try for the next station in line.

Pascal was worried about Rams's condition. The captain hadn't taken well to his medication, and had remained unconscious most of the time. Could he have calculated a wrong dosage? Suspecting that he had done so, he reduced the dose. As a result, Rams stayed awake, but was in a constant, low level of pain. They had to get him to a decent medical facility soon. Without his intervention, *Thorn* might have become a twenty-first century Flying Dutchman, sailing Jupiter's vast seas with the ghostly crew of Louella and himself. He owed this man a lot for saving him from spending eternity as Louella's constant companion, and that required far more gratitude than he could ever express.

After carefully reviewing the data bank of possible destinations, Pascal selected station CS-17 as their next most likely target. After a few minutes of intense calculation, he predicted that they would intersect her track just eight hours ahead of her, five days, fifteen watches, hence.

That meant that, once they got in front of her, all they had to do was simply reduce sail, slow below wind speed, and wait for the station to creep up behind them. It was a simple plan, and one that wouldn't require special handling.

Twenty hours before they arrived at CS-17's track, the radar alarm hooted loudly, bringing Pascal to high alert and Louella staggering sluggishly from her cabin, her broken arm forcing her to move carefully down the passageway. In the past few days, she'd banged it often enough to learn the painful lesson of keeping it held closely to her chest. Even the drugged Rams was awakened by the clamor.

"What the hell is that?" Pascal exclaimed, pointing at an indistinct shadow on the screens. "Louella, see if you can crank up the gain." He fought to keep the image centered in the screen by manipulating the sail controls and the wheel.

"Don't touch… gain," Rams wheezed from his pallet. "Too much noise out here. You'll wipe out whatever… we have. Try infrared instead. Maybe you can get a better picture with that."

"Can't. It's too far away to use the IR—and the damn sonar doesn't help either! Oh no, there it goes…"

Louella reached Rams's side just as the hazy shape disappeared completely into the sparkle of background noise. "What was that? What did we just miss?"

Pascal scowled at her. "You should be sleeping, not up here in the cockpit."

"Can't sleep with that stupid alarm clanging," she shot back, her weariness evident in the lack of conviction in her voice. "What did you see?"

Pascal described the faint image that had raced across the radar screen, and his inability to resolve the image into anything he could comprehend. "If we had some decent equipment…" he began.

"*Primrose* has… best equipment on… planet," Rams mumbled from his bunk. "Cost… a bloody damn fortune. But can't run a tight schedule… without it. Won't find better gear on any ship on the planet," he finished in a rush.

"Then why couldn't we see what that thing was?" Pascal demanded, angry with frustration and the lack of rest that kept him from concentrating.

"Environment's the problem," Rams explained. "Old man Jupe puts out… lot of radio noise—magnetic field or something. Too much noise for radar, even with the double encrypted digital radar I use… Best I can 'see' is 'bout a klick."

"Which must have been just about the distance of that thing we passed," Pascal said, shaking his head to clear it.

Louella was still scowling at the instrument panel. "One kilometer for radar, and the double damned infrared's only good for close range work; about a hundred meters or less. Since the docking sonar is only good for five hundred meters or so, its like sailing blind on a dark night in the fog!"

"Gotta depend on your inertial," Rams said with a whisper of finality.

"You heard the man: Depend on the inertial," Louella repeated, as she staggered back down the passageway. "Wake me when it's my turn at the wheel."

"So what was that thing we saw?" Pascal asked doggedly as she left. "Was something really there, or was it just a radio ghost?"

"Don't know," Rams replied softly, his voice fading as he fell back to his drugged sleep. "Out here you… trust your inertial. You gotta trust… data."

The next day, the inertial indicated that they had arrived on the track of CS-17, and were leading it by nearly six hours.

Louella started sailing a waiting pattern, criss-crossing CS-17's predicted track while heading the ship in the same direction as the station. Pascal anxiously scanned the three sensor screens for the station's arrival each time they crossed her predicted track.

After ten hours of anticipation, CS-17 still hadn't arrived. According to the inertial's readings, the station should have been right on top of their position, yet both the radar and sonar showed nothing there except clear seas, roaring winds, and the perpetual hiss and crackle of radio noise at the limits of their range.

"Trust your inertial," Pascal muttered angrily under his breath each time they crossed the empty track.

"If the station isn't here then where could it be?" Louella demanded when she took over the watch. She was as frustrated as he at the lack of contact after nearly a day had passed. "Could the station master have altered the station's course for some reason—to avoid the storm or run a rescue mission?"

Rams grimaced with the pain in his leg. They needed him conscious and alert for this discussion, so Pascal hadn't administered the scheduled shot of sedative.

"The stations' positions are the only stability we have down here," Rams said through clenched teeth. "It's only the absolute predictability that makes sailing possible. No station master would ever vary his track by a millimeter, even if his life depended on it, because every sailor is dependent on that station being exactly where he is supposed to be at all times. No, the station wouldn't have deviated from the track for any reason."

"Then something must have happened to it," Pascal said slowly. "Maybe the storm moved it to a different track. Hmm, with that much wind force, almost anything could be possible."

Louella snapped her fingers. "That's it! I'll just bet that's the ghost you nearly ran into earlier—we must have passed the station without realizing it." She turned to Rams. "Is there any possibility that your inertial equipment is out of kilter; that somehow it is giving us the wrong readings?"

Rams shook his head weakly from side to side, obviously trying to clear his head. "Not possible. The inertial has a better pedigree than King of England. Remember, I'm staking my life on it every time I set sail. I calibrate it with the station's master system before I leave port. No, it can't be wrong—just not possible."

"Then, somehow the damnable storm must have moved the station off course, off track, whatever, and that's why it isn't where it's supposed to be."

"Brilliant deduction, Louella," Pascal injected. "But what can we do about it? Should we try to catch up to it?"

"Can't do that. Don't know what track she's following. Haven't a prayer of finding her." Rams took a deep breath before continuing. "If the storm blew the station off her track, then the master's probably fighting like mad. He has to get her back on track: Probably working the sea anchors, ballast tanks, whatever to move her. Even if we use her last position, we can't predict the line he'll take. Take more than dumb luck to find her. We'd never know how far below or above her track she'd be."

Louella sighed, and made a small adjustment to the tiller. "So what do you suggest that we do?"

"Simple," Rams smiled groggily as he climbed out of the pilot's seat and stumbled toward his bunk and some much needed rest. "Find 'nother station."

By the end of his next watch, Louella had decided on the station that they could intercept soonest, and set them on the intercept track. The station she chose, CS-12, was farther to the south and an eighth of the way around the planet, far enough from the track of the storm not to have been affected. With proper trim and a little luck, they could transit the distance to her track in little over a week or, with fair winds and some luck, a little less.

"We won't starve before we get there," Pascal remarked when he saw her sail plan. "I think we have enough food and water on board to last us. Just the same, I'm worried about our host. Rams's leg is definitely looking worse, and the amount of sedative I've got left in the medicine chest is running dangerously low. We have to get him to a doctor as soon as possible."

"I agree. Be a pity to lose him after he rescued us. Say, our air looks good, too," Louella said, squinting at the tell-tales on the instrument panel. "We've enough reserves to spend another two weeks out here before the atmosphere in here goes stale on us. As long as we don't run into any more problems, we shouldn't have any trouble reaching CS-12. Piece of cake."

"Sure," Pascal replied with a worried glance at their rescuer. "Let's just hope we all survive long enough to eat it."

The following days were an endless blur of watch on watch at the wheel, trying to keep *Primrose* on her track, and squeezing every bit of speed they could out of the ship. Pascal took to talking to Rams in the long quiet hours to keep himself awake, telling the captain of the races he had run, talking about the lean years before being hired by JBI, when he and Louella had bummed around the world, their clothes their only possessions. He spoke of the clear air of a winter's crossing, the stormy clouds of a southern storm, the crystalline brilliance of a spring night far from land, and the smooth hissing silence as a ship's bow sliced the waves.

The one thing he never spoke about was the gut-wrenching fear he had felt when he brought Rams back to *Primrose*, and the shame that still burned inside him for his craven, cowardly behavior. Louella might think he was some sort of hero, but he knew the truth of what had happened, he knew absolutely certainly that he was, at heart, a sniveling little coward, afraid of the deep dark that was anxious to pull him to its bosom.

The return to his bunk at the end of each watch was a brief respite, a welcome relief for his poor body. He could hardly wait to lay down and release the truss that bound his lower body and protected him from rupturing himself in Jupiter's constant two-gee drag. Usually he fell asleep in seconds, only to groggily wake at the chime to return to the wheel and relieve Louella.

But occasionally he could not rest. In those periods, he recalled the terror he had felt when he was outside. What if Louella found out that his cowardly fear had nearly caused him to kill himself and the captain? Would she laugh at him, belittling him in that taunting way of hers, if he told her? Yes, he thought sadly, she would do exactly that. He had no choice but to hide his cowardice from her and Rams. He just wished that he could hide it from himself as well.

He had nightmares of falling endlessly into Jupiter's bottomless depths and being crushed slowly in her enormous embrace. There was no rest from such dreams, and he usually awoke bathed in the stink of fearful sweat.

Ten days after the near encounter with the wayward station, the winds, which had been generally westward, suddenly became gusty, shifting thirty degrees to the north, varying in strength each time they quartered back to the west.

Once, *Thorn* started to drift away from *Primrose* when the winds gusted, only to slam back and strike broadside as the wind shifted. *Primrose* shuddered with the force of the collision. A moment later, far below, *Thorn*'s keel, with the huge rock attached, smashed into *Primrose*'s, and sent a vibration racing upward that made the hull ring.

The chunk of rock embedded in *Thorn*'s keel had been a gift from the storm, one of the valuable bits of flotsam the storms occasionally brought up from the depths. It was these rocks that made Jupiter's miners risk searching the edges of the hurricanes despite the dangers. A single rock could bring a fortune for its metallic content, and a modest profit for the volatiles that it might contain. By the standards of the trade, the one caught in *Thorn*'s keel was enormous, ten times the size of the largest one Rams had ever heard of.

"Any more surprises like that and we're liable to flounder," Louella remarked as the vibrations dampened. "I'm not sure of how much punishment this ship will bear."

"We ought to cast *Thorn* off," Pascal suggested. "*Thorn* and that damned rock's a danger to us. Besides, we could to make better time if we weren't burdened by the tow."

"*No!*" Rams shouted from his bunk. The reduction of the dosage meant that he was conscious more than not. "Can't do that to me… won't let you steal my future."

Pascal knelt beside him. "Captain, be reasonable. You need medical attention soon or you'll never be able to use that leg. What good would all the money be if you can't walk?"

Rams coughed. "Not 'bout money… 's about freedom: owning my ship free and clear; being able to steer from port to port without worrying about the bank waiting to seize it. About having enough profit to get a decent crew, 'nough to put something aside for when I can't fight the damned gravity any more."

He pushed Pascal's arm away and turned his head toward Louella, stretching a hand out to her. "This is about having *Primrose* as my own for the first time. Can't you understand that?" he sobbed before lapsing back to unconsciousness. "Can't… you… understand…"

Pascal couldn't understand Rams's concern. He'd always sailed on someone else's boat; sometimes as captain, but mostly as crew. Ownership had never mattered to him; it was being able to sail the ship, to direct her course, to trim her heading was all he cared about: There always had been far more ships needing trained captains and crew than there were capable people. Ownership wasn't important.

"I understand," Louella remarked unexpectedly from the passageway, breaking his chain of thought. "We'll do everything we can to save her, won't we, Pascal?" The tone of her voice told him that anything other than agreement would create a hell of a row.

"It's insane," he replied with as much emphasis as he could muster, as he let her slip behind the wheel. "We're liable to have a hull rupture if *Thorn* smashes into us again! We'll never make it to the station unless we cut the damn tow loose and get rid of *Thorn* and that damned rock! It's stupidity to try to save them when our own survival is at stake."

Louella snorted in derision and twisted the wheel, heading *Primrose* back into the wind. *Thorn* was pushed away as the head wind rushed between the two hulls.

"I'm putting us on a new course. If we sail close to the wind, *Thorn* will stay on our lee side and away from *Primrose*. We won't have any more bumping."

"That's crazy. That is completely off our planned course! We might miss the station entirely!"

"Pascal, you bitched the same way when we were trying to work our way around Cape Horn in that storm back in '79, and I got us through that, didn't I? Now, instead of complaining, why don't you try to figure out what this new course will do to our arrival time."

After a few minutes of playing with the inertial and the computer, Pascal announced that they would arrive too late, twenty hours behind the station.

Louella considered for a few minutes. "If we come up behind her, then we can go on a broad reach and catch up to the station. Hey, our speed has to be faster than the station. We can catch it in maybe thirty hours or so. That'll only add another day or so to what we originally thought. Close enough, and it saves the tow for the Captain." She nodded toward Rams, who had slipped back to sleep while they argued. "That should be good enough reward for saving our skins, eh, Pascal?"

Pascal couldn't argue with that: He just hoped that their supplies would last.

And the captain, of course.

Rams's condition was getting worse by the hour. Pascal had peeked beneath the bandages, saw the swelling around the break, felt the heat radiating from the wound. Obviously there was an infection present within the leg, probably around the break. He'd been giving Rams the antibiotics until their supply ran out. The supply had never envisioned a journey this long, he thought, and now Rams was paying the penalty.

"We need to get him to a doctor soon," he told Louella when she returned from her all-too-brief rest. "I think an infection is setting in, and I don't have anything left to deal with it."

"How far away is CS-12? We should be crossing its track this watch, shouldn't we?"

Pascal started, the discovery of Rams's problem had driven the approaching station completely out of his head. That was the trouble with exhaustion: it was so damned hard to keep your mind focused, so hard to remember anything. "Yeah, we should hit it sometime in the next few hours. Then all we have to do is catch up to her."

Louella slipped into the seat and placed her hands wearily on the wheel. "Piece of cake."

"Trust your inertial," Pascal replied mirthlessly with a final glance at Rams. He headed for his bunk and a few blessed hours of relief.

He awoke with a start. An alarm was ringing shrilly somewhere. Was it time to go to school? No, that was the dream. He shook his head to clear it, and realized it was the radar alarm. They must be near the station! "Damn Louella," he cursed. She must have let him sleep right through the watch, doubling her own burden to lighten his own. He tightened the truss, stood, and moved toward the cockpit, checking the time as he did so.

Wait a minute; he hadn't been asleep more than four hours! What the hell was happening? The station was still hours away. What could they have run into?

"It's another damn ghost," were the first words Louella spit at him as he entered the cockpit. "Come on over here and see what you can make of the displays."

"Looks like something really big. Could be the station, just like the last one. Trim us up a couple of points higher, would you?" Louella twitched the wheel slightly to turn *Primrose* closer to the wind. Their speed picked up slightly, and the radar image started to clear.

"Doesn't look like a station," Pascal announced as the outline clarified. "Come around another ten degrees. Yes, stay on this heading and we'll be able to pick it up on the sonar."

An hour later, they still couldn't make out what they were seeing on the screen. The image showed something larger than the ship by a factor of ten, but looking like nothing they'd ever seen.

As best they could make out, it was roughly cone-shaped, with the blunt end facing the wind. Whenever they got close, a slimmer projection appeared at the leading end, seeming to lead upward.

It was Rams who figured it out. "It's a drogue," he explained. "One of the sea anchors the station uses to hold itself in place. They're usually a klick below though."

"What the hell is it doing at this level," Louella demanded. "I though those things were hundreds of meters below the stations, not on the level the ships used."

Pascal thought hard. "Maybe we aren't where we're supposed to be. Perhaps we are way down below where our instruments tell us we are."

Louella stared hard at the display, trying to work out her own conclusions. "You think there's something wrong with the altimeter? Oh shit!"

"What's the matter?"

"The altimeter isn't absolute. It just figures out the altitude by the buoyancy of the ship—it's an approximation."

"So we aren't as high as we should be? That doesn't make any sense. If the outside pressure was lower, then the station would be as affected as us." Pascal replied, fighting to hold the logic of the problem in his mind.

"*Thorn*'s dragging us down," Rams suggested. "Rock and ship are ballast, too. Holding us down."

"Why didn't I think of that," Louella exclaimed. "Crap, all we have to do is rise to their level to dock with her."

With that, she reached out and flipped the heater switches that would vaporize and vent a portion of the ballast and lighten the ship. "Shouldn't take more than a few minutes to evacuate some ballast. Hey, that's strange…" Her forehead crinkled in thought as she stared at one of the displays on the console. Finally, she spoke.

"Pascal, honey, I think we have another little problem."

After extensive systems checks, repeated attempts to get *Primrose*'s heaters to work, they concluded that the heater circuits within her keel must be faulty.

Louella said it first. "The question isn't how did it happen; it's what can we do about it? How can we get the ship up to the station's altitude?"

"Need to get down there and fix the circuits," Pascal suggested after a few minutes of intense thought. For some reason he wasn't thinking too clearly, probably because of the lack of rest and the pressure of their predicament.

"I think the drag of the tow is holding our speed below that of the station at this angle of attack. We're losing way relative to the station. We need to quarter away to build up enough to catch it again," Louella said in a tired voice.

So saying, she let the wind take *Primrose* on a slanting course away from the station, building their speed once more. Back and forth they passed under the station, careful to avoid the lines that held the drogues in place, and trying the radio with each pass, but getting only static for their troubles. There was no way they could tell whether the station was aware of their plight or not.

Meanwhile Pascal had crawled forward to loosen the hatch to the lower deck and the heater connections. He had to check several times, because he kept forgetting what he had done. As far as he could tell, the heaters were working properly. He could even feel the warmth through the housings with his hand.

So that meant the problem wasn't the heaters, he reasoned slowly. Therefore, it had to be the vents. They must have been damaged whenever *Thorn*'s rock had smashed against their keel. Maybe one of the collisions had warped them into uselessness. No way of telling from here. Wearily, he climbed back up and made his way to the cockpit to tell Louella the sad news.

"I knew we should have cast *Thorn* off when we had the chance," he said once he got his breath back.

"Too late to reconsider that now," she replied, too tired to even argue the point. Instead, she appeared to be deep in thought. In a few minutes, Louella came up with a truly frightening solution: Pascal would simply go over to *Thorn*, and switch on her heaters. That would provide enough lift to bring the both of them to the station's level.

"Maybe I should raise *Thorn*'s sails, too," he suggested dryly. "Or even sail the damned thing up to the station by myself."

The sarcasm was lost on Louella, who was as tired and worn down as he. "Did you forget that we lost the sails, dear? No, just see if you can lighten the load for us."

"Maybe if we just cast off the tow," he began.

"Not after bringing it all this way you won't!" she shot back. "We're going to save both of them!"

Pascal wasn't sure if she meant *Primrose* and Rams or *Thorn* and the rock. Not that it mattered—he still had to go out on deck and dare Jupiter's fatal siren call once more.

He hoped his bowels would hold this time.

lowly and with great care, he suited up and returned topside, clipping two safety lines in place as Louella flipped on the lights. Very carefully, he worked his way to the edge of *Primrose*'s deck, clamping a death-like grip on a stanchion to anchor himself in place.

After a few moments in which he tried to steel himself for the task ahead, he looked at the gap between the two ships, the chasm that had no bottom, a chasm into which he could easily fall forever...

No, he shook his head to clear out the thought. He couldn't let the fear control him. He had a job to do. But his guts told him differently, as did his trembling legs.

Thorn was still drifting off to the port side, but she was significantly below *Primrose*'s level, giving the tow lines a steep downward slope. Why hadn't they noticed that she was pulling them down? Was that something else they had missed because of their fatigue?

Maybe he could do what he had the last time; tie himself to the tow rope and slide down to *Thorn*. It would be easier than last time with the slope so steep. Wait, maybe it was too steep; so steep that he would break his legs from the impact of hitting the other deck under two gees!

But what if the tow line parted when he hit? With his legs broken, he wouldn't be able to hold himself in place—he'd slip over the edge and into the dark chasm that...

Damn, why did his thoughts keep returning to that nightmare? Once more, he tried to clear his head of the nibbling fear, even as he threw another line around the winch for added security.

Perhaps he could rig a second line to retard his fall, paying it out as he lowered himself down the line. That would keep him from hitting too hard, but it would also make the time he hung over the deep, black emptiness even longer—increasing the risk of the line breaking and letting him fall, fall... He shook his head, dismissed the thought, and began rigging the lines.

He first put a short loop around the tow rope, then anchored both ends to his suit. He then attached a second loop, and a third, just to make sure. Next, he detached another line, put it around the winch, and secured one end to his belt: That would be his retard line, one he could pay out through his hands and control his slide.

Just as he had before, he said a short prayer before lying down under the tow line and testing the harness he'd created. Satisfied that it would hold him, he released a meter of the security line and felt himself start to slide down *Primrose*'s curving side.

Through the narrow field of his helmet, he could only see the tow rope and the spider's web of lines that supported him. He concentrated on letting only a small amount of line at a time through his gloves. With each downward lurch, the fear started eating at the edges of his mind, fear that he kept trying to suppress, of the depths that could so easily draw him down, down, down. A shudder of stomach-wrenching fear tore at him as he rocked somewhere above the vast chasm, paralyzed by his fear, unable to move. Tears welled up in his eyes, and he felt his sphincter spasm. He was shaking so hard that it was difficult to think.

The longer he stayed here, he finally realized, the greater the chance that the line would break and send him to his death. With great effort, he forced his hands to relax for an instant and release another meter of security line, so that he could continue his slide toward *Thorn*.

Except he didn't move. The released line drooped limply on his chest. Panic filled him. The retarding line was jammed. He was stuck here! He would stay here forever, dying suspended above Jupiter's crushing depths!

With the desperation of the damned, he reached up to pull at the tow line that was supporting him, desperately hoping to get himself in motion, but the tow line was just out of reach; he had made the harness too long!

And the call of the depths was intensifying, increasing his risk, increasing his fear. The sour smell of urine and emptied bowels inside of his suit told him that his body had submitted to the fear even more than his mind.

What could he do, he wondered with sudden clarity of mind; just lay here in his own shit and piss and tears until the lines snapped and ended it all? Yes, that could be an appealing option—a few minutes of terror and then the sweet release of death, final and complete! Finally there would be an end to this fear, these nightmares, this cowardice that he had lived with for so long.

But, another part of his mind protested, that would also doom Rams and Louella, two people he had an obligation to save, and one of whom he just realized that he loved. He couldn't kill them just because of his own cowardice.

Then he noticed that two of the safety lines were crossed on the tow line. They had jammed while he lay there letting himself submit to the cowardly voice within. All that he had to do was untangle them and he'd be able to continue.

After struggling to reach the lines, he finally concluded that there was no way to reach the knot. The only way to undo the tangle was to untie one end of one of them and pull it through. All he had to do was remove one of the safety lines that kept him from falling into the depths at his back.

Did he have the courage to try, or was he too cowardly to take the risk? That was the question. He tried to move one hand toward the line. It froze into immobility, captive of the fear inside, divorced from the urging of his conscious mind. He tried to force his hand to move, to grasp the line and loosen it, but it remained as it was.

At that point he realized that this was an irrational fear, something born in the primal, reptilian depths of his brain. There was nothing he could do about it; his fear wasn't a conscious choice so much as the way his brain was wired. At that it was as if some liberating wave passed through him, releasing him from his false perceptions, releasing his hand from the clasp of his deep-rooted fear.

"Either way, I die," he said, and quickly, before the fear within could take control, undid one of the ends at his side.

As the supporting line came loose, he fell backward with a stomach-wrenching lurch. His legs were held as his upper body dropped. The safety line whipped out of his hand, and he felt himself fall down, down, down… to clang viscously against the deck of *Thorn*.

"I did it! I did it!" he shouted joyously, reveling in his success. He clambered to his feet and looked back at the gap he had crossed. With a sudden feeling of relief, he realized that he had crossed more than the physical chasm; he had crossed a threshold within himself. Discovering that he could do what he had to, despite the gnawing, debilitating fear inside of him, meant that he wasn't a coward. A coward would have submitted to the fear and hung out there until the lines parted. No, he wasn't a coward at all, he finally admitted to himself.

And, now that he had conquered the real enemy, taming the *Thorn* and bringing them both into dock would be a trivial matter. He headed for the hatch and his future, clipping his safety line securely in place with every step.

Just because he wasn't a coward didn't mean he should take chances. Jupiter's depths still called to him, and the smell inside his suit warned him that the fear was still a gnawing reality.

*T*horn seemed terribly cramped when he crawled back inside and made his way to the console. They had left the ship open to the atmosphere so he had to squeeze his suit into the tiny cockpit and the pilot's chair. The switches were widely spaced, and he could easily move them with his gloved fingers.

No matter how many times he tried the heater switches, *Thorn* refused to gain any altitude relative to *Primrose*. After the tenth try, he remembered that they had lost all of their ballast—that had been one of the problems after that rock slammed into their keel.

Damn, how could he have forgotten something as significant as that? Both Louella and he must be more fogged by fatigue than they thought. Now he really was in a pickle; he had no way to make *Thorn* rise and, worse yet, there was no way for him to get back to *Primrose*. He hadn't the strength to climb up the tow lines in a two-gee field nor, he admitted freely to himself, the nerve.

A quick check of his air supply showed that he had less than a day before it ran out. "Lou, we have another problem," he said into the radio, hoping that she could hear him through the popping, crackling noise.

After she replied, he quickly explained *Thorn*'s status. "As best as I can figure it," he said slowly, "there's only one way that you two can make it to dock; I have to cut *Thorn* loose and let *Primrose* run free. *Thorn*'s dragging you down: Without her weight, *Primrose* will be able to make station."

As he said those words, he was surprised at his own sincerity. He really was willing to sacrifice himself for them. A great inner peace came over him with the knowledge that he could face his certain death with such calm detachment. Where was the quaking coward who had shit himself on the line? Where was the little man who feared the depths more than his own death? Apparently, his cowardice wasn't the only thing he'd lost on the way down.

"You damn fool! That's suicide for you," Louella shot back. "There has to be a better way. Can't you lighten the load? Maybe toss something overboard?"

Pascal replied sarcastically. "Sure, nothing to it. I'll just drag a few tons of metal out the hatch and toss them over the side. Shouldn't take me more than a few months, that is, if I had the equipment."

"At least you haven't lost your sense of humor," Louella responded dryly.

"Yeah, that's one thing I didn't lose on the way down here. Listen Lou, I already thought of that possibility and discounted it. It just won't work." His voice dropped to a more serious tone as he said, very slowly so that there would be no misunderstanding; "Trust me, Louella, this is the only way to save you two."

"Damn it, Pascal, I can't let you throw away your life," Louella shouted. "Why don't you see if you can cut the keel loose from the housing—better to lose the rock and save you." She paused for a moment and then added, "and the ship, of course."

"Won't work. No tools, no way of squeezing into the lower hold in this suit, besides, there isn't enough time." He explained the condition of his air supply.

Rams's weak voice came on. "Wait a minute. You don't have to cast away. Just lengthen the tow lines. Add more line and see how far the ship sinks. Might be buoyant at a lower level—ain't no P12 layer, y'know."

Pascal considered that suggestion. Perhaps Rams was right; if he rigged all of the line on board to the tow, he could gradually let it out until *Thorn* stabilized. Damn, they could have done that from *Primrose* and he wouldn't have had to come across in the first place! Another bitter tribute to their deficient, sleep-deprived thought processes.

But, he continued to reason it out, what if *Thorn* didn't find a level where she was floating? In that case, she'd continue to exert the same drag on *Primrose*. Unless *Thorn* floated, there was no way that *Primrose* could escape.

But he still had the option of cutting her loose if that didn't work. Wearily, he rose from the pilot's chair and began to climb out onto the deck. There was no sense telling either of them that he was considering that possibility; he'd just do it when the time came. As he worked on making the lines fast to the winches, he wondered what it would be like to sink into Jupiter's seas. At least, he added with a smile, he wouldn't be falling.

Something loomed out of the dark, whipped beside the ship, and disappeared into the dark behind him. He'd no more than a brief glimpse of something huge and conical. It almost looked as if some giant bucket had been...

He slapped his head, and the helmet rang with the impact of the armored glove hitting the metal. There was no need for them to lose *Thorn* after all! The solution had been in front of them the whole time!

Slowly, knowing that the survival of them all depended on his safety now, he returned to the cockpit and keyed the radio once again.

"You need to cut as close to one of the drogues as you can," he explained to an incredulous Louella. "Get in front of it and let off so that *Thorn* slips inside. With a little bit of luck, the drogue will hold *Thorn*. Then I'll cast off *Primrose* so you can get to dock. After that, you can have them haul in the drogue."

"Pulling *Thorn* and you to safety," Louella finished for him. "That's freaking brilliant. But do you think I can steer the ships well enough in the dark? I'm as likely to smash you into the drogue as not."

"You're the best helmsman I've ever sailed with," Pascal replied warmly, hoping she could hear the admiration in his voice over the crackling, popping link. "I'd trust you with my life."

"Which you are going to do," she responded without a trace of humor in her voice. "Stay off that deck on our approach. You hear me, you little twerp? Stay inside and conserve your air. I don't want to lose you now."

"I hear you, captain." Matter of fact, you'll have a hard time getting rid of me from now on, he added to himself as she cut the connection. There was still a lot of time to wait before he could get out of this stinking suit.

Instead of doing as she wanted, he stood on the deck and peered into the darkness. The lights illuminated the side of *Primrose* and etched the thin tow lines that held the ships together, a thread of light that bisected the chasm he had crossed. For the past two hours, he had watched Louella switch the sails, changing the heading to get in front of the station and into position on one of the drogues. When she backed the sails, he knew that she had picked up a drogue on her radar, and was steering the ships to intercept.

He looked across the stern, wondering when he would be able to see the maw of the approaching bucket, and if *Thorn* would hang up on one of the drogue's lines instead. If that happened, he'd cast off the lines in an instant to keep *Primrose* from floundering. There was no way he would let her be trapped.

It loomed out of the dark like a great fish, its gaping whale mouth making the *Thorn* a mere minnow in comparison. Pascal didn't hesitate: As soon as he saw the drogue, he loosened the tow lines and watched them whip away. *Primrose* shot away, rising like a rocket, its light dwindling into a mere star in the inky blackness above him.

And then even that point of light disappeared as *Thorn* was swallowed by the huge drogue and an absolute darkness descended. Pascal braced himself for the impact when *Thorn* hit the rear of the drogue. He prayed that his safety lines would hold, that he wouldn't be thrown off the deck. He dropped down and held on with both hands while he braced his feet against the traveller bar.

Contact was more like a soft kiss than a harsh crash. There was a slight bump, then a grinding noise as *Thorn* swung around until her broad side rested against the wall of the drogue.

Pascal turned on his light so he could find his way back to the cockpit, and noted that the deck was canted at an angle. This puzzled him for a moment until he remembered that the top of the mast was probably touching the low wall of the drogue and forcing the entire ship to one side. They must have come to rest in the very tip of the huge bucket, the very safest place he could be. Now he had only to wait for them to haul their catch up to the station. A piece of cake, as Louella would say.

The young elevator pilot who had delivered them to the station several weeks before smiled in recognition as Pascal and Louella climbed out of the connection tube and eased themselves into their seats.

"Have a good race," he asked innocently, as he readied his elevator for the long trip back up the cable to synchronous orbit, where their transport back to Earth and Jerome Blacker's wrath awaited.

Pascal glanced at Louella, smiled, and answered. "Let's just say that this race was one of our best."

Louella glared at him. "Pascal, you are so full of crap! The only one who came out ahead was Rams, God bless his grasping, greedy heart. Damn it, we lost the frigging race, gave away *Thorn*, cost JBI a bundle, and almost killed ourselves. This race was an unmitigated disaster from the beginning to the end."

Pascal continued to smile at her. Yes, the great Jupiter race had been all of that, and more. But without it, he wouldn't have become the man he now knew, and accepted. He reached over, took her hand, and squeezed it gently.

"It was all of that, Louella, and," he added sincerely, "I wouldn't have missed it for the world!"

Chapter Four—Mars

The wind blew soundlessly across the red-gray Amazonis landscape. Arching high above the station's masts were the fluttering telltales on the tug's sails. Halsey "Sands" Ribblokenni barely gave them a glance as he headed for the dispatcher's shack. His mind was more on Tuesday night's race out on the Tiblia Planitia. He was in third place in the latest series and, if he managed to win the next race, he'd move up to second.

For the third time in as many days, he hoped Paula would be able to make it up from Anson in time to see him speed across the finish line, turn upwind, and spill the tiny morsel of Martian air that drove the buggy's wing. In his mind's eye he rehearsed leaping from the saddle, racing to her, and proposing over their suit-to-suit link.

That they wouldn't be able to manage more than a sterile embrace as they touched helmets didn't trouble him at all. Waiting to propose until they were back in atmosphere lacked the drama he felt the moment required. Besides, delaying that willing, accepting kiss would make it all the more passionate.

Yes, second place was definitely within reach this time, after working so hard at tightening the rigging and figuring out how to remove another quarter-kilogram from the frame. That alone would give him at least an additional half-meter per second. Even that was an advantage, where most races were decided by mere seconds.

"Got a heavy load this morning," the dispatcher said in greeting. "Got six tonnes of air tanks heading for OpOne." Outpost One was located a few hundred kilometers southwest, across the high planitia. "Bad news is that there's strong headwinds blowing. I had them put the big sail on the tug for the load you'll be pulling."

Sands groaned. With a heavy load and a headwind, he'd be on the trail for ten hours at least. "How strong?"

The dispatcher glanced at the gauge. "About one hundred, but that will rise as the day warms up." Sands had to grin at that. The warmest it ever got on the plateau was still sixty below freezing, and that only in midsummer.

Outside, he did his walk-around of the tug. It was far different from the light, slim racing buggy he owned. Instead of a single wheel at the prow, this clunky machine used a two-wheel fore-tractor. The rear outrigger wheels were large, nearly as wide as he was tall, and splayed outward at the base to maximize the huge soft tires' footprints on the sand. Just behind the rear seat were the attachment points for the cargo pod. He checked to ensure that the pins that secured the tug to its load were locked in place.

Rising above his head and passing over the cargo pod was the huge gaff-rigged sail—nearly eighteen hundred square meters of aerogel fabric supported at the top edge by a spar projecting at a sharp angle from the tall supporting mast.

The gaff rig was a compromise between balance and power. A traditional sail would be so large that it would tip the tug in the slightest breeze. The gaff brought the center of the sail's mass lower with no decrease in sail area. A lateen rig, on the other hand, would lower the center even more, but be harder to maneuver.

Had there been a nice following breeze instead of this near headwind, they could have had a nice, steady ride. As it was, they'd have to quarter back and forth the whole tiresome way.

Jack, his linesman, finished checking the lines he'd control from the rear seat. His job was to make certain that each ran smoothly through the five sets of pulleys that gave him the mechanical advantage he needed to handle the long boom.

Sands dropped into the steersman's seat and hooked his suit into the life support gear. "Check," he said as soon as he activated the link.

"Whenever," Jack replied as he buckled in. "I'm ready."

Sands felt a jolt as the electric pusher moved them into position behind the cargo pod and began to push them away. The winds on these plains were so light that wind power alone was insufficient to overcome the inertia of the cargo pod. The pusher at least got their speed up to where the wind could sustain their movement.

As the tug began to move—more from the force being applied by the pusher than from the light wind striking the sail—Sands turned the wheel to bring the tug into the wind. Jack let the boom swing free until it captured the wind and stopped fluttering.

They were on their way.

Four hours along the cleared trail, and the landscape was as boring as ever. The wind was blowing so steadily that Sands had only had to quarter twice since they left, but not so far as to leave the cleared trail. The sun was high in the southwest, but it would drop below the horizon two hours before they reached their destination. Sands hated sailing in the dark, but there was no way they could avoid that, given Mars' short winter day.

He noted that the telltales were streaming evenly along the sail's surface to indicate a smooth airflow. Jack was obviously doing a good job of trimming. They were getting close to the edge of the cleared trail, so he'd have to quarter back in a few minutes.

"I could use a drink about now," Jack said to break the monotony. "Maybe some good Earth beer."

"If you're going to daydream, why not imagine scotch?" Sands replied. "I drink nothing but the best in my daydreams."

"Yeah, I think—What the hell is that?"

Sands felt the tug lean under a sudden fierce gust of wind before the right rear wheel lifted off the surface. At the same time, Jack let go of the sheet and let the sail swing wide to ease the pressure.

Sands swore. Where had that blast of air come from? It was too early in the season for squalls, and they were too far away from the hills to have a downdraft.

Sands turned the tug off the wind to bring the wheel back down. As the left wheel touched the loose drift sand at the edge of the cleared trail, he felt the mass of the cargo pod fighting the change of direction.

He had to keep the cargo pod out of the loose sand or they'd lose all their forward momentum. The forward wheels threw aside showers of dust as they dug into the turn. The right wheel lost contact with the surface as the whole tug leaned in an extreme heel to the left.

Jack was fighting to spill wind, but the tip of the sail was dragging in the sand and could not be let out any more. Sands wrenched the yoke, desperate to turn upwind.

Suddenly, Sands saw a rock where no rock should be. As the fore truck hit, the yoke twisted out of his hands. He felt the tug tilt farther. His belt snapped, and he flew along the sail, sliding away from the nearly vertical tug, ripping the thin fabric as he tumbled. His world was a whirl of sail, sand, and hard blows before the huge cargo pod rose above him and then descended.

"Paula" was the only word he had the time to utter.

Louella was still fuming over losing the Jupiter race as they waited stationside for the transfer ship to arrive. The small shuttle would carry them out to rendezvous with the ship as it transited through near-Jupiter orbit. The ship had already looped twice to intersect Io, skimmed Jupiter to pick up speed, and flew outward to Europa. On this pass, it would be near maximum speed on its way to Callisto as it left on its way to meet Mars in the eternal planetary ballet. These big ships needed all the gravity boost they could get to cover the distances without wasting fuel, and every near pass to one of the moons improved their speed.

"Blacker is going to ream our ass over this, Pascal," Louella complained as they gazed for the last time at the rosy orange arc of Jupiter they could see through the portal.

They made an odd couple, Louella, a large black woman, and Pascal Dumay, a slight Frenchman. One would never know they were experienced ocean sailors who had just completed a harrowing voyage across Jupiter.

It was hard to believe that they had been sailing in Jupiter's atmosphere just a few short weeks before, daring the winds, and damn near losing their lives in one of those ships that were a combination of dirigible and submarine. The only good thing about it was how the experience had cemented her friendship with Pascal.

Friendship was the only term for it. The bastard was wasting his good looks and cute accent charming the most attractive crewman instead of ministering to her needs. With only two crewmen, and one of them past his prime, she found herself in a different competition with Pascal.

What was it going to be like on the eleven-month trip to Earth?

The shuttle run was misery. They had to spend over three hours crammed asshole to elbow with four other passengers in a can barely large enough to contain them. It was hot, smelly, and nearly as uncomfortable as *Thorn*'s cabin had been.

"Have to speed up to match the ship," the pilot shouted over the constant bang of the engine as it built up pressure and fired over and over again. "She's doing nearly 5,000 kps by now. We'll pass her this loop, and she'll catch up to us on the next. Any of you want a peek as we pass, you'll have to squeeze up here in the bubble. Only one at a time, though."

Louella used her strength and size to assert herself so she could catch a fleeting glance at the confusing array of spars, tanks, lines, panels, and god-knows-what conglomeration that constituted the interplanetary transport as it whipped by them and diminished in the distance.

It had looked nothing like the fancy passenger ship they had used to reach Jupiter. Of course, back then they were being treated as the great JBI sailing team, celebrities almost, and in the good graces of JBI. Now they were just a pair of losers who had to return to Earth by the most economical means. She was absolutely certain Jerome, the young penny-pinching bastard who ran JBI, was behind this downfall, but there was nothing she could do about it.

Rendezvousing with the transport was more like a controlled collision than a graceful ballet. The jarring connection and sudden acceleration rattled Louella's teeth.

"Sorry, I was a few kps short there at the end," the pilot cheerfully apologized. "But we actually made it without killing anyone."

She couldn't tell if he was joking or not.

Pascal was pleasantly surprised to find how commodious the transport's passenger compartment was. Everyone had a private cabin, which was to say a three- by two- by two-meter compartment stacked like tubes around a common open volume on one deck of the PassCan, as the crew referred to it.

The can was the third largest cylinder that made up most of the volume of the ship, the second largest being the cargo pod, and the largest the fuel tank. The three were spaced along the central axis like a string of pearls. At the forward end of the PassCan were amenities and a magnificent view of the heavens. At the base were the passenger and crew cabins, life support, and maintenance bays. In the center was the water ring, a torus the center of which was the refuge where all would repair should the sun throw off a sheet of high-energy particles that the water could absorb. For the normal radiation, they all had to continue the damn drugs that tasted like ten-year-old milk.

Thirty-odd passengers were already aboard, having transferred on at Europa and Io. They appeared to be a mixed lot in age, gender, and appearance. Some looked hardened, as if they had seen far too much for their young age. Others appeared more settled, satisfied with their lot. One pair were obviously a couple, although Pascal could not understand what a rugged looking guy like that saw in his scrawny companion. Well, we all have our tastes, he thought. One of the men from Europa looked promising, and had even smiled when their eyes met. That was encouraging, he hoped.

Dining was done in shifts, with each shift determined by some program a psychologist had probably designed to ensure that cliques did not arise to disturb the delicate balance that having so many people together in such cramped space would otherwise generate. This was fine with Pascal.

Tonight's dinner companions were the odd couple from Io, Haley something or other and her companion, Matt.

They were prospectors, they told him. Both of them were heading to Mars, she to return to her home and he to follow her. Both were effusive about the wonders of the place.

"You haven't seen anything until you've stood atop Olympus Mons and gazed at the stars," Haley said. "I did that a time or two." Pascal wondered how anyone could gaze in wonder atop a damn mountain. The thoughts of being on something that high sent shivers down his back.

"So, how was Io," he said to change the subject.

"Smells like wet farts," she replied. "Mars is better." She smiled and added, "Smells like dry ones."

"Io was beautiful and dangerous," Matt said. "Like Haley here." The big oaf grinned like he'd just bestowed on her a glorious compliment. "Fire and ice," he added, and got an elbow in the ribs along with her smile.

"I actually spent most of my life on Mars," Haley said. "Prospecting, mostly, although I did run one race down the big one."

"She means Olympus Mons," Matt explained. "Rode a fancy Mars bike, and nearly killed herself doing it."

Haley blushed. "Well, there were two of us, so I can't take all the credit."

Pascal was horrified. It was bad enough to climb mountains and risk certain death, but to deliberately fly down the face of one on a bike was insanity.

Haley must have read the terror on his face. "It wasn't that bad. Mons has a shallow slope—only about five degrees at the steepest part. Not at all like those tiny things on Earth. Matter of fact, if you stood on the side of Olympus, it would look just like a slightly inclined plain, except for the chasms, craters, and piles of rocks. Not at all what you'd imagine a mountain would look like."

"Thank God," Pascal said under his breath.

"Have you heard the big news?" Matt asked later, as they were eating the entree. "Jerome Blacker, the boss man at JBI, died last week. I caught the news upload just before dinner."

Pascal was shocked by the news, but wasn't surprised. It was obvious from their last meeting that the elder Blacker was nearing his end. The watery-eyed senior member of JBI's management team had appeared to be a physical wreck with his thin buzzard's neck, mottled skin, and a slight trembling that declared declining health. Jerome had looked older than his hundred and ten years—and at some point even his great wealth would not stay the grim reaper.

"How did it happen," Pascal asked. He'd liked the old man on their few meetings, and felt a pang of sorrow at his passing.

Matt shrugged. "Heart attack, stroke, something sudden. I hear JBI's in complete disarray, trying to figure out how to run the empire without him."

Pascal wondered about that. "But his son was running the company anyway. I don't imagine the loss of his father would matter that much."

Matt put his knife down. "Son? Did I say that? No, the old man is still kicking. It was his son, the young Jerome, that died."

Louella was waiting in the lounge with her dinner partners when she saw Pascal emerge from the dining space. There was a strange look on his face as he rushed to her.

"Have you heard," he asked before she could say a word. "Blacker's dead—heart attack or stroke or something." Before she could jump to the same, but wrong, conclusion he added. "Not the old man—the son, Jerome, was the one who died."

"The penny-pinching bastard who put us on this cheap-assed transport instead of a decent liner?" Louella shot back. "Well, good riddance. Maybe we'll get better treatment now that he's out of the way." She reached into her pocket and held out a flimsy. "Maybe that news has something to do with this request we have from JBI. They want us to listen to a bloody too-damn-expensive conference call this evening."

Louella fumed at the delay enforced by the slow speed-of-light transmission that made the conference call an agony of delay and deliberation. With a ten-minute delay between exchanges with the JBI agent back on Jupiter, the term "conversation" took on a new meaning. It was more like making speeches at one another without the benefit of immediate feedback. Every misunderstanding took so long to correct that both sides were being very verbose in whatever they said.

So far she had learned that the JBI dinosaur was in panic mode, its body of thousands of employees and managers trying to cope with their sudden and unexpected loss. The majority of the company still operated normally, but eventually, without a head, the body would fail to coordinate its actions and begin to die.

She learned that the news of Jerome's death had sent the price of JBI stock tumbling, with repercussions throughout the solar system due to the interrelations of system-wide corporations. Soon, other companies would be affected.

Old Blacker had even had his set piece to open the conversation, although Louella suspected that it had been pre-recorded. "Lots of good publicity on the Jupiter race," he'd said. "Your rescue gave us more news share than the winners. Gave us good legs in the PR front. Need to have more of that.

"Now we have to keep JBI in the news so people will forget about Jerry's loss," Blacker continued, his voice lacking any trace of remorse. "My damn flyspeck accountants tell me that we need to staunch the cash flow. We need more good publicity to restore JBI's good name and stock price. News that will make people believe we are still a forward-thinking, risk-taking company worth investing in."

"Fat chance," Louella said to herself. "No way I'm going back to Jupiter for another damn race." She and Pascal had nearly lost their lives when the combination dirigible and submarine that "sailed" the upper atmosphere of Jupiter had lost its sails and been cast adrift. Had it not been for the fortuitous meeting with *Thorn* and her pilot Rams

Potswamynada, they would have become Jupiter's Flying Dutchman, doomed to sail the red seas of Jupiter forever.

"There's a new race I want you to sail," Old Jerome continued, bringing her thoughts back to the present. "GeoGlobal and First Mars are sponsoring entries with some local talent, none of whom have your experience. It'll be an easy win and won't take much time off your schedule. My people on Mars will send you the details. Expect great things out of you. Make me proud."

A new race? The Honda Global wasn't scheduled for another year, and he certainly couldn't expect her to run the Grand Vendee again. She had nearly lost her life drifting on an upside down racer in Earth's Southern Ocean four years ago, an experience she didn't want to repeat.

So, what race could it be? And would she have time to regain the skills and feel for blue water sailing after they reached Earth?

For that matter, did she really want to get back into competitive sailing once more? After her adventures on Jupiter, sailing the Earth's seas would be safer, but would also seem tame. Too tame, perhaps. Maybe it was time to settle down and get on with her life.

Pascal was as puzzled as Louella over Blacker's statement about a new race. He thought he knew all the world-class blue-water races that were scheduled over the next two years, and none of them were of a stature that would garner JBI the type of publicity old Jerome needed. What would it be?

The details came in the form of a massive download that had the rest of the passengers grumbling over the loss of their own time on the machine. The crew had to parcel the download into multiple files so that the reading stations could handle it.

The first sixty gigs were a complex contract that neither of them could understand, so arcane was the language JBI's lawyers had formulated. It was only when they looked at the attachments that they realized the huge bonus JBI would provide if they won the race. What's more, even if they did not win, the salary they would receive would more than compensate them for any lost time from whatever they had planned.

"I could build my own sailing school with that kind of money," Louella said.

"And I could finally buy my ranch in Arizona," Pascal sighed. "Or a villa in Marseilles."

The dates of the race were puzzling. Their ship wouldn't reach Earth orbit for another two months, yet the race was scheduled to begin in forty-five days. How was that possible?

The second download had included a surprising location—Mars. There was only one tiny fact the JBI staff had overlooked.

"How can there be a fucking sailboat race on Mars, for God's sake?" Louella exclaimed. "There's no freaking water, no seas, not even a damn pond."

The download also provided their contact's name, berthing arrangements, and even their departure dates for Earth after the race. Obviously JBI's planners had covered everything needed to ensure that they would satisfy their contract.

Pascal had brought up a map of Mars and checked out the locations. "I see no possible settlements near this race location," he said. "Near the equator just east of Arsia Mons, it says." It looked like a flat plain—an unlikely place for open water. An accompanying satellite shot showed nothing but an empty, rose-colored plain of lava flows.

"It looks like a damn desert," Louella exclaimed over his shoulder. "How the hell can you sail on fucking sand?" She paused, turned to Pascal, and said, "I think we need to do a little research."

Pascal knew from the tone of her voice that she could already feel the lines in her hands as the red sands flew beneath her. "There is a woman on board who said she raced on Mars," he said, recalling what Haley had said over dinner. "Perhaps we should talk to her before we make any commitments."

Haley was less than informative about sailing on Mars. "Nothing I ever heard of," she said. "Atmosphere's so thin I doubt if it would be possible, and this spot is pretty high up—about eight or nine klicks above the reference normal. Sailing, you say? Well, that's the most foolish idea I've ever heard. We have more productive things to do on Mars than waste time on something as stupid as sailboat races."

Pascal squeezed Louella's hand hard before she could let loose a skin-peeling torrent of invective that expressed her utter contempt for those who thought sailing was stupid. "But wouldn't you say the same about mountain racing?" he replied.

To her credit, Haley blushed. "Well, I guess so, but the Tai Chan race is sort of a tradition we've turned into a race, so it's a little different. Besides, I was getting paid good money for helping out."

"As are we," Pascal continued, his fingers still digging into Louella's arm. "But right now we need to know more about Mars. Are the winds strong, and do they change direction quickly? How frequent are the sandstorms, and how bad are they?"

"Wind's so slight you never feel it on your suit," Haley replied. "Which is why I can't figure out how anybody could use it to sail. Sandstorms might whip up a breeze, but they aren't that frequent, and mostly in the spring. They're worse at the equator, but some might occur further north. I think I heard the wind speed increases with altitude, but that wouldn't matter much since the atmosphere's so thin."

"Barely comes up to your knees," Matt injected, repeating a joke long grown old.

Haley continued. "Most sandstorms aren't strong, but they sure are abrasive. Spend a few weeks getting hit by them and you'll have your suit polished to a high shine."

"Sandblasting does that," grinned Matt. "Are you going to let your girlfriend speak now?"

Pascal jerked his hand away from Louella's arm as if it had suddenly turned into a snake. "Girlfriend?" he said incredulously.

"Don't make any assumptions about us," Louella said angrily. "Pascal's my crewmate, and that's a hell of a lot closer relationship than being married, most of the time. Now, will one of you tell me where I can find out more about these Mars sailing, uh, boats?"

The ship's library held an amazing amount of material on Mars and its atmosphere, but little about sailing in any form. Neither was there any hint of any large body of water.

"I sure would like to know what the devil they're smoking," Louella said, after reviewing the material about the Martian atmosphere. "The pressure only ranges two or three millibars, hardly enough to raise a decent wind."

Pascal scanned further down the reference. "Maybe that's why the typical wind speeds are under ten meters per second. Even the dust storms only get up to 30 mps!"

"This whole venture is starting to seem ridiculous," Pascal replied. "It has little to do with sailing as we've known it. Without water, what is the point of it all? I thought the Jupiter race would be interesting, but all we saw was the inside of our cabin and the black outside of the ships. I might as well have been in a simulator for all the thrill of sailing it gave me."

Louella cocked her head to the side. "You mean it was all for nothing?"

Pascal hesitated for a moment before responding. "Not entirely. There were some moments…"

"Like saving my ass and Rams's? Like overcoming your fear of heights? Like finding out that we actually mean something to each other? Was that all for nothing?

"Come on, Pascal; you won't have to worry about falling. The area looks pretty flat, for God's sake, and how much wind can there be with hardly any atmosphere? Whatever they're talking about will be a walk in the park compared to what we've been through. Hey, the money they'll pay is more than we could get from the suits for the best race on Earth."

Pascal considered. The Martian desert looked quite unlike Arizona's, whose flat, distant horizons, rich colors, fantastic sunsets, and distance from the ocean had great appeal. Arizona's high plains were cold at night, but the temperatures didn't plummet as low as negative one hundred degrees Celsius. Even in the daytime, the Martian desert would barely reach minus twenty degrees, and that was on a warm day!

On the other hand, Louella had a point. With the money they'd already gotten for racing *Primrose* and the bonus they might receive if they won this ridiculous Martian race, he could do anything he wanted. He could build a home far from the ocean, far from anyone who knew anything about sailing, far from anything in his life to this point. He could finally be free to do as he pleased.

"I will do it," he said. "But only for you."

"I don't like your contract terms," Louella said to the JBI representative on Mars. They had gotten close enough while they went over the background material that the delay in transmission was a mere forty seconds, barely noticeable after their earlier experience. "We'll need complete outfitting, training, and expert advice if we are going to compete in this race."

"That's all been taken care of," the rep replied. "All you have to do is agree to land at Marsport. We've scheduled everything for you."

"We want JBI to arrange first class passage to Earth after the race," Louella demanded. "Yeah, and a bigger payment. I don't have a lot of faith that we'll be able to earn the bonus, given our lack of experience with this"—she choked to suppress a giggle—"Martian sailing thing."

"I'll download a video," he replied angrily. "See if you can contain your amusement until then."

The download brought some sense to the situation. It was a short movie that showed a group of wheeled triangular frames with huge sails tearing about a rose-colored plain at incredible speeds. Pascal was amazed at how the mechanisms managed to actually accelerate after they turned into the wind. "How is this possible?" he asked. The winds of Mars had to be too slight to drive such contraptions, yet he could not deny the images before him.

When they returned to negotiations the next day, the dry JBI man looked as if he had not moved a millimeter from his earlier position. Did JBI now have virtual executives, Louella wondered?

"Mr. Blacker has complete trust that you will do your job," the rep said as soon as he saw they were on line. "The amounts we've offered are quite generous, and far more than you could get elsewhere. I should point out that you have been off the race circuit for nearly two years, and would have a hard time getting backing for ocean racing."

Louella swore silently. It was too damn true. It would take her a long time to restore the network of backers and financiers she'd need to finance a race team. "Generous? You're asking us to risk our lives sailing on an unfamiliar Martian desert. I think that deserves more than the pittance your employer offered." She just wished she had a better idea of what she was talking about.

"Piffle. It isn't that dangerous. Besides, Mr. Blacker made it quite clear that you were to participate in this race," the rep replied. "Mr. Blacker is not a man to be trifled with."

"We're not his damn employees," she shot back. "Tell Jerome that he can stick his Martian race up his ass if he expects me to delay my return to Earth for so little money. I want the damn bonus regardless of where we place, or we're not coming down to Marsport."

The delay this time was noticeable—nearly a full four minutes, far too little time for the representative to contact Earth for advice, but enough time for a quick conference. "I am authorized to offer a third of the bonus as incentive," the answer finally came. "You'll get the remainder only if you win."

Louella wondered if she should push the man further to see just how far he would go. But that long delay said that he had executed a carefully calculated comparison of cost against the benefits of publicity. JBI's managers put a price on everything they did, and this was no different.

"Deal," she said, after making him wait a few minutes. "I'll tell my agent on Earth to sign the documents." Scott, her agent, would crap in his pants when he saw the numbers and found out what she'd be doing for it.

T he passenger compartment of the shuttle to the Martian surface was cramped, smelly, and obviously well worn. The hatch handles were burnished to a bright finish, as was every place a hand could rest. "Polished by the dust," the pilot explained as he shoved Pascal into his seat and pulled the safety harness entirely too tight for comfort. Ordinarily such close proximity to the cute pilot would have been welcome, but the fact that both of them were encased in protective surface suits made the closeness less than enjoyable. "Dust gets into everything, and there's not a vacuum made that can get it all up. You'll have to learn to live with it when you get below."

The reason for the excessively tight harness became abundantly clear as the shuttle dropped to the surface. To Pascal, it felt more like a controlled fall than a glide. The jarring landing took at least three bone-crushing hops before it settled into a bumpy roll. "Not bad," the pilot said cheerfully. "We didn't lose our wings this time."

Wings? Was this stomach-clenching drop from orbit what passed for a glide, Pascal wondered? There must be even less atmosphere than he imagined.

He got no glimpse of the landscape as the passengers trundled through the tunnel and into the 'port. Dull gray partitioning and a strip of lights above gave the tunnel an industrial look. There was a gritty feel to the floor and, when Pascal glanced down, he saw the coating of reddish dust the pilot had described.

At the end of the tunnel, a pair of efficient attendants helped them out of their suits and pointed the way to the electrostatic barrier that was supposed to keep the dust confined to the tunnel.

"If you will come this way," a studiously polite young woman asked, and led them to a waiting electric cart. "We've booked you on the train to Bilbis Patera. I'm to accompany you." She glanced at her watch. "Sorry for the rush, but headquarters told me to get you to the Jovus Bubble as quickly as possible.

"Here are your schedules for the next week," she continued as she handed across a pair of databooks. "You'll have plenty of time to read them later, on the Biblis Patera train. It's quite a long trip—nearly nine hundred kilometers."

Pascal had been trying to take in the sights of Marsport as they raced along in the open cart. Marsport was the largest settlement on Mars, but wasn't much to look at from what he could see. The passage showed him nothing but low ceilings, narrow passageways, and few, if any, windows. Perhaps they were passing through the lower regions of the settlement, he thought, and the living areas were above them.

That thought disappeared as they dove down a ramp and passed through a larger volume containing what appeared to be a small park. It resembled nothing more than the center section of a huge shopping mall, but less glamorous than many he'd seen. "I wanted you to see our beautiful Central Park, and not the less appealing parts of the settlement," she said without a trace of sarcasm.

They continued along another set of low hallways. "Ah, here we are," she finally announced, as the cart stopped before a large hatch.

A pair of clamshell doors retracted as they approached, to reveal a platform beside a long line of large wheeled cars. At the head of the line was a squat tractor, dwarfed by the size of the cars.

The woman indicated one of the cars, and opened the hatch to a small compartment with six plush seats. "This is our private car," the woman said as she flicked the doors closed. "Please, make yourselves comfortable. We will be leaving shortly."

Pascal hardly heard her. The sight through the large windows beside the train revealed a stark orange landscape. Beyond the rows of cargo containers, industrial cranes, and piles of materials, stretched a horizon that seemed to rise into the distance. He tried to make sense of the sight. "Since Mars is smaller," he said, "shouldn't the horizon appear closer than it would on Earth?"

"You're looking up the slope of the old man," the woman said as she leaned over him. "That's Olympus Mons, the biggest mountain in the solar system. It's so huge that the top of it is actually below the apparent horizon, which is really the side of it. Blows your mind, doesn't it?"

She was lingering close entirely too long for his comfort, her breast brushing his shoulder as she pointed. She rested one hand on his arm.

Louella snorted. "You're wasting your time, honey. Pascal's not the type you could get friendly with."

The woman blushed as she stood back. "Sorry, I had no idea that you two were…"

"We're not," Louella replied abruptly, realizing that the woman had made a second wrong assumption. Three strikes and you're out, she thought. "They didn't brief you on who we were?"

The woman appeared flustered. "No, they just told me to accompany you to Jovus. I imagined that you were two of JBI's scientists. I escort a lot of them through here."

"Scientists is not the word for us, honey. Jesus, don't you see the news? We're the team that sailed JBI's boat on Jupiter."

In reaction to the blank look on the woman's face, Pascal spoke up. "We had a few problems and had to be rescued. It was all the news a few months ago."

"We're here to race some Martian sailors," Louella replied. "We're JBI's sailing crew."

"I don't pay much attention to the sports news," the woman sniffed, her voice dropping a few degrees. "Taking time to care for JBI's important guests takes all of my time."

"Strike three," Louella exclaimed.

The train's trip to the Bilbis was less than interesting. It wound between large dunes and the walls of chasms for hours at a time. They'd been told that the tug could pull the train at a steady forty-five kilometers per hour, but with all that emptiness it felt as if they were hardly moving. When they started, she'd glimpsed industrial structures, storage areas, and construction sites. Marsport was expanding across the landscape, and not in an attractive way. In less than an hour, however, all traces of mankind disappeared, save for the markers of the train's course.

Phobos cast a faint glow that produced few shadows as it raced across the night sky and too quickly disappeared to the west, not to appear for another four hours. After that, there was nothing interesting at all.

Louella tried to sleep. Thirty damn hours on a train—what a waste of time.

The tedium of the long trip was boring, and after the limited conversation with their boring companion, Pascal had fallen asleep. With nothing else to occupy it, her mind came back to her future.

What would she do if she did stop sailing? Would she hang out with a gaggle of old sailing buddies? Settle down and admire her mantel full of trophies? Both options seemed too damn settled for her liking.

Maybe she could run a sailing school? She wouldn't need to struggle for money, not if she won this race, so she could do it for the love of sailing alone. Maybe it was high time she contributed more to life than this constant fight to finance her boat and crew, and then to drive them across the line to win.

It was something she had to seriously think about.

Jovus Bubble turned out to be a dirty pink balloon sitting atop a crater. Inside was a jumble of structures—one could hardly call them buildings—of various sizes. The terminal was an open set of platforms on either side of the train's berth.

Louella was surprised to see some familiar faces among the crowd on the platforms, especially Georges Franchard and Randy Holiday. She hadn't seen them since before the big Jupiter race that Georges's team had won. Both had fought hard against her in other races, as well as the Super, back on Earth.

"Finally found you, did they?" Franchard laughed when he spotted them. "I thought as much when I saw your names on the entry list last week."

"We didn't know you would be here," Louella shot back. "Wait! What did you say?" Last week would have been before she signed her contract. "Obviously, refusing JBI wasn't really one of my options," she said ruefully. "But why are you here?"

Randy gave her a boyish grin. "We'll sail anywhere if there's enough money involved—First Mars offered to sponsor me when they heard JBI was going to enter."

"I still think it's a stupid idea," Georges said. "I can't see how anyone could be interested in a race where there's hardly any wind at all. Might as well sail in a vacuum," he sneered.

"But GeoGlobal's offer changed your mind, didn't it?" Randy injected. "Besides, look on the bright side—we get a free tour of Mars."

"I'll miss the Volvo next year because of this," Georges complained.

"We've all been away too long to build a team for the Volvo," Louella said. "The Jupiter race took us out of the running. Crap, who knows what new tech they've thrown on those boats by now. No, I think this Mars race is probably the last sponsored one we'll be able to get. After this, it's all dinghies and day sailing for us old salts."

"I'll miss those beauties," Randy sighed wistfully. Louella wondered if he was referring to his thirty-meter racing machines or his former string of adoring female fans.

Randy's glum face brightened when the JBI woman returned. "We're leaving for Pavonis as soon as they recharge the train," she said. "Please return to the car."

"These are our friends," Louella said. "Why don't they ride with us?"

"I'm afraid that would be against company policy," the JBI woman sniffed. "Especially since these two are with JBI's competitors."

"Randy Holiday," Randy said smoothly, sliding up to take her hand and looking intently into her eyes. "I hate the thought of us being in competition on anything."

Louella could see the Randy magic working on the woman's libido. Had to be his damn aura or something. That line wouldn't work in a cheap bar on a slow night.

"I don't imagine it would hurt," the woman wavered. "That is, if Mr. Dumay has no objections...."

"Oh, I might," Pascal said with a smile, twisting the knife in Randy's gut for a moment. "But not this time."

The scenery between Jovus and Pavonis was little different from what they'd observed on their first leg; dry orange-tinted sand covered with rocks of all sizes. In the flats each pebble seemed to have a drift of fine sand behind it, shaped by the wind into elongated teardrop forms.

"Well, that proves that there is some wind," Pascal remarked when Louella pointed them out. "If it can move sand, it could fill a sail."

"Yeah, but enough to push a... buggy?" Georges stumbled over the word. "You'd have to have a pretty big sail for even a small amount of weight. I'd think the force to weight ratio would be too low to do anything meaningful."

"But still, they move," Louella replied, thinking about the video of those fast contraptions. "You can argue theory all you want, but the fact remains that these Martians are managing to sail, despite your common-sense arguments."

Pascal laughed. "Can't argue with facts, Georges, so sit back and enjoy the scenery."

Here and there they could see traces of human activity scattered across the landscape; a pit where someone had prospected, tracks in the ever-present dust leading off into the distance, and the occasional discarded piece of trash—it seemed that even into this remote desert, humanity had brought its worst habits. What was not seen were any sign of human habitation or, for that matter, a structure of any size.

As the top of the Jovus bubble faded from view behind them, the horizon began to appear normal, that is, if you ignored the fact that it was much closer than that they'd seen from the decks of their boats on the open ocean—about twenty miles away instead of the thirty-some they were used to. For moments at a time, it appeared that Mars was rolling beneath the stationary train.

While Georges, Pascal, and Louella found the sights fascinating, Randy pursued other interests.

Their guide giggled as he whispered in her ear.

Sands saw the black woman wrinkle her nose in disgust as she and a slender man stepped into the common room. He waited as they glanced around, obviously looking for him. He did nothing as they figured out whom to approach.

"You Halsey," Louella asked as she came near.

"Call me Sands," he replied. "Have a sit."

"We're the—" Louella began.

"No need to say. Obvious you're newcomers from the funny way you walk and talk. I guess you're the so-called expert sailors who are going to show us dumb Martians how to race."

"We were told you could give us a few lessons," Pascal said, before Louella could explode over the obvious slight. "We've never done any land sailing before, much less here on Mars."

"Not many Earth-bound have," Sands said. "Now, all of a sudden, three big companies are throwing all kinds of money at it. Why is that?"

"JBI wants publicity," Pascal offered. "I guess the rest jumped in for the same reason."

Louella interrupted. "Which has nothing to do with what we need at the moment. We've got a month to practice before the race. We need to know everything there is to know about racing on this desert," she waved a hand toward the outer shell.

"Yes," Pascal said. "For one thing, how in God's name can there be enough wind to move a boat in this thin atmosphere?"

"Buggies," Sands sneered. "They're called buggies." He sipped his drink and made a face. "Marquilla," he explained, raising his drink. "It's an iced local brew with something the chemists swear tastes like lime. Personally, I think the stuff tastes like alcoholic rat piss. Want to order one?"

Pascal hesitated, but Louella spoke up. "Damn right, I need a strong drink to wash the taste of this place out of my mouth."

Sands signaled for two more. "That's the dust. You get used to the taste of it after a while. After fifteen years, I hardly smell it any more."

Louella screwed up her face after one sip of her drink. "Christ, this tastes terrible."

"You should taste it without the lime," Sands suggested. "It's worse."

"You still haven't answered the question about how you manage to get the boats... er, buggies, to such high rates of speed," Louella asked. "With a surface pressure under ten millibars, how can Mars have any kind of wind force at all?"

Sands took another sip of his Marquilla. "I hate this stuff, but can't afford Earth scotch, even with what JBI is paying me to help you."

"So why do you drink it," Pascal asked.

"Takes the edge off," Sands explained, and slapped his leg. "Cheaper than aspirin."

Before either of them could ask what he meant, he started to explain the winds of Mars. "You're right about the atmosphere's density being a lot less than anything you'd find on Earth, or Jupiter, for that matter. Mars is close to a vacuum by those standards.

"But there is an atmosphere and the air does move. A physicist told me that the force was about 1/100 of a wind on Earth traveling at the same velocity."

Louella screwed up her face. "But doesn't that mean the Mars winds have to be traveling a hundred times faster? I haven't heard any evidence of hurricane force winds anywhere on the planet, and it would take that to move something the size of your buggies."

Sands smiled. "Good logic, but wrong. Look, the amount of air pushing a sail depends on both the mass of the air and its velocity. What moves the buggy is the kinetic energy of the wind."

Pascal leaned forward and interrupted with rising excitement in his voice. "The kinetic energy is density or mass times velocity squared!"

"Right you are!" Sands grinned. "So if you do the math, you see that our wind only has to move ten times as fast as an Earth wind to get the same effect."

"Well, I'll be damned," Louella threw back the rest of her drink, coughed, and said, "How about another round? I think I might get used to this."

"You stopped competing a couple of years ago," Louella said, after they finished another few rounds and were on more friendly terms. "Why did you do that? JBI said you were once the best land sailor on Mars." Maybe his answer would help her understand her own future.

"Got stepped on by a dinosaur," Sands replied, and slapped his leg when he saw their puzzled expressions. "My transport's cargo pod flipped and crushed my legs. Since then, I've been making do with these sticks. They're great for walking, but I no longer have the kins for sailing."

"Kins is something you'll have to explain."

Sands shrugged. "Kins means Kinesthetic, if you prefer to use big words. You have to use your whole body to sail a buggy. You have to feel the tension of the sail on the frame through your legs, and the resistance of the wheels with the yoke. You'll have to understand the vibration from rolling across the surface with your ass, and learn to use your whole body instead of depending on the senses you've probably been using."

"So I have to wiggle around like this to sail?" Louella said and shook her butt.

Pascal snorted. Throw a decent looking guy at Louella after a few drinks, and she started making moves. Just for once, he wished she could shut down her libido.

And maybe give him a chance at the guy. He thought Sands was awfully cute.

"So you stopped racing," he asked, to get the conversation back on track, "when you lost your kins?"

"I still sail." Sands tossed back the last of his drink. "So 'won't race' is a better way of saying it. No sense racing a buggy if you can't compete. Crap, I can barely keep up with the kids, let alone another racer.

"So I teach a little, drink a lot for the constant pain, and... try to think of reasons not to take a walk out on the plains without a suit." There for a second it sounded as if he started to state some other factor, but stopped himself.

"So why help us," Louella asked. "Sounds as if there's more to your reasons than the money." She reached out and put her hand on his arm.

Sands shook off the gesture. "Reasons? Look, this is probably going to be the biggest damn sailing race Mars has ever seen, and I want to be part of it. The best sailors, guys I used to beat regularly, are going to be in this race.

"You want to know why I'm helping you? It means that maybe, with your experience and my training, you could have an edge. I want to win, even if I have to do it vicariously. Does that answer your question?"

Pascal grinned. "Bien. So how do you think we can beat more experienced racers? I assume it won't be easy while we're wearing suits weighed down with air bottles and water jugs."

"Every sailor will have the same handicap," Sands explained. "The buggies will all have the same frame construction and rigging, so it'll be what you would call a one-design race.

"Look, I'll work with you on how to run the buggy, show you a few tricks with balancing the sail, and fill you in on the tactics these guys might use against you. That might help you keep up, but barely. It's going to take all of your experience with wind and sail to do better than that. Look, JBI's betting that your blue water experience and the skills you learned sailing on Jupiter will make handling our little buggies easy."

Pascal was certain he knew the answer to that challenge. He had no doubt as to who would adapt better to this environment. He sailed scientifically, calculating the best heading based on readings of barometer, wind gauge, and telltales. Louella, on the other hand, sailed instinctively, feeding off her senses to trim the sails and set the rudder. He'd clearly be at a disadvantage in this race.

"When's our first practice," he asked, anxious to prove his point.

P ascal's first impression of the buggy was that there was hardly enough of the thin metal frame to support the amount of sail he was told it would carry.

The buggy's eight-meter frame was a triangle of tubing, attached at each corner with flexible joints. The three sides were connected with half a dozen cross braces. A single mesh wheel supported the front of the buggy while two more, larger wheels, splayed from the rear corners and raised the rear a good meter higher than the front end.

In the center of the outer frame was the mast step. Rising from this was a fifteen-meter mast that tapered from base to tip. The mast supported a long spar at the top and a boom that extended at least five meters beyond the rear of the buggy, its weight balanced by a counterweight forward of the mast. Wrapped along the length of the boom was a bundle of plastic sheeting. "That's the sail," Sands said, when he noticed where Pascal was looking.

"What keeps the whole thing from falling over?" Pascal wondered aloud as he gazed upwards.

"Despite their appearance, the spar, boom, and sail together weigh less than a hundred kilograms," Sands replied. "The counterweight balances that weight, so it has nearly no effect on the buggy."

A saddle was mounted on a rail about midway between the mast and the buggy's rear end. Directly in front of the saddle was the steering yoke. The frame's rails supported a confusing array of lines and pulleys. He tried to relate these to the rigging of the sailboats he was familiar with.

In his mind's eye, Pascal could see how four of the lines running through the pulleys could be used to control the sail, but was puzzled by the others. "Why those extra pulleys," he asked, pointing at the lines to either side of the saddle.

"They'll control your position," Sands answered. "You adjust the lines to shift your weight from side to side. You'll need to shift to keep the buggy level. That counterweight won't provide all the balance you need when the sail is full and the boom swings wide."

Now that he mentioned it, Pascal noticed that the saddle slid side-to-side on short rails, and was pivoted to allow the rider to lean to either side. Sailing this rig was going to prove interesting and exhausting if it required as much body movement as Sands suggested.

Pascal lowered himself into the saddle. "Too much room for my butt," he smiled, wiggling around.

"Not when you've got your suit on," Sands replied. "Besides, you'll be strapped on the saddle to keep you from slipping off. Could break a leg or tear your suit."

Pascal shuddered; a torn suit or cracked helmet would be deadly on this hostile planet. "That ever happen to you," he asked, glancing at Sands's artificial legs.

Sands shrugged. "Sort of: the safety strap broke when my tug flipped over."

"That what you meant when you said you'd been stepped on by a dinosaur? Was that what you called the cargo pod?"

"No," Sands said. "The tug went off the trail and hit a rock. That's what tipped the tug, the rock." He paused. "Funny thing was that the rock turned out to be a meteoroid from ancient Earth. That's why I said a damned dinosaur did this to me."

Throughout the conversation, Louella had been walking around the frame, stooping to examine this feature or that.

He was used to the way men checked out Louella on the sly, not realizing that she went out of her way to parade her assets when she found a man interesting, which she was obviously doing in this case, and rather more than usual.

Pascal noted that not once had Sands so much as glanced at her. At the same time, he realized that Sands hadn't paid that much attention to his own less obvious signals either. Something was definitely wrong.

L ouella's first attempt to sail Sands's buggy was a disaster. The supine position that put her ass a few centimeters above the surface was unfamiliar, as was the awkward steering yoke, so different from a sailboat's wheel. Her first glance at the huge sail looming over her head made her fearful that any shift would overbalance the buggy.

"The sail's weight is negligible," Sands insisted when she mentioned this. "You could easily hold every square meter of that fabric in one hand without straining, it weighs so little. Don't worry, the counterweight will keep you somewhat level when she's full of wind."

The "somewhat" worried her.

Despite Sands's insistence that there was a nice breeze, she could see no evidence save the fluttering of the sail as she unfurled it from the boom that appeared too slender and flexible for so much material. Despite its appearance, the entire assembly only massed a hundred kilograms, and weighed less in Mars's weak gravity.

"Take the buggy straight out and turn downwind," Sands suggested. "Don't turn or pull the sail in until you get a feel for it, or you'll tip over."

Louella doubted there was enough wind for that to happen. She could barely feel the tension of the sail as she rolled across the hard-packed surface of Arsia Sulci. The buggy picked up speed, but was still moving at what seemed a snail's pace.

She played with the yoke that controlled the front wheel of the buggy. The buggy was quite responsive to her slightest movement, a quite different feel than what she got from moving a sailboat's rudder. When she had gained more confidence in the degree of movement, she turned the yoke enough to bring the buggy closer to the wind, and pulled the sail tighter. The buggy immediately picked up a surprising amount of speed for such a small adjustment.

Suddenly, before she could react, the buggy heeled to one side. She threw her weight to oppose the buggy's tilt, attempting to twist so her feet could press against the downwind rail. She fumbled to release the sail, only to see its tip touch the sand momentarily, before the entire buggy slewed into the wind and slowed. The sail fluttered uselessly above her. She was of all things, in irons—a tyro's mistake.

"Weight and balance," Sands shouted over the radio. "You have to shift your whole body before you adjust the sail angle."

"I got that much," Louella replied curtly. Damn, she felt like some novice on her first day of sailing. The reaction of the buggy to her moves was so different from what she thought she knew.

Or was it? The effect of wind angle on the sail and the propulsive force it exerted on the buggy was no different than the forces acting on a real sailboat. Sure, the buggy balanced differently than a sailboat, but that was something she was certain she could get used to. She had only to learn where the border of safety was: that thin line that separated disaster from success, the point where you skirted the edge to gain as much speed as possible to win.

As Sands had said, she had to find those edges if she expected to win.

Pascal's experience was much the same. He had been watching Louella's awkward movements and the resulting actions of the boat.

Must remember to call them buggies, he chided himself. The trick seemed to be shifting your weight gradually and averting sudden movements. The frame was so light in comparison to the sail area that the slightest change in weight distribution altered the balance.

An hour later, he realized how difficult that philosophy became when encumbered by suit, heavy air tanks, and assorted gear that kept his frail body safe from the Martian harshness. "Hard to move," he grunted to Sands over the radio.

"Try to rotate your body around your belly," Sands instructed him. "And try to keep your legs straight down the center line."

That instruction puzzled Pascal, until he realized that rolling onto one buttock while keeping his body stiff controlled the buggy quite easily. Better still, it was easy to make small corrections by doing this. "Thanks," he radioed.

The play of wind on the sail was about the same as any breeze on Earth, or Jupiter, he recalled ruefully. On a normal sailboat, the sail propelled a boat both through the action of the wind as it passed across the sail's surface and the pressure exerted by the wind on the face of the sail.

He played with different sail settings as he raced back and forth across the surface. As he was trying to find the stall angle, where the wind pressure was equal on both sides of the sail, he noticed something strange.

At an angle that should have been so close as to decrease his speed, the buggy suddenly sped up. Thinking it was a sudden gust, he waited for it to die. When it didn't, he tried to figure out why. There certainly had to be a good physical reason for this amazingly different behavior.

In his experience, as a boat turns into the wind, the angle of attack lessens but the apparent wind speed—the difference between the actual wind speed and that experienced by the sail—actually increases. Turn too much into the wind with an extremely low angle of attack, as he had been trying to do, and the increased drag and diminished degree of efficiency of the sail should cause a loss of accelerating force and bring the boat to a dead stop.

But with these buggies, that did not happen until the sail was directly into the wind. Somehow, perhaps due to the light weight of the contraption, or the lack of friction on the surface, the buggy actually took advantage of the apparent wind and increased its efficiency. Amazing!

He performed a few more runs to test his theory, and perfecting the angle that gave him the greatest speed.

The third day of practice was better. Louella'd quickly become familiar with the differences between the feel of a boat slapping the water and the buggy's wheels rolling across the hard-packed sand. Turning across the breeze was difficult, but turning to the wind was easier than she expected.

She was feeling quite confident when Pascal blew by her as if she were standing still.

"How the hell are you doing that?" she screamed over the suit-to-suit link. She was pulling as close to the wind as she should, but getting nowhere near the speed he exhibited. He certainly hadn't had more practice, so where had he picked that technique?

"Pure physics," he replied cryptically. "Stifle that damned intuition of yours and think about the force vectors you are dealing with."

"That makes no sense whatsoever," Louella replied with heat. "There's just the damn wind, sails, and buggy. It's no different than a sailboat."

She thought hard as she watched him move into the wind. His sail wasn't luffing when, at that angle of attack he should be at a dead stop. What kept him from losing speed? Curious, she pulled her own sail tight, cutting the wind at an angle she was sure would make her lose the bubble of near vacuum these Martians called a wind.

Almost immediately, the buggy accelerated. Instead of a flapping sail this close to the wind, it was as if she'd been hit with a gust. That had to be it: the apparent wind was actually boosting the sail's efficiency. She could sail closer to the wind than she ever had on Earth!

After a few more experiments, she realized that the relatively low weight of the buggy in relation to the huge sail surface, plus the trivial amount of drag from the wheels, made the buggies act so differently.

A few turns later and she was not only keeping up with Pascal's buggy, but was beating him on the turns. He was obviously unwilling to tilt too sharply for fear of a spill. Now it was his instincts that were the problem.

"You're strapped in, for God's sake!" she radioed. "You can't fall out even if you flip the buggy. Besides, the mast will keep the buggy from going completely turtle."

"I know that," he replied. "But knowledge does not overcome one's inclination."

"Well, you'd better learn to ignore that if you want to win this race."

"You're both being too cautious," Sands told them over drinks after their practice. "These buggies are a lot tougher than you might think.

Despite what your eyes tell you, all that sail up there and the mast hardly weigh a thing in comparison to you and the frame. The center of gravity is just about even with your helmet. That means you could tilt the whole thing about sixty degrees before you overbalanced. In a strong wind, you could probably get up to seventy-five degrees."

"No way," Louella exclaimed. The idea of sailing with her body nearly parallel to the ground was scary enough. It had to be downright frightening for Pascal. It would be even worse when he had to lean away from the direction of turn.

On the other hand, she thought, maybe a stronger breeze would make it easier to perform an inside turn if she had the wind pushing on the sail to help counterbalance. Maybe she could push those angles further, maybe up to eighty-five degrees?

It was worth trying.

As the weeks sped by, there were both exhausted from Sands's strenuous training schedule. There was scarcely enough time in the evening to grab something to eat before turning in.

"It's the oxygen," Sands told them. "You're breathing a richer mixture in your suits. That dries you out and burns energy."

"So why do that," Pascal asked. "Why not breathe the same air as we do here in the bubble?"

"Economics," Sands replied. "Oxygen is waste product of some of our industrial practices. Costs more to add the nitrogen, helium, and other crap we normally breath."

"Well, I've been breathing too damn much," Louella chimed in. "I need a break. We both need a break."

"I think you both deserve some time off. Tell you what, make a night of it, and we won't start practice until after noon tomorrow."

"Gee, thanks coach," Louella mumbled. "Now, excuse me, I think that guy over there is giving me the eye, so I'm going to see what he has in mind."

Pascal glanced in that direction. The man she was talking about was a beefy construction worker with biceps and broad shoulders. A little on the rough side for his taste, but probably energetic enough to satisfy Louella.

"My tastes are quite simple," he said, after Louella had left. "I think I will just sit here and get bloody drunk on those horrible Marquillas. Pity Mars has no vintners."

"Oh, we have wine," Sands answered. "But it comes out of the same labs that do the lime juice. Somehow, I doubt that someone with your background would like the product."

Pascal shuddered. The thought of drinking the mass-produced factory "wine"—something that was little more than alcoholic grape juice—was bad enough, but laboratory wine? "I'll stick with what I can stomach," he replied.

Sands's story finally came out over too many drinks of a late night long after Louella had left with her beefy companion.

Pascal felt comfortable enough with Sands to admit to the horrors he'd felt during the Jupiter race, when he'd jumped across the deep dark gulf separating their own from the rescue ship. The fact that he'd had several lines tied to him and was actually more fearful of what Louella might do than his own fear of heights went unstated. It made a better story, too.

"I spent eight months in the hospital," Sands told him. "They had to rebuild my pelvis before they could attach these damn sticks." He slapped his legs for emphasis. "Good for nothing but walking, and that kept me from working the tugs."

"So what do you do," Pascal asked. "Living on Mars costs a lot. You on some sort of charity?" He'd already encountered the oxygen and water taxes on everything he'd bought or used.

"Isn't charity that keeps me going," Sands continued. "InterPlane Transports had to offer a nice retirement so I wouldn't sue their sorry asses for not maintaining the tug. Martians don't like incompetent people, and think worse of those whose sloppiness puts others at risk.

"The incompetent jerks rigged more sail than the payload required, and not by a little, either. Crap, they put up double the amount needed, which was why a little gust turned into a catastrophe. I lost a lot in that accident."

From the way he said it, Pascal knew he was not talking only about his competitive racing or his job. "What else did you lose," he asked softly, realizing the reason for Sands's apparent indifference to Louella's earlier overtures. Perhaps, without *les pendants*, there would be no desire.

"Something like that," Sands grunted, threw back the dregs of his drink, rose, and walked away without another word.

A woman at the bar came over and sat down. "I was hoping the eunuch would leave soon. Buy me a drink?"

Pascal's first reaction was to blow her off, both for the usual reason, and because she had just insulted someone he was starting to think of as a friend. But perhaps he could get some more information from her first.

"Sure," he forced a smile. "What did you mean by that comment about Sands?"

She held up two fingers to signal the bar. "Shoot, everybody knows his sad story. Can't get it up anymore; hell, he don't even have anything to get up, for that matter."

That confirmed his earlier supposition. "So what's the sad story," Pascal probed, as he resisted the urge to leave.

She got her drink from the barkeep and sat back at the table, smiling flirtatiously. "You're all right, sweetie. What say we make a night of it?"

Despite his disgust at her crudeness, Pascal held his anger in check. "Later, maybe. What else do you know about what happened?"

The woman pouted, obviously disappointed in his answer. "Let's see, right after he got out of the hospital, he broke off with his girlfriend. Said that she needed a real man, not some damned broken wreck she'd have to nursemaid the rest of her life. They had some screaming arguments everyone in the bubble could hear." She took another drink. "Me, I would have left him like that." She snapped her fingers. "But Paula, that was her name, kept trying."

"So, what happened," Pascal asked. "Sands didn't mention a girlfriend."

"Oh, he finally drove her away, or maybe she just came to her senses. Went over to Marsport, I heard. But that's enough talk about Sands. What say we get a bottle and go to your place for a little fun?"

Pascal threw down a handful of scrip for the drinks. "I think I prefer my own company tonight, darling. Sorry."

"Time to go!" Sands announced after their final practice. "We have to get up to Ophir Station in time to have a few practice runs on the race course. We leave tonight, so grab your kit and meet me at the train."

"What's the freaking rush?" Louella demanded. "Why tonight instead of tomorrow morning?"

"Because tonight is when we can catch the supply train out of here, instead of waiting for shuttle the day after tomorrow. We'll have an extra day to acclimatize to the race area and rest up from the trip," Sands replied. "Now, grab your gear, and let's go."

Louella stared out the narrow ports of the so-called passenger compartment as the train trundled on its fat mesh wheels beneath the star-studded skies of Mars. The tiny cabin was far different from the comfortable train they had taken from Marsport to Jovus.

They were crammed with four other passengers knee-to-knee so tightly they could smell each other's breath. Ordinarily, she would not object to being this close to so many muscular construction workers, but they had all gone to sleep as soon as they got aboard.

The cargo pods behind them were, according to what she could gather, crammed with expandable habitats, life-cycle support modules, and furniture. Sands said the four men could throw up enough habitat to house twenty people in a single day, which seemed awfully rushed to her. She'd hate to have her life depending on some hastily constructed shack in Mars's harsh environment.

Unlike Sands, Pascal, and the construction crew, she could not relax, much less fall asleep. She was starting to have doubts about this entire venture. What was she thinking of, racing these silly buggies? This wasn't what she trained for all those years. Her proper place was on the big boats, bringing sheet to wind and blowing by her competitors with some imaginative tactic. She was water, not sand; wind, not a faint breeze. In God's name, what was the sense of doing this, anyway?

Well, the money was damn good; that's what she thought. Still, the whole point of this was unclear, insofar as it related to the progression of her life, her inner goals, and what she hoped to accomplish before something killed her. Maybe this whole venture, from the day they accepted the Jupiter race to this, was a bad career move. She probably had better things to do.

She just wished she could figure out what they were.

The scenery she could see in the supply train's lights was pretty dull. Occasionally, she'd see the foot of a hill, the edge of a chasm, or simply an endless succession of random rocks. Dull, dull, dull! Even the faint rosy light from Phobos casting its fleeting shadows as it raced across the sky failed to hold her interest. The second time it came over, she hardly noticed it at all.

It would be dawn by the time they reached their destination.

Before dawn, before the feeble rays of the sun could provide enough heat to dissipate the thin coating of hoarfrost that lay white on the ground, they reached Pavonis Station. It was only a waypoint where they took on additional cars and a second tug. The passengers used the break to refresh, grab some warm food, and stretch their legs. It was hardly enough to counter the stiffness from the long ride and prepare them for an even longer leg to Ophir Station and the highlands.

Ophir Station turned out to be a dull gray dome sitting on the flat plane and surrounded by a dozen or more smaller domes, Quonsets, and tall, upright cylinders. Snakelike, flexible tubes connected them, some to each other and some to the main dome.

"We'll be adding these habitats over there," a beefy construction worker said as he leaned over her to peer out the window. He was pointing at a clear area not far from where they were heading. "Place was just a weather station or something before we brought all this crap up here for your race."

"Really?" Louella took the opportunity to rest her hand on his bicep. Nice and firm, she thought. She pointed at the cylinders. "What are those for?" She wasn't that interested, but it was nice having him so close.

He put a hand on her shoulder as he leaned further to see where she pointed. It was unnecessary, but a definite signal. "Oxygen generators," he replied. "They're sitting on top of some deep bores. I think they bring up CO_2 and break it down into oxygen and something else."

He didn't sound very bright, but damn, he had a nice chest and broad shoulders. Maybe she could make her brief stay up her at Ophir Station a little more interesting.

She was about to set something up when the seal broke and fresh air rushed into the cabin. "About damn time you lazy bums got back," a woman in a set of work coveralls and a hard hat yelled. "Come on, we got a tight schedule today, and we're half a day behind schedule as it is. Move it."

"See you later, Charlie?" Louella said to his back, and got a grunted "Maybe," in response.

No sooner were settled in their habitat just off the main dome than Sands shifted into lecture mode, going over the same material he'd been harping on the week before, only now that they were here, it seemed more real, more relevant.

"The winds are going to be stronger than those back at Jovus basin. Now that the season's getting toward Martian winter, the whole geothermal balance is changing. The wind could sometimes reach better than a hundred kilometers per hour."

When Pascal blanched, he added, "The race sponsors have assured everyone that there's good weather for the race."

"You won't have any winds close to that this early in the season— maybe sixty or seventy kph at most. That should push the buggies to a nice twenty or thirty klicks; scary, but manageable. Being able to reach those speeds is one reason for being this far north and out here on the planitia."

"That's hardly reassuring," Pascal added. "Especially since my ass will be almost dragging in the sand. Couldn't they require a little less sail, or add weight to the buggy to keep them from tipping?"

"No, you'll use the same sail sets you've been practicing with. The increased wind will let you run a tighter line than you've tried so far, but it'll still be controllable. Hey, don't worry," he said when they frowned. "Everybody's got the same rig, so your opponents are equally disadvantaged."

Louella couldn't help noticing Sands's uncommon stiffness whenever he moved. The cramped conditions during the long train ride must have played hell with his legs. Had that been a fleeting grimace of pain on his face? Should she say something, do something to help?

"The race will be three times around a one-hundred-kilometer course," Sands continued, apparently unaware of Louella's close observation. "Depending on wind direction, the course will start to either the north or northeast. There will be a standing start—none of that positioning you do with sailboats to get advantage. The staggered start line will give everyone an equal chance at the wind. The thing to remember is to keep your tacks as long as you can, so you don't lose time or momentum on the turns. Thirty klicks up the course, there will be a yellow flasher where you turn right."

"Starboard," Louella and Pascal corrected him in unison.

Sands grinned. "Whatever. Thirty klicks along that line you'll find a green flasher for the next turn, to run downwind for another thirty. That's the slowest leg of the course, and the one where you have to use every bit of strategy to stay ahead of the others."

As he spoke, the tiredness from the trip seemed to disappear. His entire demeanor changed. It was easy to see how excited Sands had become about the race. Vicarious participant he might be, but that obviously hadn't quenched his competitive spirit.

"The last turn is marked with a flashing red beacon. From that point, it's ten klicks to cross the start line again, and make another run around the course. You have to do that three times to win."

"Will the wind be steady or shifting," Louella asked. "It's a nine-hour race, so will the wind change as the day warms up? Will they adjust the markers during the race if the wind changes?"

"Those are all good questions," Sands replied after a moment's thought. "Past experience up here is that the winds quarter about twenty degrees or so. They pick up in the morning and calm down later, when the planitia reaches some sort of thermal equilibrium." He paused for a moment. "But storms have blown up this time of year, and sometimes the wind dies completely."

Louella grinned. "That's comforting. What the devil do we do if the wind dies—do they stop the race and make us get out and push?"

Pascal weighed in. "Yes, we can ill afford a race delay that will make us miss our flight back to Earth."

Sands shrugged. "That's not my problem, is it? I don't control the weather. All I agreed to do was get you two ready to race, and give you some training and a few hints about tactics and strategy. Running and winning the race is up to you."

He gazed out the window at the passing landscape. "One more thing: pay careful attention to the surface beneath your wheels. Stay away from anything that looks like a drift. Drive onto drift sand and you'll quickly lose speed. Catch one wheel in loose sand and you'll probably spill. At the speeds you'll be moving, that might be disastrous."

"Sounds like the voice of experience," Louella said. "Wasn't that what happened to your legs?"

Sands turned away to gaze out the window. "Yeah, something like that." There was a catch in his voice. All the buoyant excitement and animation he had been exhibiting drained from his posture.

"Let's go for a walk," Pascal said, and took Louella by the arm in the awkward silence. "I need to talk to you privately about our contract."

"What the hell was that all about?" Louella hissed as they walked away. "There isn't anything to talk about on contracts."

"It was what you said," Pascal said.

Louella pulled her arm from his grasp. "It was just a simple question."

"He's sensitive about the accident," Pascal answered, and looked back to make certain they were out of Sands's earshot. He then told Louella all that he had learned of Sands's sad tale.

Louella was silent for a few moments before she answered. "So, what are we going to do about it?"

Pascal stopped. "What do you mean? He drove her away. I can't change that."

"No, but maybe we can do something else. It doesn't take a genius to see how miserable and alone the man has been. If somebody doesn't do something, he'll probably kill himself before too long."

"It's not our problem, Louella."

"Really?" she answered, and Pascal realized that she was right. You always looked out for your teammates.

The next day, Louella and Pascal joined a dozen other sailors, including Randy and Georges, on the electric cart for a tour of the race course.

"We'll be moving slower than you can expect the day after tomorrow," their guide announced from his seat at the front. "We'll go down the center line. The boundaries of the course—that is, those areas that have been cleared, extend about one kilometer to each side. Pay attention to the soil conditions as it changes from hard pack here at the start to a granular mixture close to the first marker, and then goes back to hard pack for most of that leg. On the following leg, you'll see some drift, but not enough to kill your speed. The final leg is mostly hard pack."

"So why are we taking this tour if we already know what the surface is like?" Randy asked. "It's taking valuable time away from the practice I really need." A few of the Martians smiled, no doubt sensing an easy victory over this obvious novice.

Louella smiled as well. She knew Randy's tactics started long before a race, and his declaration might just be an opening gambit.

"The first landmark," the guide continued, as if he had not heard the remark, "is Crepis Patera, that you can just see peeking over the horizon. That's the direction you want to head to find the first marker."

"Why do we need to know that," Pascal asked. "Won't we have our gps and inertials?"

"Those instruments are allowed, but what if your equipment goes out? That mountain will still be there and," he smiled, "there won't be any clouds to obscure it."

Only the Martians laughed.

The rest of the tour was equally exciting as the guide noted points of sail, changes in surface quality, and the path the sun would follow over the course of the day. Some took notes, others nodded in agreement, as if they already knew all this, and some slept. Randy continued to complain about his lack of practice and how the tour was wasting the time he needed to learn how to sail in these weird Martian conditions. "I'm an ocean sailor," he complained. "Not some damn scooter driver."

Halfway along the third leg, the cart rocked violently as sand and dust rattled against its side. In seconds it was over. "Wind gust," the guide said, and licked his lips nervously. "Nothing you need to worry about. That's a very rare occurrence." The darting of his eyes and the whiteness of his knuckles on the rail belied his words.

Louella knew it had taken a strong wind to exert that much force in this weak atmosphere. She doubted her buggy could survive that strong a gust.

Pascal leaned over. "Do you trust Weather to be honest? I think the sponsors have too much invested in this race to call it off."

"Not lying, but certainly shading the truth," she answered. "The reports this morning didn't say anything about wind gusts. Think they got Weather to ensure the race isn't delayed?"

Apparently the same thought had occurred to many on the tour. As angry questions were thrown at the guide, Randy's voice rose above all the others. "I am not risking my freaking neck on this race if we have to face winds like that. It's just too dangerous."

"Damn straight." Several others rapidly agreed with these sentiments. "No way I'm racing." It was obvious from the angry scowls and disappointed faces that there would be at least three withdrawals this evening.

Louella was absolutely certain that Randy wouldn't be one of them.

Ophir Station was getting crowded as each train brought more people in from Pavonis. Some of the crowd appeared by the cut of their clothes and their gorgeous companions to be high rollers.

Their appearance and behavior set them apart from the modest working clothes of the sailors and their crews.

With so much wealth evident, there had to be some serious betting going on, Louella thought, and wondered how she and Pascal were doing in the odds.

"You and your Earth buddies are getting three to one against," Sands informed them when she asked. "Zhang Wu is the top racer on Mars, so they're giving him even odds to win—Zhang's a tough competitor. Two of the other Martians, Pavel Zhubinsky and Peer Jackson, are getting way better odds than you."

"Glad to hear how our sailing reputations are respected," Louella remarked dryly. "Have you put some cash down?"

Sands grinned. "I put a couple hundred on you to place. I might put up more if your odds get worse."

"What're his strengths and weaknesses," Louella asked. "If you want us to give this character a race, you'd better let us know what we're facing."

Sands screwed up his face in thought. "He runs right on the edge of disaster. Always hauls the sail too tight, and likes to bank the buggy on the turns. Those tactics allow him to maintain a good speed through the turns. His biggest weakness is that he's very impatient and takes risks. He cuts the markers a little too tight in my opinion and tacks too damn quickly."

Louella had a history of racing against people who followed pretty much the same tactics against her. To beat them, you had to be as strong as they and take advantage of their weaknesses. Now she had to think about how she could do this in these conditions. "So, if we crowd him, he might get more reckless?" she mused.

"If you can catch him," Sands grinned. "As I said; he's good."

"I think it's time for a strategy session," she replied, and waved Pascal away from his friends. To get into the details, they needed more privacy than this gathering afforded. There were a lot of things they had to learn about their competition. From what Sands had just said, skills alone were not going to win this race.

The next day, the officials allowed the sailors to use the course for practice. The wind was blowing steadily from the north, although nothing Louella could see or feel told her that. Even with the suit's external microphones turned up high, she could not hear the howling of this so-called wind.

She rolled her buggy to the starting line. About half of the sailors were queued up, waiting for Georges and Randy to start. From their history, she knew Georges and Randy would be challenging each other the entire way around the course. It was their nature.

Georges shot off the line and quickly caught the wind, expertly driving to the best line in moments. Randy, on the other hand, fumbled with his gear, backwinded the sail, and took minutes to get straightened out. Louella wondered if this fumbling was another of his psychological tactics, or if he was actually as inept at this as he appeared?

From the obvious amusement of the other sailors, she suspected the former.

She waited as one after another buggy left, until only she and Pascal remained. They wanted to run last so they could test some of the ideas the three of them had generated the night before. Better that the others not see their moves too early, she'd suggested. "We'll come late to the line."

She loosed the sail as the buggy ahead of them disappeared into the distance. She glanced up at the feathery tell-tales at the top of the mast and the rear of the sail. A minor adjustment brought the sail into the wind, and her buggy began to roll. Pascal paced her on the downwind side and slightly ahead of her, to keep away from the wind spilling off her sail.

As soon as they were well away from the starting line, she hauled the sail as tight as possible, and let the buggy take its own line toward the right side of the course, following Pascal. The buggy's speed steadily increased as the angle to the wind lessened, until the right wheel lifted from the sand.

Louella threw her weight toward the high end to bring the wheel back to touch the surface. Now she could actually feel the force of the wind on the sail through the lines in her hands, and sense the vibration of the buggy in her seat. At this extreme speed, the buggy stopped becoming a contraption in her mind, and became a living creature vibrant with life and eager to race.

She was approaching the right boundary, where the hard-packed sand changed to a more granular texture. She turned the yoke, loosened the sail, and let the wind fill the sail. She'd lost sight of Pascal for the moment.

On this tack, the side of the sail couldn't use the apparent wind and lost of lot of its efficiency. She could feel the speed diminish. "Have to keep these tacks short," she reminded herself of Sands's advice. She started mentally laying out the series of long and short tacks she'd have to use to maintain the greatest speed.

Pascal was now well behind her, probably because he was afraid of leaning too far, she thought. So much for his theory of science over intuition.

She let the buggy race at this modest pace back across the course. She saw another buggy in the distance as she did so. Red suit, she noticed. That would be Randy for sure. It looked as if he was having no problem handling his buggy now that he was out of sight of the others.

The turn downwind was a surprise. She had to shift all the way to the right to counterbalance. As the huge sail deployed to the other side, she watched the large counterweight swing across the bow.

The sail was a marvelous sight in the rosy glow of the morning sun, and made her think of the dark red sails of the fishing dhows in the Mediterranean. Of course, this sail was colorless and nearly transparent, being barely a centimeter thick film of aerogel. A sail like this wouldn't last the typical breezes on Earth.

Pascal passed her. Damn, she had to stop daydreaming and get to work. She hauled a tighter line and followed him. Where had he tacked the last time? How would she tell if he was about to change? She watched carefully for some sign.

She saw the slight shift of his body and immediately yanked the yoke, pulled in the sail, and threw her weight to the outside of the turn. The buggy tilted dramatically, and then slammed down as she cut back across the wind.

She glanced back. Pascal was a fraction of a length behind her, catching all of the disturbed wind off her sail and falling further behind. Great tactic, she thought. I'll have to use that on what's-his-name, Zhang Wu?

Sands was waiting at the lock when they returned. "Let's look at the recorders," he said without preamble, as he accepted the data plugs from their inertial guidance systems.

"That was a good move there," he remarked at the way Louella had cut off Pascal's tack as they replayed their actions on the course. "Zhang won't be so obvious, however, and others have used that tactic against him. A better strategy would be to stay upwind of his line so that even if he tacks first, you can still recover."

He had even more advice as they went over their performance meter by meter. "Stay to the far right of the lay line," he advised at one point. "Watch for the drift sand here," and, "Give yourself lots of room at the markers—you've got a lot of sail behind you, and hitting the marker with the sail will put you out of the race."

"Disqualify you," Pascal asked.

"Destroy the sail, more likely," Sands replied. "Now, let's run through the entire recordings once more."

Louella groaned. It was later, and she and Pascal had things to do. Things Sands shouldn't know about.

Pascal slowly dragged himself from the bunk and staggered to the washstand. All of the unfamiliar physical moves he'd employed to control the buggy were finally taking a toll on his body. He was stiff in places he didn't know he had places.

Later, after doing his exercises to work most of the kinks out and having a dry breakfast, he headed for the dome's garage. This far north at this time of year, the sunrise wasn't until nearly eight hundred, Earth time. The race wouldn't start until ten—giving them enough time to finish before dark.

Sands was already at work on the buggy. "I'm replacing the lower sail line," he remarked as he tossed a coil to one side. "I spotted some fraying, probably from the pulley we replaced yesterday."

The sail was unfurled, and hung limply in the still air of the garage. It appeared to be nothing more than a thin, milky cloud, a wall of mist, instead of a cascade of barely substantial fabric. Pascal accepted one end of the new line from Sands, and clamped it to the grommet at the end of the boom. Sands ran the other end through the pulleys, and cinched it tight to the hold-fast at the saddle.

When that was done, Sands began to lower the spar as Pascal rolled the sail, until they had the entire sail secured against the boom. A steady pull on the string would release and raise the sail. He wouldn't do that until they were outside.

As Sands went over to work on Louella's buggy, Pascal began checking his suit, lubricating the wheels, adjusting the yoke connections, and ensuring that every mechanical and electrical component of the buggy was properly tuned for the race. There was no place for spares on the buggy's open frame, so everything had to work perfectly.

When those tasks were completed, he looked around the vast garage. Ten buggies filled the great space, and all but three were being feverishly worked on in preparation for the race that was to begin in less than an hour. He waved to Georges and Randy across the way, nodded to those closer, and then looked at where Louella and Sands were working on the counterweight.

Curious, he wandered over.

"Moving the counterweight forward will give me greater mobility," Louella argued. "Puts more pressure on the front wheel, and that'll give me more swing when I shift sail."

"We've tried that in the past," Sands countered. "The only reason everyone doesn't do it is that it makes the whole rig unstable when you're running downwind. All that pressure on the sail with the weight so far in front will tend to lift the rear end."

"So I'll put my fat ass on the rear rail to bring it back down," Louella scoffed. "What's so difficult about that?"

Sands sighed in exasperation. "For one thing, you'll have to remove your safety harness and get out of the saddle. Not only is that dangerous, but it means that you'll have to eventually get back in the saddle. You could lose your line if you take too much time. Worse, you risk falling off."

"I'll be careful," Louella said with confidence. "Don't worry about me. I know what I'm doing, so let's adjust the counterweight and stop wasting time."

Sands sighed again. "Well, let me show you the best way to position it, then."

They'd drawn for positions along the starting line. Pascal was second, Randy in the fourth position, Georges next to him, and Louella seventh. Zhang Wu, ever the lucky one according to Sands, had drawn the number one slot, closest to the windward side but farther back along the staggered starting lineup.

The wind was blowing to her back from the southeast, according to the telltales. The officials had separated the buggies far enough apart so that the sails would not block each other's wind. That consideration would disappear once they were underway. She'd have to keep an eye out until the group spread out.

"Five minutes," the starter announced over the common link. Louella checked her lines, snuggled in the saddle to check the fit, and made a final adjustment to the safety harness. The sail was to the far side and fluttering slightly, as if eager to grab the soundless wind and run with it.

"Just a minute, baby," Louella mumbled, and placed her feet on the crossbar. She rested one glove on the yoke and flexed her fingers. The countdown was starting.

"Fifty seconds," the starter said. "Forty… thirty…"

Someone bolted across the line. Louella knew that would cost the eager beaver a one minute delay penalty. Tough luck. She couldn't see who it was, since her view was obscured by an adjacent sail. She hoped it hadn't been Georges or Randy.

"Ten, nine, eight…" Louella began pulling the line that brought the sail against the wind. She had learned from practice that it would take at least five seconds for the sail to overcome the buggy's inertia, so she had to time it right.

"Three, two," the voice crackled. "*Start!*"

Louella felt the buggy roll forward as the sail filled with air. She wondered what this start might sound like if she wasn't in a damn suit? She hadn't realized how much she missed hearing the crack of the sail as it ballooned under a stiff wind, feeling the rush of air across the deck, hearing the sounds of water beneath the hull and the distant cries of crews cursing and shouting as they maneuvered for position.

Instead, there was only the hiss of her air recycler, the creak of the suit's pressure joints whenever she moved, and the hiss of her suit radio, all so unlike the racing she'd done most of her life.

This isolation from nature had been the same on Jupiter, where she'd been cut off from the physical reality in which she sailed, having to depend upon instruments to tell them what was going on outside, in the black depths of Jupiter's atmosphere. Yes, this experience was similar in that respect.

On the other hand, all of her other senses were alert. She felt the vibration of the buggy's wheels as it rolled along, the continual tug on the sail line, and the bite of the front wheel transmitted through the linkages to the yoke. She had her kins, as Sands would say, and she had to make the most of them.

She glanced to her right, along the line of racers. One was easily outdistancing the others, but she couldn't tell who it was. Zhang's orange suit on the buggy closest to the right edge of the course was starting his turn.

"You've got a clean line," Sands shouted over the radio. "Take advantage of it. Cut closer to the wind, and you can move closer to the lay line."

Without hesitating, Louella shifted her weight and turned the yoke, bringing her buggy across the front of the sailor nearest her and neatly cutting him off. All she glimpsed was his large counterweight swinging over her left wheel, and then he was gone. Have to keep a closer watch, she thought, and cursed the limited view provided by her helmet.

The wind shifted again, so she turned onto a broad reach, with the wind coming more from the side. This set of the sail slowed her, but she realized that it would set her up for an early tack with a longer and faster one to follow.

Zhang remained slightly ahead of her on the course, paralleling her track, even though he appeared to be far to her rear. It was position along the lay line that mattered, not the way things appeared to her.

Several of the others had also made their turns. Time to concentrate and keep the pressure on, she thought. It's only the start, and there's a long distance to go. As on Earth, most races were lost by a moment's loss of focus, a matter of seconds in many cases. She wouldn't let that happen this time.

She felt the metallic taste of competition in her mouth, felt the sweet thrill of mastering the elements in her gut, and heard the roar of her heart hammering in her ears as she made an adjustment to her sail. This was what she lived for, to win and show everyone that she could beat the best.

Even on this god-forsaken, rusty, dried up, prune of a planet.

At the two hundred kilometer mark, the only sailors in Louella's sight were Randy, Pascal, and that damned Zhang, who had managed to stay ahead of her the entire way. No matter how she shaved and risked, he was still a full thirty seconds ahead of her, according to the inertial. What could she do to catch up? Sands's strategy was to put pressure on Zhang, but she couldn't do that if she couldn't catch him in the next hour.

A beep sounded in her ear. It was the air alarm again, or maybe it was the reservoir signaling that it was full. Damn, she knew she shouldn't have drunk so much coffee this morning on top of the amount of water she'd been sucking down. With the catheter, she couldn't tell how much she had been passing.

She checked the indicators. Everything looked green except for a small blinking light near the bottom of her helmet that was crying for attention: air supply marginal, it told her. Damn, she had been concentrating so hard on the race that she'd forgotten to switch tanks. She took one hand off the yoke and threw the valve over to the second tank. Be a hell of a stupid thing to do, she thought, run out of air out so close to the finish. She laughed at the double meaning of that phrase as she recalled the languid doldrums during the Super Grand Vendee race years before.

She'd drifted for days in the tropical sun without a breeze, certain that all of the others were streaming past her on more favorable winds. The surface of the water took on an oily appearance when there was no wind, broken only by the occasional splash of a fish jumping to escape a predator.

She hadn't even been able to use the radio to find out where the other racers were. Without a wind, there was no way to recharge the batteries that powered the radio, and she needed the solar to keep the microfridge cool. No, she just had to sit here, sweating in frustration as she waited for the still air to change.

That happened in racing and was frustrating. Did she miss that unpleasant aspect of sailing? Maybe if she thought about the bad as well as the good, she might rethink continuing to sail.

The hiss of fresh air stopped the light from blinking as she brought her attention back to the present. She was approaching the line. From that point, she'd only have a hundred kilometers left in the race.

The sun was at a low angle to the west. There were only about two hours left before nightfall. There hadn't been much change in the wind since the start, although it did die down a bit when the sun was directly overhead, or as near to overhead as it could get at this latitude.

Zhang had already crossed the line for his final circuit, with Pascal close behind. How had that little frog pulled ahead of her? She sure hoped it wasn't his knowledge of physics, or she'd never hear the end of it.

She cut the line marker close, and pulled her buggy into the wind, letting it hit her sail. From the course the buggy was taking, the wind must have shifted more to the west, perhaps a sign of the post-sunset cooling in the east. Well, if the wind stayed steady, she might be able to make the next marker with only a single long tack.

Trouble was, Zhang and Pascal would probably follow the same strategy. She'd have to close haul and run on the edge of a spill if she was going to catch up to them.

The buggy's right wheel felt as if it lifted a fraction off the surface. Good, she thought, as she loosened the safety strap and shifted as far to windward as the saddle would allow. Sands had said that she could run at a sixty-degree tilt if she had to, and this looked like the time to test that idea.

She kept one hand on the yoke and leaned backward as far as she could to counterbalance the force on the sail. At this point on a tiny one-design sailboat, she'd be hearing the wind whistling in her ear and feel the spray off the bow. Not here. The only physical indication she had was the sight of the surface flying under her and the tension in her legs as she fought to keep the buggy level.

She pulled the sail all the way in, putting the bottom corner behind her. The counterweight nearly scraped the ground. As the right wheel lifted off the sand, the yoke fought to turn the buggy toward the wind.

Louella pushed the yoke the other way, turning the front wheel so that it was rolling partly on its side. Only the enormous pressure of the wind on the huge sail kept it from turning. The slightest failure of attention at this point would take her off the thin line she was sailing.

She only hoped the risk was giving her the edge she needed.

By the time she reached the marker for the turn, she'd cut Zhang's lead by half. She was close enough to see the curly script on the back of his helmet that could be his name for all she knew. Pascal was to her right, setting up for a wider turn downwind. He was probably thinking of stealing Zhang's wind if he could. The size of these sails made that a distinct possibility, and highly effective in this weak breeze.

Louella let the sail loose as she moved back to the center. The buggy immediately veered to the left, making a sharp turn for the downwind leg. Zhang was still in the lead. She caught a flash of sunlight reflecting off his visor as his helmet turned in her direction.

"You know I'm coming for you," Louella grinned. "Now we'll see who's the best damn sailor on Mars."

The front wheel seemed heavier as the wind was directly to her back. As Louella leaned back to throw a bit more weight on the rear wheels, she had an idea.

Without hesitation, she released the belt and pushed herself off the saddle to sit on the rear crossbar. She had to lean forward to maintain her grip on the yoke. "Where's a damn extension when you need one?" she cursed. Why hadn't anyone thought to put a long arm on the yoke for situations like this?

But she realized that she did have an extension: her legs. If she held onto the bar with both hands, perhaps she could steer with her boots. There wasn't a great need for accurate steering on a downwind run, where the wind kept you straight. Better not slip, though. If she tumbled off, the buggy would continue on, and she'd probably have to wait a long, embarrassing time for someone to pick her up.

She felt that doing this had given her a knot or two more speed, but she couldn't tell. Any closure with Zhang was so slow as to be indiscernible. If she was running faster, she probably wouldn't be able to tell until they got closer to the next turn, twenty kilometers further on.

During the long run downwind, Pascal had been maneuvering closer to Zhang's rear, running a long line that put him directly between the direction of the wind and Zhang's sail. He was still too far back for the blocking to have any effect, and they were too close to the next turn for it to help Louella at all.

Behind Pascal, Louella had spotted three other buggies, Randy's among them. Maybe so obviously discounting his skills had given him an advantage over the Martians, she thought. But, perhaps not. It would be nice if three of Earth's sailors finished in the top four.

Her arms and legs ached after holding this awkward and tenuous position for so long. Her water bottle had gone dry long before, and she was dying for the drink that awaited her at the finish. No different from other races, she thought. Physical discomfort came with the territory.

She flexed her fingers, mentally preparing herself for the coordinated moves she'd have to make to position herself for the next turn.

First she'd have to take her boot off the yoke while leaning forward to grab it. At the same time, she'd have to lever herself with the other hand to get back onto the saddle. She could do that while running downwind, but not too far before the turn, or she'd lose what little she'd gained. If anything went wrong, she wanted to minimize the time to recover.

If she could regain her position on the saddle, she'd have to haul the sail in so it didn't hit the marker. Cutting it that close was the only way she could carve another few meters off of Zhang's lead. It was obvious from his tendency toward the south that he was not going to take a similar chance.

Louella looked beneath the sail to watch the marker post's approach. "Careful, careful girl," she told herself. At this speed, a fraction of a second's delay would be too much.

There! Now! She quickly hauled in the sail and threw herself to the left as the post whipped by. The boom flew overhead as the wind hit the other side of the sail to turn the buggy on the final leg.

The chance she'd taken seemed to have paid off. Zhang's course was nearly parallel to her now and only a half length ahead. In a sudden act of bravado, she lifted one arm and waved at him.

He did not wave back.

The run along this leg was boring. Their speed was only half of the upwind leg, owing to the diminished efficiency of their sails. Louella wondered if she could use Pascal's blocking strategy to get between Zhang and the wind, and then dismissed the idea. To do that, she'd actually have to drop behind him and lose the distance advantage she'd gained at the turn. Best, she thought, to simply maintain her position, improve it if she could, and beat him on the final turn.

Most likely, he'd cut early toward the marker in hopes of cutting her off. But to do that, he'd have to turn sooner and lose some of his forward momentum. Would that loss be enough to pull far enough forward to cut him off instead, she wondered?

She tried to picture their relative positions and possible lines of turn as they rolled ever closer to the marker. Maybe, if she drifted toward him, he might worry about tangling his sail and pull away. No, that wouldn't work; she'd screw up her own buggy if they did tangle.

They were both running as close to the wind as they could so there seemed no possibility of… Wait, why had she slowed all of a sudden?

A quick glance at the telltales told her that the wind had shifted westerly. She loosed the sail, and glanced over to see that Zhang had been equally surprised and as quick to respond. They were now running away from the line they'd been on before.

If this continued, she'd be in an even better position to tack ahead of him, she thought, and checked to see how far they had to go. The blinking light was a few hundred meters away and closing rapidly. Seconds were all she had to decide.

Louella gauged the turn with as much precision as she could, neatly coming into the wind below Zhang. Now she had the advantage—three meters along the lay line, at least.

A quick glance up the course toward the finish line told her that she was on a direct line. There would be no need for a tacking duel. It would be a piece of cake from here on in.

At first she thought the rosy glow near the finish might be the lights from the bubble. No, there wasn't enough atmosphere to disperse the light like that, so what could it be?

Zhang had suddenly turned his buggy dramatically to the west, and was increasing their separation. What was he doing, for God's sake?

Then it struck her: Dust! The glow was the late evening sunlight reflecting off a cloud of dust. There had to be a huge gust of wind to raise that much debris—maybe even a sandstorm!

How strong would it be, and from what direction, she wondered as she turned to follow Zhang's lead. He must have encountered this before, she knew. Had she lost her advantage? No way to tell on this tack. He appeared ahead, but where were they on the lay line?

The wind stiffened, a fact she could only detect by the increased pressure on the line in her glove and the suddenly greater speed of the buggy. From what she could tell, she was moving about forty or so, maybe more.

The buggy's speed kept increasing as the glow came closer. Now it was obscuring the stars close to the eastern horizon and was a good thirty- or forty-degrees wide. Hell of a storm, as Pascal had phrased it when they hit that disastrous blow on Jupiter that shredded their sails and set them adrift. "Jesus almighty," she exclaimed, and hoped the same thing didn't happen here. She'd hate for something like this to happen so close to the finish line.

A glance to her rear showed her that Pascal had only just turned upwind. Randy and the others hadn't changed course yet.

Louella estimated that they had come at least half a kilometer off the lay line. Could she turn now and take advantage of that wind, or was it too soon? A second tack in a sandstorm might be impossible, if not downright dangerous.

Over the years, she had come to know the features of the winds. On balmy days, little puffs of wind chased across the oily surface of the still water. She'd always imagined them as atmospheric haystacks, each with its own center and peripheral winds—miniature and low-powered hurricanes, almost. Would this storm be any different? If not, perhaps skirting the high winds on the edges and driving around it was the more cautious path. The wind was coming to her side, so the rest of the storm's winds should be running in the opposite direction. Perhaps she could take advantage of that? It would mean cutting into the face of the cloud and possibly guessing wrong.

Should she chance it? Zhang was still running to the west and not watching her. He obviously hadn't thought of doing something similar yet.

The buggy leaned slightly as the wind shifted once more. Worth a chance or not, she debated, even as her hand turned the yoke while her other hand pulled the line tight.

Well, if she was going to hang up her sailing career, she might as well do it with a bang. She was going to finish this race even if she had to drive through a sandstorm. She was going to do this for Sands, and even for those miserable money-grubbing bastards at JBI. No fucking dried-up world was going to get the best of her.

The boom snapped across the buggy with a speed that alarmed her as the buggy turned into the wind. The right wheel lifted off the sand as the front wheel once again tried to turn her away from her line. She threw her body to the rising side of the buggy as she let the boom swing wide to reduce the sail's exposure to the wind. Even at that, her speed continued to increase.

Her forward vision was reduced even further as the cloud obscured more than sixty degrees of the horizon. Down the course she saw Pascal and the others continuing west, now that they realized the danger. Not a single buggy, not even Zhang, was following her lead.

Was she making a serious mistake? Was winning this race really so important that she had to risk failure if she chose wrong? Was winning so important?

All her life, she'd been competing with others. Even in the Annapolis sailing school where she'd learned the intricacies of competitive racing, she'd been fighting to do better than anyone else. Her size and strength let her win more races than not, and crewing on some of the long, but minor races—such as the Bermuda—during her teen years had honed her skills and sharpened her desire to defeat whoever stood in her way.

That edge, that driving urge to declare herself a better sailor, had gained her a measure of success as well as a great deal of personal satisfaction. Just the same, she'd never achieved financial stability, as witnessed by the way she'd been struggling to finance her racing when Blacker backed her on the Super, and later on the Jupiter race. Had all her struggles to quench the urge been worth it?

After all, what had all that success gained her? After this race, after they got back to Earth, she'd be too long out of the racing circle. After this race, she was sure she was never going to race again. There was only a slim possibility that she would be able to race the big boats again after two years away.

The wind tipped the buggy beyond the seventy-degree tilt so that she was looking between her boots at the surface. She saw the tip of the boom skim the ground, and realized that, if she didn't adjust sail, the buggy was going to flip. As she arched her back as far as she could, throwing all her weight off the right rail, she felt her shoulder brush the edge of the right wheel.

For a long moment she hung there, poised on the lip of disaster. Then, as the weight shift worked, the buggy's precarious angle decreased, and it returned to a controllable angle.

The near disaster had pumped Louella's adrenaline levels. Her heart was pounding in her chest. The sound of her breathing was loud in her ears. Her every nerve tingled with excitement. She became acutely aware of every vibration of the frame and wheels, and felt the sail's snap in the breeze through her fingertips. She realized she was running that winning edge she'd been looking for and, with that awareness, all her doubts and fears fell away. For the first time since she set foot on Mars, she felt right with the planet. She was in complete harmony with the wind and the sail, the surface and buggy. They were a single organism, racing across the sand, and flying toward the finish line.

On she flew, one with the wind.

Sands stared in frustration at the dead radio in his hand. The damn dust was playing hell with reception, and all he was hearing was static with an occasional bit of garbled speech.

What was happening to Louella and Pascal? Why had the stupid hardheaded bitch turned toward the sandstorm, instead of running the edge like Zhang? Was she determined to destroy her sail and their chances of winning? Why wasn't this radio working, damn it!

As he stared at the dark screens, he heard a sound behind him, a soft footfall, hesitation, and then another cautious step. He turned.

"Hello, Sands," Paula said softly. A shy smile lingered on her lips.

Sands caught his breath. He had nearly forgotten how her presence affected him, how the sight and smell of her so easily overwhelmed him. For a brief moment, the appearance of her so close brought back memories of other days and better times, times when he had been a whole man.

"What are you doing here?" he said, when he finally wrenched his mind back to the present.

"Somebody told me that you needed me," she replied. "It's good to see you again."

"I told you that…"

Paula took another step forward and placed a finger on his lips. "I know what you said, and I also know what your girlfriend said about it."

"Girlfriend?" This was getting increasingly weird. "I don't… I never… Who are you talking about?"

Paula pulled a flimsy from her pocket. "Pascal," she said. "She told me how much you needed someone to hold you close and keep the bad nights warm." She cocked her head to the side. "If I were the jealous type, I'd actually think she was in love with you. She even paid for the trip. She's very sweet, I think."

Sands desperately tried to keep a straight face. "She isn't… I mean, he's…" Words failed him.

"You never were very good with words," Paula said, and gave him a hug. "Do I feel better than her?"

Sands could hold it back no longer. Gales of laughter poured out of him as he hugged Paula tightly. Just the feel of her in his arms told him how he had lied when he drove her away, how he had wasted all those years feeling noble for giving her up.

The radio squawked. "Sands, damn it, Sands, can you hear me?" Pascal's gravelly voice cursed. "Where the hell is Louella?"

Sands toggled the switch. "I can hear you, Pascal, loud and clear."

Now it was Paula's turn to laugh.

Pascal had just turned to avoid the dust cloud when he saw Louella cut back toward it. What was she doing? Zhang was obviously following the best strategy by skirting the edge of the air bubble that was driving the swirling cloud, and using the edge winds to drive himself forward. He had a better line, being closer to the stiffer winds, and was gaining ground.

A quick glance behind showed him that Randy had figured out the same tactic, and was closing fast. Less than twenty meters separated the three of them.

Sands might know something about these sandstorms, if that was the word. At this altitude, it would probably be called a dust storm instead. "Sands," he called, and got no reply. He called again, but got nothing but hissing. The dust must be blocking the transmission, he thought.

Louella had nearly disappeared from sight into the obscuring cloud. She was tilted over at an impossible angle, and he knew she was probably screaming with joy at the rush that came from taking a risky line. One of these days, it was going to kill her, he thought. "But not here. Not now."

His own tactic of sailing close hauled was working. He was now visibly closing on Zhang's sail on the windward side. A few more meters, and he could block the wind as he roared past.

Zhang jibbed toward Pascal's line to block, but the separation was too much to close in time. Pascal's sail's leading edge was now cutting the wind to the trailing edge of Zhang's sail.

Zhang immediately realized the danger he was facing, and veered away. The closer he was to Pascal, the greater the theft of wind would be. His best chance of maintaining speed was to get far enough off of Pascal that the turbulence was minimized.

Pascal expected that, and adjusted his own line to stay close to Zhang so he could block if the other tried the same maneuver on him.

Louella had completely disappeared into the cloud that continued to drive to the west. "Sands," he radioed. "Sands, damn it, Sands, can you hear me?"

He heard Sands's voice. "I can hear you, Pascal, loud and clear." The rest of what he was saying was drowned by laughter.

He didn't get the joke.

Visibility was down to a few meters. How can so little wind raise so much dust, Louella wondered, as she drove further into the cloud. Swirling winds buffeted the sail. Speed diminished, and the right wheel slammed back to the surface. Louella watched the telltales and counted: about ten seconds a shift, she estimated. This would be just like sailing in a thunderstorm, only she didn't have to worry about lightning here.

The trick in this type of wind was to trim the sail to the average direction and not try to drive through it. She counted ten after the last buffeting blow, tightened the sail slightly, and loosed it as the next gust hit her. The buggy rocked in a steady rhythm as the wind alternated from side to side, but she was making steady forward progress.

At least she thought she was. For all she knew, the cloud could be taking her at right angles to the line she'd been on. No, the instruments said she was still true to the finish line, still on her path to success.

Suddenly the sail ripped, a small tear near the center that quickly spread toward the luff.

Not now, she cursed. Not so damned close to the finish. She let the sail out to relieve the pressure, and managed to slow the tear, but not by much.

How close was she? Visibility was marginal, but the instruments showed her only a hundred meters from the finish. Did she have enough momentum to cross the line in time?

The sail fluttered. Even the lessened pressure failed to stay the spread of the tear. Part of the sail trailed from the boom, dragging in the dust, while the remaining shreds flapped uselessly from the spar like flags of defeat as the buggy ground to a halt.

She was lost.

Pascal could not believe his luck. He was maintaining position on Zhang as they neared the finish along the edges of the dust cloud. A few moments before, he had noticed that the visibility ahead was getting better just as the wind shifted more to the west. From his position, he could ride the back edge of the storm's haystack and stay close to the lay line, effectively blocking Zhang from any further advance.

The line was only two hundred meters away when the wind died.

The sails on both buggies hung limp from the spars as they rolled along on sheer momentum.

Pascal looked at the telltales for any hint of a breeze, any sign that he could get enough wind to get across the line as the dust cloud continued to the southwest. He was moving at barely two mps when he spotted Louella's buggy up ahead, *sans* sail. He wondered how had she managed to sail through the center of that storm?

"Sands, what do I do?" he cried. It wouldn't be long before he ground to a halt less than a hundred meters from the finish. Was this how he was going to end his racing career, sitting at a damn stop on this dust-dry planet?

No, by all that's holy! He was not going to let it end this way! He freed himself from the pesky belt and climbed off the buggy. Louella had the truth of it during one of their briefings when she asked if she'd have to get out and push. Well, when the wind died on Earth, there was nothing you could do about it.

But here you could push.

Louella was cursing continuously at her poor luck. As the dust cleared, she spied two buggies racing to her left. All that trouble, and she'd not even get to finish, she thought. Hell of a way to go out: sitting on her ass like some spectator.

Then the Gods smiled on her. The wind died, and the two sailors slowed to a dead stop. A few moments later, she watched in amazement when one of the sailors got out of his buggy and started to push. The other quickly followed suit.

She recognized Pascal's suit on the lead sailor. The little twerp was trying to push himself to the finish. The trouble was that the larger Zhang was rapidly catching up.

"Is that legal?" she radioed Sands. "Are they going to be disqualified?" Perhaps if they were, she could do the same to get across the line that was at once so close and yet so far. No, she'd never make it in time, she realized.

"Nothing says you can't do it," was Sands's reply as she climbed from the buggy.

Without another thought, Louella raced to help Pascal. "Sands said there's nothing in the rules about pushing," she radioed, as she put her hands on the rail and added her strength. "Don't mind if I help, do you?"

"That's what teammates do," Pascal replied. "They help one another."

That had been true from the beginning of their strange relationship. From the time he'd rescued her from certain death in the Southern Ocean, through the arduous training regime they'd had in preparation for the Jupiter race, and during the daring rescue by Rams on the *Thorn*. In every case, they had worked together to overcome adversity, to pull success from certain failure, just as they would to get this damned buggy across the line to win the Martian land race.

That's what partners do.

The news services were all over them as they entered the main dome, along with several officials arguing vehemently with Sands and some dark-haired woman about the rules.

Someone ran up with a flimsy from old Jerome. "Great publicity for all of us. Put Mars back in the news. Stock up five points." That was high praise, considering the source.

Most of the reporters had already interviewed her earlier, gathering all the backstory they'd need in the event that she managed to win the race. She was certain they had done the same with all the other competitors.

"What was it like," they asked. "How did this compare with your races on Earth and Jupiter?" "What will you do next?"

"One of the joys I've always felt," she began slowly, as they hung on every word, "was the smell of the ocean, the wind in my hair, and the taste of salt spray on my lips. I had none of those on this race, but the thrill of competition, the need to run on the edge of disaster, the praying that the chances I had to take would work, and knowing that I was competing against the best," she nodded to where Zhang was chatting with his own coterie of reporters, "that is the same no matter where you sail.

"You ask me how it compares? It is always the exhilaration of mastering the winds, the joy of running a true line, and the feel of being one with the boat that will always be the same, whether it is on Mars, Jupiter, Earth, or any place else where a sailor can put sail to wind."

With those words she knew she would never stop sailing, not until she was too old and too frail to climb on board.

She was a sailor.

About the Author:

Bud Sparhawk has published one mass market paperback novel: *Vixen* (Cosmos, 2008) and two print collections: *Sam Boone: Front to Back* (Foxacre Press, 2001) and *Dancing with Dragons* (Wildside Press, 2008). Several collections of his published works are available through Amazon and Smashwords in Kindle and iBook format.

He is a three-time finalist for the Nebula award (all novellas): "Primrose and Thorn" (*Analog*, May 1996), "Magic's Price" (*Analog*, March 2001), and "Clay's Pride" (*Analog*, July/August 2004). His work has appeared in two Year's Best anthologies: David Hartwell's *Year's Best SF #11* (Eos) and Gardner Dozois' *The Year's Best Science Fiction, Fourteenth Annual Collection* (St. Martin's Press).

His short fiction has appeared frequently in *Analog Science Fiction and Fact*, *Asimov's Science Fiction*, *Daily SF*, *Clarkesworld*, as well as anthologies and podcasts. He has published eight stores in his Shardie series in *Asimov's* and in the *Defending the Future* anthologies (Dark Quest Publications.) *Analog* published five of his Sam Boone series as novelettes and short stories.

Bud's non-fiction articles have appeared in *The SFWA Bulletin* and *How to Write Science Fiction* (Dragon Moon Press, 2007) as well as sailing articles for *Chesapeake Bay Magazine*.

Bud resides in Annapolis, Maryland, where he writes a weekly blog on the pain of writing at http://budsparhawk.blogspot.com/. His personal web site is http://www.budsparhawk.com.

About the Cover Artist:

As a traditionally trained artist, George Krauter has always been interested in science fiction. In the early 1990s he began painting covers for *Analog Science Fiction and Fact*, eventually creating several per year. As his commissioned work increased, he began using digital media.

Over the years George has created illustrations for the magazines *Analog*, *Asimov's SF*, *Science Fiction Age*, *Byte*, *Scientific American*, *Omni Comix*, *Astronomy*, *The San Francisco Bay Guardian*, *Fortune*, *American Metal Market*, Stanford University, and many others. As the 1990s ended, George began teaching various 2d and 3d software in San Francisco at both the Academy of Art University and the Center for Electronic Art.

In 2005 he moved to Los Angeles, where he fulfilled a lifelong dream of working in the Visual Effects industry on feature films and commercials.

CPSIA information can be obtained at www.ICGtesting.com
Printed in the USA
LVOW07s0318250415

435997LV00004B/47/P